Night Falls on Chicago

Kaycee Nilson

Night Falls on Chicago

ISBN: 978-0-9847215-9-7

Library of Congress Control Number: 2012930637

Cover design by All Things That Matter Press

Dedicated to my Mother

She believed when no one else did.

Acknowledgments

First, I want to thank my husband and family for the sacrifices and support they gave during the writing of this book. Many thanks go to my husband for helping me to edit as well.

Words alone cannot express how much I am grateful to the "Authors of Horror Fan Club" for their advice, as well as to the club members for wanting more and more of the story.

I would also like to thank the members of the "South Park Fan Club" who backed me, and urged me to continue on to make my dream a reality.

PROLOGUE

No one knew exactly how old the ancients were, or how their lives began. Some said that they were simply born vampires at the beginning of time and through the centuries learned their craft and how to survive in the mortal world. Some thought they evolved much like mortals, only at a faster rate. Still others claimed the ancients came from another world, or another dimension. But wherever these immortal creatures originally came from, all agreed to one fact: the ancients were incredibly old, and could have walked the earth long before mortal man.

In the beginning, there had been many, and they had ruled the planet. Through the centuries many had been destroyed. Mortal man simply could not accept the existence of a superior being walking amongst them, and, reacting out of simple fear, killed any vampires they came across. Some of the ancients were destroyed at the hands of their brothers and sisters out of vengeance or struggles for power. Now, only a small handful of the ancients remained.

Other immortals, those made by the ancients, were not nearly as powerful. They had similar abilities—flight, self-healing, blinding speed, and incredible strength, among others—but the power held by the ancients was exponentially greater.

It was rumored that at one time the ancients had formed a council, who initiated a set of rules and regulations for all vampires to live by. It was known simply as "The Code", and was designed to keep the immortals from being discovered by mortals. Those who refused to follow the Code were destroyed by the council. When new vampires were born or made, they were taught the Code, and learned to live by it.

The mating of the ancients occurred only once every ten years, during the lunar eclipse known as "Blood on the Moon". When two ancients, pure blood vampires, mated, the resulting offspring was another pure blood. Although these children did not possess the knowledge of the beginning of time, they were still considered to be "ancients". The mating of an ancient with a vampire who had been made was forbidden by the Code. Although the union would draw power from nature into the ancient involved, the resulting offspring of such a union always resulted in a child who, although still immortal, was physically deformed, mentally unstable, or simply lacked all ability to live under the rules of the Code. These children were known as ghouls, and were sought out and destroyed by the ancients at every opportunity.

It was said that an immortal prophet, in years past, well before the ancients began their mating rituals, had predicted which of the ancients would mate, and produce pure blood offspring to continue the shadowed reign of the immortal world. During the Blood on the Moon, all ancients would feel the urge to mate, but two would be drawn inexplicably together. To this day, each of the prophecies had come true.

ONE

The sun dipped low into the western sky, throwing brilliant colors of purples and reds across the majestic city skyline. The tall towers with their glistening steel and glass stood proudly against the cool wind blowing in from Lake Michigan to the east bringing a small relief from the heat of the day. The masses that work inside the buildings began to scurry like rats toward the buses waiting at the corner, the taxis filling the streets, and down into the subway systems that rumble through the bowels of the city to begin their commute from their daily humdrum jobs to their evening humdrum homes. Just another day in their ever-humdrum lives.

Just look at them down there, thought Elizabeth in disgust as she peered from her shadowed perch high above the bustling city street. Not a thought in their heads other than how to pay their mortgages and what to cook for dinner. Slowly, as she watched the flow of humanity, she began to feel the hunger. It was a hunger that she had felt as long as she could remember. It was a hunger that haunted her dreams. A hunger that came as quickly as the tides, and as predictably as the setting of the sun. A hunger that could never be entirely quenched. The hunger could only be satisfied temporarily — with her next victim.

Once the masses dwindled and the sun had slipped completely beyond the horizon, Elizabeth focused on which of the remaining mindless drones below would become her first victim of the night. Those still in groups were quickly discarded. There would be too many witnesses. Those in a great hurry were forgotten. It was too much effort to try and slow them down. Those who looked a little too wealthy were cast aside. Too many others would be looking for them. The homeless and street people were left as a last resort. They just weren't appealing.

She noticed a well-dressed man walking down Michigan Avenue's "Magnificent Mile", past the street vendors still selling their cheap trinkets trying to make a quick buck, past the horse drawn carriages offering romantic tours of the city, past the musicians with their beat up violins, corroded saxophones, and drum sets made of plastic pails, and past the over-priced stores and shops that screamed for tourists to spend more money in a day than they earned in a month.

With his head hung low, the man walked aimlessly, ignoring everything around him, with no real direction in mind. He had the look that Elizabeth always searched for. It was the look of someone with no place in particular to go other than an empty one-bedroom apartment, with no one waiting for him when he got there. It was the look of the defeated, the beaten down, and, most importantly, of the lonely. It was the look of someone who wouldn't be missed or searched for.

There's my bitch, thought Elizabeth as she watched the man trudge further down the block.

Elizabeth looked ahead of the man, searching for the best place to make first contact with him. It had to be somewhere unnoticed by others on the street. And, more importantly, it had to be somewhere that would not seem suspicious should she suddenly appear out of nowhere. She noticed an alleyway that exited onto the street just ahead of where the man was walking. There was a small storefront right next to it. It would be as good a place as any.

With the agility of a cat, Elizabeth sped down from her perch and across the busy street. She was so fast that hardly anyone noticed her fly past. She became just another blur in the tired minds of those just trying to get home. Elizabeth quickly slipped around the block to the far entrance of the alley, and through it past the dumpsters filled with refuse from the day's business and the few homeless people who were too weak and fragile to get themselves out onto the main sidewalk to beg for the change they needed to buy their next bottle of whatever liquor was cheapest that night. She came to the end of the alleyway just before the man reached it, blended into the shadows of the doorway to the store that had been already closed for over an hour, and waited patiently. This was her favorite part of the game, toying with her victim before she made her move.

As the man passed in front of the store, Elizabeth stepped from the shadows and coughed slightly. Something about that cough made the man look toward her. What it was, he couldn't begin to guess, but there was something about this woman who suddenly appeared by his side, something he couldn't put his finger on. But he knew in that very instant that it was something special and something appealing.

Elizabeth walked seductively toward the man, her strawberry-blonde hair shimmering in the light of the streetlights that were slowly coming to life as the sky darkened. She made sure she never lost eye contact with him. It was one of many ways she could control her victims. He felt himself staring into her incredible violet eyes, and although it made him uncomfortable to maintain such intense eye contact, the power of her gaze would not allow him to turn away.

"Hello," she almost breathed into his ear. "Would you like some company?"

The man was shocked at first, thinking he was being accosted by a prostitute. But prostitutes were unheard of in this part of town, especially on Michigan Avenue, where the tourists and the wealthy shopped.

Elizabeth sensed his anxiety and quickly changed the expression on her face to a look of pleading for help and tried to reassure the man. "I'm lonely. I just moved to this city and I know no one. I saw you walking down the street and I thought you looked nice. And I thought that maybe you would like to stop into a bar around the corner and have a drink with me."

The man thought for a minute about the empty one-bedroom apartment he had waiting for him at home. He pictured himself spending yet another evening alone in front of his 13" TV screen, watching reruns on late night television. He pictured his beat up brown recliner, with the stains from years of beer spills, and the rips and tears in the fabric from the restless nights when he fell asleep in that very chair. He pictured the uninviting darkness and the drab walls, and remembered the all too familiar smell of cooked cabbage that continually penetrated the walls from the apartment next door. If a man's home is his castle, he thought, I must be living in the dungeon.

"Sure, why not?" he said to his new companion. "I have nothing else to do anyway, and no one waiting for me at home. And besides, after the day I had, I could really use a drink myself."

He introduced himself to Elizabeth as Paul, and she slipped her arm into his as they began to walk around the corner to the bar that Elizabeth spoke of. She had been there dozens of times, always with the newest victim, but she couldn't tell him how familiar she was with the place. After all, she did "just" move to the city.

They looked liked a perfect couple. Paul was in one of his nicer suits. It was navy blue and made of fairly high quality linen, although seen close up it was rather rumpled and well worn. It was a look that perfectly complimented his dark tousled hair, and deep blue eyes. Paul had the ability to look more successful than he actually was, and hid his lonely, shabby, empty apartment life from most of the people he came across. Elizabeth looked stunning, as usual. Dressed in her favorite black leather duster over a skin tight, form-fitting leather cat suit, she simply glowed with charm and grace. She had to be careful not to attract too much attention to herself, or she would become too memorable, and be forced to find a new place to hunt for victims.

They made their way to a dark, rundown neighborhood bar. Elizabeth preferred smaller, out-of-the-way, sparsely occupied places. Fewer people around meant fewer who would remember her later.

After walking down the short flight of stairs to the basement-level bar, Paul found himself leading his new friend around pool tables and fool ball tables toward the back of a bar with walls exposed right to the bare brick. There were the obligatory neon beer signs hanging here and there, but the place had more the look of a typical basement storage area than a welcoming tavern. A few locals, regulars, were shooting pool. If Paul and Elizabeth had stopped to watch, they would have seen that the players were playing very poorly, with balls bouncing off of the hard rubber rails instead of falling into the pockets. A couple of drunks who could barely stand were off to the left, tying to play a game of darts on the electronic dartboard.

Just what this town needs, Paul thought. Another couple of guys all boozed up, throwing what could be considered a lethal weapon.

The small DJ stand next to the door was unoccupied, apparently on automatic pilot. There was some current hit playing that neither Paul nor Elizabeth recognized. The bar itself was surrounded by mismatched barstools, each with a seat made of a different material, color, and apparently from a different era. About the only thing the barstools had in common with each other was that they were all bolted securely to the floor. No one was going to walk off with one of these highly prized seats. And if they got drunk and fell off, at least they wouldn't take the stool with them and cause more damage to it.

There were a few scattered drinkers sitting at the bar doing little more than staring at the television set in the corner. The local baseball team was playing and had captured the attention of everyone present, including both bartenders, each of whom had been surgically enhanced to help fill out their skin tight T-shirts bearing the bar's logo splashed across the front. Apparently youth and plastic surgery were prerequisites for being hired. Actual bartender experience and knowledge was not necessary.

"Can I take your order?" a surly waitress popping bubblegum and wearing a shirt matching those behind the bar asked the pair after they had made themselves comfortable as far from the regulars as possible.

Paul ordered a Gibson without even thinking about being a gentleman and letting his lady friend order first, or asking what she would like. Elizabeth was used to being treated with more gallantry, but she brushed it off, since it really didn't matter to her if her victims had manners. She simply turned to the waitress and ordered a Cosmopolitan.

They sat and made idle chitchat while waiting for their drinks to arrive, even joking about the deco they discovered on their table. It was from the 1970's, and looked like it had barely been cleaned or repaired since then. Quickly running out of subjects to discuss, Paul started talking about himself, a subject he was obviously fond of. Once Paul began, Elizabeth learned much more about her prey than she usually cared for.

Paul had moved to Chicago several years earlier from New York City. He did, as Elizabeth had guessed, live alone. Paul was a journalist, but wasn't associated with any specific publication or broadcaster. He worked freelance, and had just had an incredibly rough day trying to sell a story he had written about some cover-up in the mayor's office regarding the Mayor's mental health. Apparently he could not find any corroborating sources, so no one wanted to bother with his story.

Although Paul enjoyed talking about himself, occasionally he would try to turn the conversation to the subject of Elizabeth. Every time he tried, Elizabeth was able to avoid his questions by making a joke, asking a question in return, or simply changing the subject suddenly.

As the evening wore on, Paul continued to drink. He didn't even seem to notice that she had not taken the first sip from her Cosmo. As long as she seemed interested in him, he was doing fine.

The more he drank the nearer Elizabeth got to him. She would occasionally inch her chair slightly closer to his, until finally their legs were touching, side-by-side, under the table. Luckily for her, these chairs were not bolted down like the bar stools.

She took his hand and held it up to look at it. Paul's hand looked as if it hadn't seen a day of hard labor in its entire life. This was the hand of a man who had everything given to him with no effort. But she wanted to continue to compliment him and make him relax. "You've got very strong hands," she told him, the lie crossing her lips with no hesitation.

When she placed his hand back on the table, she kept her slender fingers on his arm, and slowly let them meander past his elbow and over his shoulder. She began to trace the veins in his neck with her finger. Excitement built in her as she anticipated what lay ahead. And she loved every minute of it.

She wanted to finish him off before he got slovenly drunk. If he were unable to walk easily, or got too boisterous, he would attract attention, and that would be no good for Elizabeth.

She whispered into his ear that it was time for them to go. She paid the bill with cash she had taken from the wallet she picked from his pocket and led him out of the bar. They walked down the street now lit entirely by electric lights. The evening was overcast, with Mother Nature blocking the light normally provided by the moon and stars. It was a perfect night for Elizabeth.

She led him back toward the alleyway where they first met. "Maybe we should grab a cab," Paul suggested. He had a sly gleam in his eye and he almost winked when he said, "We could go back to your place."

"Not quite yet. I'd rather walk for a bit."

Paul was having a little difficulty walking, but it was nothing he couldn't manage, so he continued on. He didn't want to upset this stunning beauty and have her leave him at the end of the night to return alone again to his empty apartment. This was the first time in many months he had the company of a beautiful woman, or any woman for that matter, and he was determined to carry it through to what he hoped would be a long night of passion, and breakfast together in the morning.

"Let's go down here." Elizabeth began leading Paul down the alleyway.

"I don't know about that. Alleys aren't the best place to be late at night."

"Oh, it looks safe to me, Mister Scared."

"It does? I think it just looks dark … and smells bad." Paul screwed up his face into a look of disgust. After dealing with the cooked cabbage from his next-door neighbor for so long, he should have been immune to foul smells.

"Oh, come on." Elizabeth gave him her best come hither, seductive look. "Besides, I've never done it in an alley. Have you?"

Paul stammered for a moment, unable to find words to express his complete shock and, at the same time, complete joy at the sudden revelation that he was about to have sex with a drop-dead gorgeous total stranger. "Uh, no, I haven't," was about the only thing he could get to squeak past his lips.

Elizabeth turned and began strolling down the alley. Paul was quick to get over his fears of a darkened alley at night and caught up to her, matching her stride for stride across the broken pavement.

Halfway through the alley, Elizabeth suddenly stopped, almost jerking Paul off his feet, and pulled him up against the side of a dumpster. She grabbed him by the lapels of his wrinkled suit and pulled him to her. She began kissing him full on the mouth. She could taste the whiskey on his breath, and was afraid for a moment that she'd let him drink far too much. She did, after all, have plans for this man.

Paul was instantly aroused. There was no foreplay. No gentle, soft kisses to start, working up a fever to the point of complete and unbridled passion. Elizabeth had shocked him again with this sudden, delightful attack, but he didn't care. He simply returned her kisses and started exploring her body with his hands.

He'd had an idea that there was a wondrous, curvaceous body beneath the leather duster she'd been wearing all evening, but he'd been unable to see it. Now his hands were seeing it for him, and it was incredible. He felt her slender waist and the curves of her hips. His hands roamed to her pert buttocks and up to the small of her back. He grew more and more aroused as he started kissing her neck, and she kissed his. One hand held her tightly as the other slid forward to find a perfectly rounded, supple breast. That perfect breast was the last thing Paul would ever touch.

Elizabeth decided this was the time.

She grabbed the hair at the back of his head and pulled sharply to the side, almost snapping his neck in the process. Oh, what exquisite pain, was all Paul could think.

She opened her mouth wide, displaying perfectly straight, perfectly white teeth — and a set of perfectly sharp fangs that quickly sank into the flesh of his neck. Elizabeth began to drink the warm liquid that flowed from the wound, the precious blood that she so craved, so needed, and so hungered for.

At first, Paul didn't realize what was happening. He hadn't seen the fangs. He hadn't felt much of anything besides the arousal in his loins, the feel of his hands on her body, and the growing passion inside of him. He was sure she was giving him the biggest hickey he had ever received, and he would have to find some way to hide it, or cover it, before starting to work the next day. But it would be a wonderful reminder of the lovely night ahead. And it would surely last longer than any relationship he had ever had.

Before long the exquisite pain began to burn, and Paul could tell something was very wrong. He realized he was growing weak, and the pain in his neck was so intense he almost couldn't stand it. He tried to pull away from the woman, but she was much stronger than he, and he was unable to stop her.

Soon, he stopped fighting and his body grew limp. She knew that the end of this feeding was almost near, and she dropped him to the pavement like a rag doll. Wiping her mouth she looked down at her victim and then with a vicious laugh, said, "So I lied. I have done that in an alley before."

She picked up the body as easily as if it were a sheet of paper and tossed it into the dumpster behind her. It landed with a solid thud among the cardboard boxes and discarded food. She reached into a pocket and produced a single match, struck it, and threw it into the dumpster, igniting the trash almost instantly. With luck, the flames would burn out before alighting anything nearby, but only after charring the body beyond recognition. Tomorrow morning, the ashen remains of Paul the journalist would make a trip in a city garbage truck to the city dump, where it would be forever buried in its final resting place.

With dinner finished, and her leftovers discarded, Elizabeth stretched her arms above her head and disappeared into the mist.

TWO

"So, what is it they want to use us as guinea pigs for this time?" Sam said between sips of lukewarm coffee.

"I dunno," Mike replied. "Some recipe they found in a magazine."

"So how about Saturday?"

"Yeah, that should be good. While the ladies are cooking up their creation, we can watch the game."

"But which game? Both teams are playing Saturday afternoon."

"Well, since we'll be at my place, I guess we get to watch my boys, huh?"

"Heh. 'Boys' is right. Compared to my south-siders, your team really is just a bunch of boys."

The friendly bantering back and forth about whose baseball team was better, the Cubs on the north side of town or the White Sox on the south, had been going on for years. It was only one of many things that seemed like it would make a friendship between Sam and Mike utterly impossible. The two were as different as night and day.

Sam had grown up on the south side of Chicago in a rough neighborhood full of street thugs, pimps, and drug dealers. His family was poor, and their tiny apartment was unbearably hot and sticky during the humid summer months, and so cold in the winters that at times Sam had to wear his winter coat to bed just to keep from freezing. His father worked days in a factory, and did odd jobs for people on weekends. What these "odd jobs" consisted of, Sam never knew. And he quickly learned not to ask. His mother worked off and on as a receptionist, or in whatever jobs her temp agency could find for her, but the jobs were few and far between, and generally lasted only a week or two.

Mike, on the other hand, had been raised on the north side, in a neighborhood known mostly for its younger, successful business community. His parents had married young while Mike's father was studying to become an accountant, both of them coming from families that were not rich, but certainly well off. Money was never anything they had to worry about. Their home was no shabby apartment. They lived in a single family home with a small yard where Mike and his sister could play without the fears faced by kids like Sam, who had to play in the streets.

Sam was a big, burly man, standing almost six-foot-three and built like a diesel engine. Mike often joked that Sam had muscles in places where Mike didn't even have places. Sam worked out once or twice a week, but staying fit seemed to come easy to him, and he didn't seem to have to worry about his brawny physique turning to flab anytime soon.

His jet black hair was cropped short, almost military in style, and he kept his moustache trimmed precisely, as if he measured each whisker to make sure they were uniform in length. He had dark skin and a square jaw that contributed to his look of strength and authority, as did his dark eyes that bellied a life of hardship and pain. When he relaxed on warm summer weekends, and removed his shirt, you could still see scars where he had been stabbed in knife fights as a kid, and other marks that served of reminders of the life he was now trying to help others avoid.

Mike was a slender man. He wasn't nearly as tall as Sam, barely reaching a height of five-foot-eleven. He was by no means scrawny or out of shape, but when he stood next to Sam, he was certainly dwarfed by the larger man. His light complexion was matched by short, light brown hair that never seemed to stay in place, and seemed to wage war against Mike and his army of men's hair sprays, mousse, and gels that he would use to try and rein it in and hold it still. Although Mike sported no facial hair, he did seem to have a perpetual five o'clock shadow that no amount of shaving could make go away. His light brown eyes, perpetually smiling, were surrounded by creases and lines that were not from a life of hardship, but from his bout with alcoholism years earlier. Although successful, his father had been a heavy drinker. His mother considered herself to be a "social" drinker, but she could certainly match Mike's father drink for drink, and often did. Mike picked up the habit at a rather young age, and became hooked quickly. He'd been through the twelve-step program, and had been sober for several years now, but the memories of things he had done while drunk were still etched in those lines on his face.

When Sam finished high school, which in itself was a surprise to his parents, he thought about joining the military. College was not an option. He was not the brightest of students, and there were no scholarships coming his way. But he wanted out of his neighborhood, and a chance at a better life. Just before leaving to sign up with the Army, he took one more look at his neighborhood, at the homes, at the suffering, and at the kids who would have to grow up in the same awful way that he had. That was the moment he decided he wanted to protect these streets, instead of fighting wars in lands across the sea. He passed over the Army, and, instead, enrolled in the Police Academy.

Mike was all set for college at that time. He had been accepted in several of the local Chicago colleges, including Columbia, DePaul, and even Northwestern, the Big Ten School located up in Evanston. But he couldn't decide exactly what he wanted to do. He had plenty of choices, so he decided to go to DePaul for a year while he figured out what he wanted to major in, and then he could transfer to one of the other schools if necessary. But during the summer before college was to start, tragedy struck, not once, but twice.

In June of that summer, Mike's sister, Lisa, was on a camping trip with some friends, and got separated from the group. As she was trying to find her way back to them, she was attacked, and became the victim of a rapist and murderer. Mike's family was in disbelief that their daughter and sister could be taken from them so suddenly. But she was gone in the blink of an eye. To make matters worse, the perpetrator was never found.

A month later, just as Mike thought he might be able to get over his grieving and move on, the second tragedy struck. His parents had gone out for the evening, when they were mugged. It was a random mugging, but instead of just giving over his wallet, Mike's father tried to fight back. It was a mistake he would not live to regret. The mugger stabbed Mike's father once in the chest, and then again to finish him off, the blade slipping between his ribs and piercing his heart. Mike's mother could do nothing but stand and scream at the sight of her husband bleeding to death on the sidewalk. The mugger had no choice but to kill her quickly to silence her and keep her from identifying him to the police. He slit her throat without a second thought, using the same blade that was already covered in her husband's blood. His plan worked, because, like the man who killed Mike's sister, he got away and was never apprehended.

Mike was not only shocked by the two attacks on his family and the deaths of his only three family members, but also at the fact that two separate criminals had committed violent murders and walked away free. It was then that he decided he had to do something about it. He called the university to cancel his enrollment, and made a call to the Police Academy.

Sam and Mike met each other during their time at the Academy, and, despite their differences, became great fiends. Others in their class referred to them as Felix and Oscar, "The Odd Couple", although they never actually figured out which of them was supposed to be Oscar and which was Felix. Sam and Mike joked that they thought they were closer to being Tom and Jerry, the cartoon cat and mouse.

Mike was almost thrown out several times because of his problems with alcohol. After the deaths of his sister and parents, his drinking became much more intense. If it weren't for Sam covering for him, helping him hide his alcoholism from the instructors, and at times just plain lying for him, Mike surely would not have graduated.

But graduate they both did. Six years later, Sam was still a uniform cop trying to protect the streets from the thugs and gangs that tormented his childhood. Mike had been moved to homicide, where, as a detective, he could use his past experience to try and comfort victims' families, all the while trying to extract information about the victim. It was something he excelled at. He managed to quickly gather information that other "less sensitive" detectives would take weeks to get.

And through it all, the two remained best friends, along with their wives.

Both men had gotten married soon after graduating from the Academy, each standing up as Best Man at the other's wedding. It was during his engagement that Mike kicked his drinking problem, with the help of his fiancée, Jane, and his friend Sam. Jane had told him that although she loved him deeply, his drinking was the one thing about him she couldn't live with, and if he didn't stop, she couldn't go through with the marriage.

Both couples lived in Park Ridge, one of the city's northwest suburbs, and got together often for meals, movies, games, and even evenings out when Mike and his wife could find a babysitter for their young daughter.

Now Mike and Sam were sitting in one of their favorite downtown coffee shops. They stayed away from the trendier, "designer" places that were springing up all over the place, and stuck to the smaller mom-and-pops.

This one was right in the heart of Chicago's Loop, near the corner of Halsted and Jackson Streets, not far from the constant rumble of the elevated train tracks that carried thousands of commuters into and out of the city each day. The décor dated back to the fifties and the coffee was just the way Mike and Sam liked it—black, and strong. No fancy cappuccinos or lattés for them.

Mike's pager went off, and before he could even read the number on the illuminated display, his cell phone started buzzing in his pocket. He pulled the phone out, looked at the display, and saw the same number as on the pager.

"Someone sure is getting anxious," Mike said into the phone without bothering with a customary greeting.

"Why didn't you answer your page?" barked the voice on the other end.

"Hey, give me a chance! The pager went off only seconds before you called my cell."

"Well, you're needed at Chicago and Rush. Get over there ASAP."

"What's going on?"

"A body was found. That's all I know. Just get there."

Mike closed the lid on the palm-sized phone without a goodbye, and looked at Sam with a shrug. "Duty calls."

"Yeah, I should get back to the park anyway. The concert there will be over soon."

"And you never know how wild and crazy those folks will get after one of those long orchestra concerts."

Mike and Sam often joked about pulling duty in Grant Park during the series of free symphony concerts each summer. Neither of them was a fan of classical music, so they tried to stay as far away from the park as possible during the actual event. After all, the people who attended were not exactly the violent types, and there was rarely any trouble. Sam would just be sure to return before the concert was over to help direct foot traffic and make sure the old ladies all felt safe from whatever it was they thought might be lurking in the trees after dark, since the shows often ended well after dusk.

Mike put away the cell phone and pager, and started patting his pockets, looking for his wallet, even looking on the floor, as if he couldn't find it.

"Don't worry. I'll get this one." Sam pulled out a five and paid for the coffee. He often paid for their little get-togethers because he knew that even on his cop's salary, his two-income no-children household had more disposable cash than Mike's detective's salaried, one-income, one-child household.

"Thanks, buddy," Mike said with a smile, to let his friend know he hadn't actually lost his wallet and shouldn't waste time to look for it. "I'll call you about this weekend."

"See ya then!"

Mike was quickly out the door and on his way to the crime scene, leaving Sam to face the old ladies and the classical music enthusiasts at the park. With a sigh, he dropped their empty paper coffee cups in the trash and headed back to his assigned duty.

THREE

Blue and red police lights lit up the buildings along Rush Street, with the block between Chicago and Pearson Avenues completely barricaded off to keep the curious onlookers and the morbid death enthusiasts away from the crime scene. Things in the area had been relatively quiet until word spread that a body had been found in a burned out dumpster. Since then, the crowd trying to get a glimpse of the gruesome scene grew until it was almost out of control, and rumors about the identity of the victim, the details of the murder, and the reasons for the location spread like wildfire.

An ambulance sat among the police cruisers, but the paramedics assigned to it were in no hurry to rush back to the hospital. After all, it had been estimated that the victim had been dead for nearly twenty four hours, and no high-speed ambulance trip in the world would result in saving the poor soul. It was obvious that the body would be leaving in a coroner's wagon instead, but they had to stick around, just in case someone else was found, still alive and able to be saved.

The coroner's wagon had already arrived as well, and after the ordeal of trying to get through the crowd without causing injuries to the innocent folks who were gathered around, found an unoccupied spot near the end of the alleyway. Max, the Assistant Coroner, was anxious to get the body moved into his vehicle and get it back to the morgue. He was a quirky fellow who felt uncomfortable around the living. Hence his chosen line of work: no live clients to deal with. But he was not allowed to touch the body, or even go near it until the homicide detectives and the forensic teams were done securing the area, searching for the tiniest of clues, and declaring the body officially turned over to the Coroner's Office.

The forensic team had little to work with at this crime scene. Nearly everything in the dumpster had been burned, and there was so much grime and filth surrounding the area that it would take a team of thirty forensic experts nearly a year to sift through each and every little particle, looking for the one fiber or hair that might belong to the person behind this crime. If the clue was there, they'd find it.

The detectives also had little to go on. No witnesses had thus far come forward. The only person to interview was Joe, the manager of the building the dumpster serviced. The first cops on the scene had tried to pry details out of him, including his last name, but it was nearly impossible. His Polish accent was so thick no one could understand anything he said—other than his liberal use of expletives.

When Mike arrived on the scene, even flashing his badge and

blowing his horn wasn't enough to part the sea of onlookers blocking his way. He ended up parking his car on the next block and fighting his way through on foot. After flashing his badge to the officer manning the line of yellow police tape and trying desperately to keep out those who did not belong, Mike was allowed through, and he walked quickly down the alley, waving and acknowledging Max on his way past the coroner's wagon.

"So, what do we have," he asked the officer who appeared to be in charge.

"Homicide, we're pretty sure. Guy was in the dumpster. We assume he wasn't sleeping there. Not even the bums do that. And then someone lit him up."

"You sure he wasn't smoking or something and started the fire himself, by accident?"

"Yeah, I'm pretty sure he didn't decide to go for a smoke break in a dumpster in a deserted back alley." The cop had a "What am I, an idiot?" look on his face, and the sarcasm in his voice was almost palpable. He kept talking as he walked with Mike over to the dumpster. "He was lying with his head down at the bottom. That's about the only reason he didn't totally burn up. Most of the trash down there was soggy and wet. Fire couldn't burn through it. His feet to his ass is pretty much barbeque. The rest is just soaked through."

They had reached the dumpster and Mike poked his head over the edge to look at the body that had been pulled from the rotting vegetation at the bottom and laid on top of the layer that had been burned to ash. The first thing that hit him was the pungent smell of burnt flesh mixed with a week's worth of rotting garbage, and he had to turn away quickly to keep from losing whatever food was in his stomach.

"Oh, and he smells pretty bad," the cop said with a grin.

"Gee, thanks for the warning."

One of the other nearby officers handed Mike a cloth to cover his mouth and nose before he peered over the edge for a second look. The cop in charge kept up his narrative of events. "Looks like whoever killed him just tossed him in, lit him up, and assumed he'd burn to nothin'. I guess they should have checked to make sure. Guy over there," he pointed at Joe, "works for the building. Calls himself the building manager, but we figure he's just a janitor with a fancy title. He found the guy today when he brought out a bunch of trash. I guess he saw the ashes, got curious, and started poking through the junk. Found the leg sticking up, called the cops, and here we are. Don't bother talkin' to him. He barely speaks English."

Mike looked over at Joe, who was speaking non-stop, using his hands to augment whatever unintelligible words were coming from his mouth.

"Any idea how long he's been there?"

"He says," nodding toward Joe again, "the dumpster gets emptied every other day, so he couldn'ta been there earlier than yesterday mornin'."

"He sure looks like he's been there longer."

"Yeah. I'd say, from the looks of him, he's been dead a couple days. Someone musta just gotten around to dumping the body. Either that, or the guy just rots really fast." The cop chuckled at his own morbid joke.

"Any sign of cause?"

"Well, there's two big puncture marks on his neck. That could be it."

"You could have mentioned that earlier."

Mike looked back into the dumpster for a closer look at the neck. There were, in fact, two neat round holes in the skin, a few inches below the ear.

"Odd," Mike said.

"What's that?"

"No blood."

"I figure it washed off in the crap he was layin' in. Or else it was cleaned up between the killin' and the dumpin'."

"Awful strange place to stab someone, or whatever was done to him. Side of the neck."

"Yeah, well, there's all kinds of wierdos runnin' around here at night."

"I guess you're right. Anyone notify next of kin?"

"Guy's wallet didn't burn up. No cash in it. ID gave his name and address as Paul somebody. Had a press ID, too, so we'll talk to the papers in the mornin' and see which one he worked for. Looks like he lived alone. We're still lookin' for family."

"Well, let forensics do their thing, and then Max can take the body."

"Shouldn't take long. Doesn't look like there's much to go on."

"You got that right. Of course, I'll still be stuck up to my ass in it all weekend trying to piece it together. So much for my weekend off."

"Hey, life's a bitch."

Mike tuned and walked back down the alley to where the cruisers and ambulance were parked. At his quick departure, the crowd seemed to sense that the body would be coming out of the alley soon. They pushed closer to get a better look, straining the yellow police tape, and the temper of the cops who repeatedly ordered them to get back. Mike paused just long enough to speak to Max, asking for a full report as soon as his customary autopsy was complete. While it was standard procedure to do an autopsy in cases where murder was likely, there were times when the family would petition to prevent an autopsy because their religion didn't allow defiling the body. In this case, with no family located, the autopsy would be performed, and quickly.

Once past the crowd, Mike walked to his car and found an orange City of Chicago parking violation attached to the window on the driver's side of his car.

"That's just great," he muttered under his breath as he tore the ticket from the window. "You'd think detectives would be exempt from these damn things at a crime scene."

He unlocked the car, climbed in, slammed the door as hard as he could and sat still, hands on the steering wheel, staring straight ahead at nothing. His mind was racing with thoughts of what those marks on the victim's neck could be. He didn't want to believe it was possible, but he couldn't deny what his eyes had just seen. And on top of it all, his weekend was now ruined.

"Well, I better head down to the park and tell Sam to forget about our plans," he said, as much to his car as to himself. He turned the key in the ignition, brought the engine to its usual sputtering start, and headed back toward Grant Park.

FOUR

Elizabeth slipped through the darkness of the alleyways, keeping to the shadows that always protected her and kept her from being seen by the homeless who dug through the dumpsters in hopes of finding a tiny morsel of tossed-away food that would serve as their gourmet dinner for the evening.

These forgotten citizens, left to rot like the trash they often lived on, were easy prey for Elizabeth. No one would ever miss them. No one would ever find them. No one would think twice about them, other than to eventually notice a decrease in the homeless population. Of course, the crooked politicians who ran the city would take full credit for the lack of bums and winos, spouting some new, unheard-of policy that supposedly helped hundreds get off the streets and find good jobs, good homes, and a good start to a "normal" life. How could they admit that the homeless were disappearing only because they were being killed off? It was almost too easy for Elizabeth.

But tonight she had other plans, and a certain destination in mind. Nothing but nothing was going to divert her from her destination.

She was headed toward her favorite place in all of Chicago, Grant Park. Besides the wonderful scenery, the Lake Michigan waterfront nearby, the view of the city skyline, and the infamous Buckingham Fountain, there were also almost always numerous potential victims around to satisfy her when the hunger arose, and plenty of places to destroy the evidence. But, more importantly, there were plenty of trees, shadows, and places to hide where she could be alone with her thoughts.

And tonight, alone with her thoughts was what she wanted.

She had heard about the body found earlier in the day, burned from the waist down in a dumpster. She was certain it was her victim from the previous night, and still cursed herself for not waiting to be sure the corpse was completely destroyed. It was that kind of sloppy mistake that resulted in her kind being discovered, and hunted. She had survived for centuries, as had others like her, by being careful, by remaining unseen and unknown. But last night it seemed she had made a careless mistake, and it bothered her.

When Elizabeth arrived at her destination, it was well after dark. The sun had dipped far below the horizon, and the half moon shone down on the treetops and paved streets. She was pleased to discover that, despite the late hour, the symphony concert was still in progress. There would be plenty of prey to choose from, and she could easily slip in and out of the sea of nameless faces without being noticed.

Elizabeth strolled nonchalantly along the narrow paved walkway that cut through the park, separating the seating area near the stage from the acre of open grass where hundreds of people set up canvas chairs, picnic blankets, or just lay on the ground listening and enjoying the music as it washed over them. The Petrillo Music Shell had been holding free concerts in the park for many years, and although the seats were standard grey aluminum folding chairs, many of them were left in place all summer long, giving the facility a somewhat permanent sense. Columns of speakers on the stage and amplifiers throughout the park made the structure useful to the city for other events as well. It was the main stage for most of the city's numerous music festivals, all of which Elizabeth made an effort to attend. The annual Jazz Fest, Blues Fest, Country Fest, Latin Music Fest, Celtic Fest, World Music Fest, and, of course, the city's largest festival, the Taste of Chicago. Centuries of life had given her a great understanding and appreciation of all types of music, so Elizabeth loved them all.

According to the program booklet Elizabeth picked up off a chair near the back, the evening had started with one of the longer symphonic pieces in the orchestra's library. That was the reason the concert had lasted so long. But this final portion of the evening was made up entirely of smaller works performed by a chamber orchestra.

Although she enjoyed and appreciated all forms of music, the chamber works were her favorite. They reminded her of times long ago, when she would attend formal balls put on by the wealthy and dance to the string quartets playing the music of Haydn and Mozart. Nights in Vienna, London, and even Rome were filled with music, laughter, and always a victim or two at the end to feed her hunger.

But the chamber music brought out the melancholy in her, as well. It brought back memories of Dominick, who spent many of those long-ago nights by her side, and who she missed terribly. And there were always thoughts of the life she had left behind when she became what she was now.

One of Elizabeth's favorite benches, set back in the row of trees that line the Jackson Street side of the park, was unoccupied. The trees around it grew thick in the summer, and shut out light from not only the sun during the day but from the streetlights at night, as well. On evenings like this, it was almost entirely bathed in darkness. The walking paths that traced the edges of the park were only a few steps from the bench, providing a close view of the passersby. The music from the stage could be heard clearly through the speakers, and the crowd of picnickers could be watched over, like a herdsman watching over his sheep at pasture.

Pushing the back of her long black leather duster aside, she sat on her bench and closed her eyes for a moment to let the music sweep over her.

Her mind began to wander backward through time. Back through the years, the decades, and the centuries she had lived. Back to that fateful night to when she was given her immortality.

* * *

The year was 1259. The monarchs who ruled Scotland had settled themselves in the lowlands centuries earlier, leaving the Highland Lairds to run their own affairs, with the clan system of the late middle ages continuing as the prevailing system of government. The only time the two opposing sides faced each other was when the king sent expeditions to stop outlaw marauders from the Highlands who tried to bring their barbaric ways down into the lowlands. The ancient Gaelic language still flourished, and bagpipes could be heard on nearly each and every peak of the majestic mountains that gave the area its rugged beauty.

The men wore kilts made from their clan's tartan; the pattern and color of checks or plaids that distinguished them from other clans. From their waists hung sporrans, leather pouches decorated with fur. And oftentimes the men carried a traditional dirk, a long, straight-bladed dagger, as well.

The Bruce was one of the leading clans of the Highlands, with ancestral lines going back nearly two hundred years to an 11th-century Norman duke, Robert de Brus. He aided William I in his conquest of England in 1066 and was given lands there, with his son being granted fiefdoms in Scotland. The fifth Robert the Bruce was married to Isobel, the second daughter of David, Earl of Huntingdon, and brother of the Scottish kings Malcolm IV and William the Lion.

The Bruce who lived in 1259 had acquired greater lands, and had indentured several families to tend to the crops that tried to grow on their rocky land, and to serve as laborers for the rest of the clan. Elizabeth's family was one of those indentured families.

She and her sisters were good-natured girls, and despite their status as indentured servants, they found time to enjoy their lives and joke with each other about which of the strapping young village men they would marry when their time came.

Their home was a small, one-room building located behind the castle that served as the Bruce clan's main residence. They were lucky enough to have their home built from stone. Other indentured families had homes made from thin wood that rotted away far too easily, and were constantly in need of patching and repair. Inside their living quarters, Elizabeth's family managed to squeeze in several pieces of furniture around the stone hearth where they cooked their meals when not working in the main castle. Besides the table around which they ate, there were also two beds, one for the mother and father of the family, and one shared by Elizabeth and her three sisters.

Elizabeth's mother and father were both heavy sleepers, especially after putting in a long day of hard work for the Bruce. But the sisters would often remain awake into the dark hours of the night, giggling and laughing, and continuing the jokes and stories they told amongst themselves to stay entertained. They were careful not to wake their parents, however, for their father had an awful temper, and if he were to be disturbed in the middle of the night, there'd be hell to pay. The sisters all knew that their good-natured dispositions had been handed down to them entirely from their mother, and learned at a young age to do everything they could to keep their father's anger at bay. It was an anger born of his situation, the life that he had been forced into. He was angry at being worked like a slave, angry at not being able to provide for his family without the help of the Bruce, and angry that his children had nothing to look forward to in life but a continuation of the same meager existence. He was not angry with his family, but, unfortunately for them, they were the only ones at whom he could lash out and release his anger. It was they who felt the brunt of his wrath.

It was one of those dark nights, the dim yellow light of the moon shining through the cracks around the window, giving just enough light for the girls to play their late night games. Their parents lay across the room; the sounds of their snoring and heavy breathing wafted through the still night air, reminding the sisters not to get too loud and awaken their sleeping parents.

Elizabeth was the oldest, having reached the tender age of nineteen, already a full grown woman, but still forced to live her life as a child under the care of her parents, simply because that was the way it was in indentured families such as hers.

She was also the bravest of the four, so when they started hearing strange noises from outside the stone walls of their home, she was the one chosen to investigate.

The first time they heard the noise, they thought it was coming from their father, and quickly grew silent, hoping he would not be overly angry at having been bothered at this time of night. But the sounds of his deep snoring continued, and the sisters breathed a collective sigh of relief.

The second time they heard the noise, they realized it was coming from outside, and quickly determined that it must be one of the village boys who had taken a liking to one of the sisters, sneaking around, trying to get a peek at the object of his affection. Elizabeth opened the door just a crack and tried to figure out which of the boys it was.

She whispered, careful to be heard as clearly as possible on the outside but not wake her father on the inside, "William, is that you?"

William was one of the boys that Elizabeth had caught staring at Colleen, the second oldest of her sisters, on several occasions. And he was just the type to sneak out of his family's house at night and stir up trouble by getting involved with a servant girl.

"Robert?" she guessed after getting no response.

Elizabeth went through the litany of names of the boys she knew to hold a place in their hearts for one or more of the sisters, be it true affection or simple lust. When she ran out of names and still had no response, she closed the door and returned to her sisters, who had been giggling throughout the entire episode, wondering which boy it was, and which girl he was after. Each silently hoped that she was the one.

"Perhaps it was just someone passing by," Elizabeth suggested.

"It's terribly late to be just passing by. We're nowhere near the paths the guards follow," Colleen pointed out.

"Well, there's no one there now."

Just then, they heard the noise again, causing the younger sisters, Mary and Anne, to huddle together in fear. It was a small noise, but loud enough to be heard. It was the sound of hard leather, like the bottom of a well-worn shoe scraping ever-so-gently against stone. It wasn't a noise that would be made by accident, but one that would be employed to attract someone's attention. And it was obvious to Elizabeth that someone was playing with them and trying to scare them, because this time the noise came from above, as if someone were scraping the roof of their home.

"Time to see who's out there," Elizabeth whispered to her sisters. She held one finger over her mouth as a signal for them to remain quiet while she discovered the identity of their intruder.

Very gently, Elizabeth opened the door just far enough to slip through sideways. The door was old, made of thick oak, and tended to creak loudly if opened too far. Having snuck out on several occasions in the past, she knew exactly how far she could open it without a sound. As she reached the outside, she looked up, trying to find some sign of the visitor on their rooftop.

With no sign of anyone above, she turned to look down the rocky path that lead from their house to the main castle, and nearly screamed when she found a stranger standing directly behind her. How he had gotten so close without making a sound, Elizabeth could not explain, but his sudden nearness sent a chill up her spine.

The stranger had a strong face, with narrow lips and a perfectly straight, narrow nose. His eyes seemed to have no color whatsoever, just complete darkness, but with a distinct coolness. His arched eyebrows sat below a high, unlined forehead that completed a face of incredibly pale, almost white skin. His dark brown hair hung straight down past his shoulders, with a small black bow tied to the end directly between his shoulder blades. He had a confident, upright stance, and seemed entirely unlike anyone Elizabeth had even met. The clan members were not blessed with this man's solid good looks, and the indentured serving families would not have his confident attitude.

Dressed almost entirely in black, the stranger seemed to float as he circled Elizabeth. She wanted to run, to hide back inside the house, safe in the security of her father's presence, but she couldn't make her legs comply. She felt as if the stranger's gaze had taken away her ability to move.

"Have you ever wished for life immortal?" the stranger said softly. His voice was like both fire and ice. The accent sounded familiar, but Elizabeth knew it was not a voice from her beloved Highlands. She recalled a Frenchman who had visited several years earlier; this man's accent was nearly identical.

"Have you ever wanted to escape the drudgery of your indentured life?" the stranger continued. Elizabeth wanted to scream, to tell him to leave her alone, and let her be. But her voice had left her, and the terror she felt made it impossible to even respond to the stranger.

Suddenly, he stopped circling her and grabbed her roughly by the shoulders. The power that flowed from his delicate fingers was unlike anything Elizabeth had ever experienced. Even the forces of her father's most terrible rages were nothing compared to this man's power. Inside, Elizabeth was struggling to be free, screaming to be let go. But on the outside, she remained still. She could scarcely breathe, and she had been rendered mute by fear.

"Have you ever wished for unfathomable power?" He looked into her eyes, reaching deep into the recesses of her soul.

Somehow, he knew the answer to his questions even before Elizabeth discovered the strength in her voice to offer her one-word reply: "Yes."

With the agility of a cat, he took Elizabeth completely into his arms, gently tipped her head to the side, and brushed her long strawberry hair back and away from her pale neck. Elizabeth had lost all sense of what was happening to her, but the fear she had felt began to melt away in the clutch of this total stranger. Even as she felt the sharp pain as fangs bit though the soft flesh of her neck and began to feel dizzy and weak from the loss of blood, Elizabeth felt surprisingly calm and unafraid.

Just when she was sure she would take her last breath, never to see her sisters, her mother, or her father again, the stranger stopped, and gently lay her down on the stone pavement. The ground felt cool, as did the air that blew softly across her skin. Elizabeth wanted to close her eyes and drift away, but felt herself compelled to watch as he dragged a long, razor-sharp fingernail across his own arm, slicing the pale skin and then squeezing the flesh until his blood began to slowly flow. He knelt next to her, and held his arm to her lips.

"Drink," he commanded softly. "Drink, and you will free yourself from this existence forever."

Elizabeth hesitantly began to drink the blood from the stranger's arm. As she felt the liquid fire flow into her, she felt her thirst grow, and she drank until he forced her to stop. It was then that she felt a sickening feeling creep through her body. Her veins burned, and she began to writhe in agony on the ground as her body jerked and twisted. She didn't understand why this man, who she inexplicably trusted, stood over her in this moment of torment and physical agony with a grin on his face, displaying each and every one of his perfectly white teeth.

"What's happening to me?" she moaned, pleading for help from the stranger as she felt herself burning from inside.

"It is only your mortal death you are feeling. Do not fight it. It will soon pass, and you will be reborn. You will become like me, a child of the night, an immortal. The night will be your playground."

As the pain began to subside, she looked once again into the stranger's eyes, which she noticed had become a bright, fiery red. "Who are you?"

"I am an immortal. My name is Dominick. And from this moment on, I am your father and your teacher."

FIVE

Elizabeth's violet eyes flew wide open as a young couple passed along the footpath near her bench. Her reverie had been broken by the soft, schoolgirl-ish laughter of the woman.

"Oh, John," the young woman giggled, "I said not until we're married."

"But, Sarah, the wedding is only a month away," he pleaded with her. "Just this one time won't hurt."

Elizabeth focused on the couple as they strolled along the path, holding hands, whispering in each other's ear, and ignoring the throng of people around them. The man was tall, over six feet, with a long, angular face sporting a goatee making him look like a beatnik left over from the 1960's. His blue cotton button-down shirt was covered by a paisley vest, another relic from years gone by.

Sarah, his betrothed, wasn't quite overweight, but the tight blue jeans and dark red T-shirt she wore were snug against her body. A mass of short, dark, curly hair topped a face that was remarkably plain. She wore no makeup to cover or accentuate her ordinary looks.

Elizabeth sniffed the air and caught the scent of something wonderful: virginity. Hmmm, she thought. Virgin blood. It's been over two hundred years since I tasted that pleasure.

Rising slowly from the bench, she began to follow, keeping to the shadows cast by the long line of trees. When the couple made their way through the crowd along the path near the front of the music shell, oblivious to the music coming from the chamber orchestra still playing on stage, Elizabeth moved quickly around the back of the building, appearing on the far side well ahead of the meandering pair, still hand in hand, still laughing softly at their own playful, personal teasing.

They reached the ramp to the north of the music shell that led downward to the park's restroom facilities. The concert was nearing its conclusion, and few people remained in the lower level. It was a perfect opportunity. Elizabeth followed as they made their descent along the cement walkway, careful not to get too close. She did her best to appear just another music lover walking to the restrooms.

Sarah kissed John lightly on the lips, passed the entrance to the men's room and walked into the women's. There was no actual door to the public restroom. Instead there was a series of short corridors, each turning ninety degrees into the next. It kept those outside from looking in and insured complete privacy for those who entered, but it also had the effect of making users of the facility feel like mice in a maze, trying to get to the cheese that waited on the far side.

As John stood waiting for his fiancée, Elizabeth slipped past him. She managed to walk directly behind him as he turned, looking at the walls, amazed at the lack of décor in the public facility.

Elizabeth entered the main area of the ladies' room just in time to see Sarah walk into the stall at the far end and close the door. Crouching down, she peered through the foot-high gap at the bottom of each square, aluminum stall. Seeing no feet besides those of her prey at the far end, Elizabeth determined that she and Sarah were now alone.

Elizabeth walked to the far end of the long line of porcelain sinks, each one more chipped and cracked than the preceding one. The steel faucets had long since lost their "stainless" status, having been overcome by rust and filth. Elizabeth couldn't imagine that people actually used these ghastly sinks to wash their hands. She hoped the water that flowed from them was much cleaner than they themselves.

When she reached the last sink, she turned and stepped toward the stall. The closed door, with its graffiti and artwork carved by some bored teen with a sharp knife, faced the inside wall of the restroom only a few feet away. Elizabeth reclined against the wall, balancing on her left leg, the right bent at the knee, her foot placed flat against the cold brick wall. She crossed her arms on her chest and waited, staring straight at the door. Patience was one thing she had plenty of, especially when it meant feeding her hunger with the purity of virgin blood. It was indeed a rarity to find such a thing in such a large city, and it was something to be savored.

The flush of the toilet told Elizabeth it was almost time. She began to feel the excitement of what was about to happen; it was so close. But still she waited, for she had been taught that, at a time like this, patience was a virtue.

When the door to the stall opened, Sarah was startled at the sight of the tall, slender woman leaning against the wall directly in front of her. She hadn't heard anyone enter, and thought she was alone. She looked down the row of empty stalls, and wondered why this woman with the violet eyes was waiting for this particular stall. Even more curious was why this woman was staring at her.

"Oh," she gasped in surprise. "I'm sorry. I had no idea anyone else was in here."

Elizabeth continued to look directly at the other woman. "That's okay. I was just waiting."

"Waiting for the stall?"

"No, my dear, not the stall." Elizabeth pushed herself from the wall to a rigid stance. "I've been waiting for you."

Before Sarah could figure out what was happening, Elizabeth flew at her, arms outstretched, reaching for Sarah's head and neck. Her mouth opened wide, displaying the deadly fangs within before they sank deep into Sarah's jugular. Elizabeth wrapped her arms tightly around the woman, holding her up so that she could drink the sweet nectar of virgin blood. Sarah had fainted at the sight of Elizabeth's fangs, and was showing no resistance. It's a shame, Elizabeth thought as she drained the life from her victim. It's much more fun when they fight back, like the journalist had done once he realized what was happening. Instead, her victim's body went limp, and quickly began to turn cold as the blood that had once pumped through her veins was drained away. It would have been an agonizing and painful way to die had she stayed conscious.

Elizabeth dropped the dead woman to the cold stone floor. She wiped the blood from her mouth, and licked the last of it from her fingers before striding to the nearest mirror, looking through the grime and filth to the reflective surface that was hidden far beneath, and fixed her hair, making sure it was all back in place.

She took two steps back toward the now still body of Sarah crumpled on the ground, intending to leave it locked in the stall she had come from. She knew there was a "Movies in the Park" event later that week, but if the stall stayed closed, no one would find the body until the flesh was gone, and any sign of Elizabeth gone with it.

Dominick had tutored her on how to live in the shadows, out of sight of those that would do her harm if she were discovered for what she was. And he taught her to hide the bodies of her victims. She couldn't simply leave corpses lying around; she would be too easily discovered. But it wasn't necessary to completely destroy them, either. Once a human was bitten and bled almost dry, the body would decompose at a rapid rate. Within three to four days, nothing would be left but the bones. Bones which could not be traced to a deadly bite on the neck.

But then she heard a noise. Thinking someone else was coming into the restroom, she had to leave fast. There was no time to hide the body. It was a mistake to leave it lying there in the open on the floor, but that was much more desirable than the alternative of being found standing over it. She might have thought differently if she had realized that the noise was only a small chunk of plaster separating itself from the worn ceiling and falling into one of the porcelain sinks.

When Elizabeth swiftly exited the restroom, she saw John still waiting for his future bride. She almost laughed out loud as she wondered just how long he would stand there looking the fool and waiting. Should she end his suffering by taking his life and allowing him to join his beloved, or should she leave him to live in misery, having just lost the love of his life while he stood, completely unaware, mere yards away?

She knew he wouldn't wait long before going to look for Sarah, and the corpse would be found easily, since she hadn't had time to hide it.

Others were heading toward the restrooms now, so someone would surely find the body, even if John didn't. And she certainly couldn't feed on every person who approached just to hide her recent kill. And, besides, all those corpses being found together in the park would make the public far too cautious, making it difficult for her to find victims in the future.

She decided to let him live, and hoped the body of the virgin would not lead to her exposure. But that didn't mean she couldn't have a small measure of fun with the young man.

"Got a cigarette?" she asked him. He had been staring at her since she walked out of the restroom, and she had stared back.

"I don't smoke," the young man replied.

With a laugh that reminded John of rustling dead leaves, Elizabeth replied, "Neither do I." She strode away, leaving him looking after her, a look of utter confusion on his face.

Thinking about the mistake she had just made, Elizabeth suddenly felt angry. She had let the thought of virgin blood get the best of her, and hadn't used the care and caution she should have. Everything around her was starting to make her feel annoyed. The mortals, the sounds of the night, the smell of the park, everything. But especially the mortals. It had been centuries since she had felt this angry, and she tried to shake off the feeling as she walked quickly up the ramp and back to the darkness of the park above.

She was shaking her head from side to side, trying to clear the feelings of anger and frustration, unaware of where she was walking, when she bumped directly into one of the police offers on foot patrol in the park.

"What's the hurry, lady?" He was one of the biggest cops she'd seen, taller than she was, with the body of a professional football player, only more muscular.

But despite his large size and brute strength, it was with great ease that Elizabeth wrapped her hands around the sides of the big man's head and twisted with a strength he would have never expected from this seemingly delicate woman. He didn't have the opportunity to appreciate her strength, however, because the vertebrae at the top of his neck had snapped with the violent twist of his head, ripping apart his spinal column, and killing him instantly.

She dropped the body, and stood over it for a moment, wondering why she had killed this man. It wasn't to feed her hunger, and it certainly hadn't been in self defense. It was an entirely senseless killing, something she had never done before.

She glanced around to see who might have noticed the act of violence she'd just committed in clear view of dozens of people. By some miracle, each and every one of them had their attention focused elsewhere. Most were watching and listening to the final strains of the chamber orchestra. Some were young lovers sitting on benches beneath the canopy of trees, oblivious to everything around them. Still others were simply minding their own business and had not been looking in Elizabeth's direction. Perhaps, thought Elizabeth, the fact that it was a cop was a small blessing. She'd learned that people tended not to watch police officers too closely out of some unrealistic fear that doing so would result in the police officer paying undue attention to them in return. In this case, Elizabeth was thankful for that particular quirk of human nature.

As quickly as she dared, still trying to escape notice, she dragged the body into the bushes that filled the area between the city sidewalk along Columbus Avenue and the inner walkway of the park. She wanted to flee, and, in her haste, she took little care hiding the big cop's body. When Elizabeth sped away from the scene, headed south toward Buckingham Fountain, she didn't notice one leg still slightly uncovered, sticking out into the walkway.

She crossed Jackson Street with such speed that the cars trying to fight their way through the heavy traffic that always marked the end of the concerts had to suddenly slam on their brakes to avoid hitting the blur that passed before them. Some nearly collided with others; several began blaring their horns, drowning out the last notes of the concert; others shouted obscenities, and gave the "one finger salute" that had universal meaning nearly the world over.

Elizabeth left behind the chaos she had just created, and slowed only when she reached the rose gardens that led the way to the world famous fountain ahead. Two paved paths ran the length of the block, allowing visitors to walk in the midst of the many various plants, flowers, and other vegetation in and around the area. The garden displayed a spectacular floral view when seen under the natural light of the sun, but Elizabeth had never been able to see them under those conditions. She had only seen them at night, lit by the moon, stars, and artificial light of the city's electric lamps.

Tonight the city's lights were not needed. The sky was clear, allowing the moon and stars to provide plenty of light for the garden. Elizabeth found one of her favorite spots in the rose garden and lay down on the ground, as far away from the pavement as possible. It was a place where she could be completely alone with her thoughts, and have no fear of discovery.

She looked up at the sky, the stars tiny pinholes of light in the black curtain, and wondered what had made her emotions suddenly turn sour. Was it the effect of the virgin blood? After all, she hadn't tasted something that pure in a very long time. She tried to recall Dominick's teachings and whether or not there was a danger to be aware of when drinking the blood of a virgin. Nothing came to mind.

Could it have been the amount of alcohol in Sarah's blood? Elizabeth had been able to taste it while she drank. Obviously, the couple had been out for an evening of music and wine. It wasn't much, but it was there. She dismissed that as the possibility for her mood when she remembered the amount of whiskey in the journalist's blood the night before. He had not had any negative effect on her state of mind.

Perhaps it was just the thrill of the kill. The excitement of the moment taking over, the blood lust making her act irrational. Was that what had happened?

Or perhaps she was just getting sloppy. If that were the case, she would have to do something about it.

No, it was none of these. She was fairly certain it was something else entirely.

In the past, she had had premonitions of events to come. They were rarely detailed thoughts, just general feelings. But they were usually accurate. And when the premonitions were of evil to come, they always put her in a foul mood. Perhaps that was what had done it. Perhaps she was feeling something evil coming again. But what could it be?

She lay there in the rose garden, her alabaster skin bathed in moonlight, and listened as the crowd broke up. The long concert had finally ended.

Life went on around Elizabeth, with a few scattered people walking through the garden for one last look at the foliage before heading home. She remained motionless, not daring to move for fear of calling unwanted attention to herself. She was glad the rose garden was in an out-of-the-way location; only a handful of people walked through. Most were headed in the opposite directions, north to the park's underground parking garage and west to the trains and busses.

Elizabeth continued to think about the reasons for her dismal mood. It had to be another premonition, but she couldn't put her finger on it. She had certainly snapped when she ran into the cop. That she knew for sure. And she hadn't been thinking clearly when she killed the girl in the restroom, either. She shouldn't have done it there, with her fiancé waiting just outside.

She spent the entire night sorting through what had happened and why, and came to no conclusions. Her final thought was that she never wanted to make another senseless and meaningless kill unless her immortality depended on it.

SIX

John looked at his watch and wondered what was taking so long. Sarah had been in the restroom for far longer than he would have expected. He knew she had had quite a bit of wine, more than she normally would have. But even that shouldn't cause such a delay. He was growing impatient staring at the worn concrete walls. He was tempted to go into the women's restroom himself, but there were other women headed that way, so he decided not to invade their privacy.

Could Sara have simply passed out? If she did, he would certainly have to tease her about it later. She'd hear no end of the story of how she drank too much wine, got tipsy and passed out in the public restroom. It would be a funny little anecdote to tell their children and grandchildren in years to come.

Suddenly a woman running out of the ladies' room interrupted John's thoughts of the future. She was screaming, "Call 911! Call 911! There's a dead woman in there!"

John didn't hesitate, but ran as quickly as he could, literally bouncing off the walls that formed the maze into the women's restroom. Somehow he knew, even before he reached the interior and saw the crumpled body in front of the far stall, that the "dead woman" was the woman he loved.

His mad dash toward Sarah's body ended and he dropped to his knees, cradling her head in his lap. He screamed and began to cry in anguish as an unworldly pain began to form in his chest, crushing his heart. The future he had just been dreaming of, his plans, and all his hopes for their life together had been destroyed in an instant.

* * *

Jeff had found a great way to watch the concerts all the way to the end and still beat the crowd that trudged en masse to the trains that would take them home. For a long time, he simply left early, missing what was often the best part of the concert. Because of his social anxiety, he didn't have a choice. He had to get ahead of the throng and get on the Red Line train headed north before too many others squeezed on with him.

The train station was three blocks from the park, and once the Chicago ELs, named for the fact that many of the tracks are elevated above the streets, began allowing bicycles on their trains, Jeff began taking advantage of it. He would ride his bike to the train, take it with him to the concert, and then, as soon as the final notes finished and the applause began, he would wheel back to the train, far ahead of everyone else.

Tonight, he didn't get that far.

He was sitting on his bike, one foot on the ground, leaning up against a metal railing along the north side of the seating area. It had become his customary spot. During the last chamber piece he strapped on his foam bicycling helmet, colored the same bright red and black as the aluminum frame of his ten-speed and the spandex shorts he wore when riding. The only part of him that didn't match his color scheme was the baggy white T-shirt.

As the final piece ended, he stood up and spun the bike away from the stage, turning the light frame easily, slid his black bicycling shoes into the pedal straps and began pedaling down the paved walkway toward the park exit at Monroe and Columbus. As he approached the exit, he moved to the outside edge of the cement walkway, avoiding the railings along the inner edge of the pavement, and began to speed past the bushes that were close to his side. His front wheel suddenly hit something, unexpectedly jarring it to a stop and sending him into a cartwheel over the handlebars.

After sliding to a stop on the pavement he stood up and brushed himself off, feeling lucky he hadn't been going faster, since a flip like that didn't require much speed to cause real injury to the rider. He was fortunate that the only thing to suffer any serious damage was his pride. A few other concert patrons had already begun heading for the exit, and most of them saw him do his unintended bicycle trick.

He picked up his bike, and, seeing no damage, took a quick peek at what he had hit. He figured the right thing to do would be to get it off of the sidewalk before it caused a fall for someone else in the stampede of folks leaving the concert. He also wanted to make sure that those who saw his spill knew that he hadn't simply fallen over. Something had gotten in his way and caused his somersault.

What he found wasn't something, but someone. There was a foot sticking out of the bushes. At first he thought it might be a bum who'd fallen asleep during the concert. But bums wouldn't have nice, well-shined shoes like the one on this foot, so he peered further into the bushes to see who it was. He couldn't see the face of the guy lying in the bushes because he was standing between the moon and the body, casting a shadow. But he could make out the clothing. It was a cop's uniform.

That would have been enough to send him calling for help, but when he stepped around the body, his shadow shifted with him, and the moonlight revealed that the man's head was turned practically backward, a large pool of blood surrounding the tears in the flesh around his neck.

Jeff spun away from the body and vomited the contents of his stomach into the next bush.

Once the wave of nausea was over, Jeff fished his cell phone from his pocket, and with a shaky hand dialed 911. He was careful not to look directly at the severed, twisted head, as if doing so would turn him to stone, like the snaked head of Medusa. But he couldn't help but glance curiously every few moments, closing his eyes and fighting the returning nausea each time.

"What's your emergency?" the bored operator said once the call connected.

Jeff managed to give her all the grisly details of what he had found in the bushes. It didn't take long for the call to go out over the radio and, in what seemed like seconds, Chicago police were on the scene.

A couple of officers drove small stakes in the ground around the body, and taped off the area with their familiar yellow "police line: do not cross" tape. Another stood guard over the body until more backup could arrive, and yet another took Jeff aside to question him about how he found the body, and what, if anything, he saw.

Soon, the customary crime scene crowd gathered. In this case, it had already been assembled; people simply had to move a few hundred feet from the concert to the scene. The forensics team arrived and began the grim job of photographing the body and collecting what little evidence they could find.

* * *

John couldn't stand the thought of leaving Sarah's body in such a filthy place as the ladies' room at the park. And he was far too distraught to realize that by moving her he was possibly destroying evidence that would help find the person who'd killed her. So while he dimly realized that he should probably wait for the police, he felt compelled to get her out of there.

He picked up her limp body and, struggling under the dead weight in his arms, pushed his way through the small crowd of women who had gathered around. He climbed the inclined walkway toward the upper level, barely able to see through the tears that flowed from his eyes.

Detective John Rojas had been on the perimeter of the crime scene around the dead police officer in the bushes, and caught sight of John and Sarah out of the corner of his eye.

John sank to his knees, still clutching Sarah in his arms as Detective Rojas approached. The detective had a hard time trying to convince the man, who was clearly in shock, to release the body and let it fall gently to the ground. That wasn't going to happen. Not yet. The man was not ready to relinquish the body he held so tightly.

"Can you tell me what happened?" Rojas spoke quietly, one hand resting on the man's shoulder.

John had a blank look on his face. The tears had momentarily stopped and shock had begun to take over. "All I know is we had some wine and Sarah had to use the bathroom. She didn't come out for a long time, so I figured maybe she passed out or was being sick. Next thing I know, a woman came running out of the bathroom screaming about a dead woman, and I went in and found her like this." With that, the tears returned, and John's entire body shook with painful sobs.

After waiting for the round of grief to subside, Rojas took up his gentle questioning. "Is there anything else you remember about your time waiting for Sarah?"

John thought or a moment, trying to hold back the tears again. "Only a woman. There was a tall, elegant-looking lady wearing a long black leather duster. She came out of the bathroom and asked me for a cigarette. "

"Can you describe this woman to me?"

John searched his recent memory. He had always been good at picking out and remembering the smallest of details. "She was tall, but not quite as tall as I am. She was slender and had flaming red hair. The most remarkable thing was her eyes. They were violet and rimmed in red. She had a laugh like dry leaves, and she moved very fast as if she was in a hurry to get somewhere."

Rojas got the attention of a member of the forensics team and motioned him over. Working together, the two men managed to finally convince John to release Sarah. The forensics team was split into groups to gather evidence in several places at once. The largest continued to work around the body of the dead officer. A couple started dealing with Sarah. A third group rushed down the ramp to the restroom where she had been murdered.

* * *

Chief David Duncan didn't usually visit crime scenes unless it was something high profile or something important to a case he was dealing with personally. But as soon as he heard that one of his officers had been found dead in Grant Park, he rushed to his unmarked car and got to the scene.

The Chief was a life-long Chicagoan, and proud to serve the city where he had grown up. But a life of deep-dish pizza, Italian sausage, and beer had given him a rather soft-edged physique. He joked that he was still in shape, "round" being technically a shape. When he sat at his desk, he could practically set his coffee cup on the ledge formed by his protruding stomach. His neck had grown several sizes, keeping him from ever buttoning the top button of his shirts, and forcing him to leave knot of his tie part way down his chest, what he referred to as "half-mast". He only raised it up to its highest possible point when he was in front of the cameras or addressing the public.

But underneath it all he was a physically strong man, and he could still keep up with the young kids recruited out of the Academy. His face might have been etched with a few more lines than theirs, a product of the stress of years on the beat followed by years in charge of the city, but most people viewed them as a sign of strength and a sign of stability. He remained a fairly good looking man, with a square jaw and a nose only slightly crooked, a reminder of the two times it had been broken while breaking up street fights. And his eyes still held the same glowing intensity as when he was a rookie cop, filled with idealism and plans to clean up the city single-handedly. It was a goal he still carried with him, in the recesses of his mind.

As he walked into Grant Park, he met Detective Mike Green, who was returning to the park to talk to Sam about the upcoming weekend and break the bad news that he'd be up to his eyeballs in reports and paperwork for the next few days. Mike had been listening to the radio and heard about the incident at the park, but had no idea as to the extent of what had happened.

The two walked together through the mass of people that had nearly formed a wall around the dead cop, Mike fighting his way through a crowd for the second time that night. When they reached the eye of the storm, they looked down at the twisted head, and the shredded flesh around the neck.

"Oh, my God!" Mike exclaimed. Through the blood and carnage he instantly recognized the face of his dear friend Sam. "That's Sam Sloane!"

"Sam?" said the Chief. "Did you two know each other well?"

Mike got down on one knee next to the body of his friend. "Yes. We went through the Academy together. We still get together on weekends. He's the one I was coming down here to talk to."

"When's the last time you saw him?"

"Not quite an hour ago. We met for coffee around the corner."

"Well, that certainly narrows down the time this happened." Although the Chief sounded cold and unfeeling with his immediate and methodical gathering of information, those that worked for him knew that the death of one of his officers was killing him inside. His quick survey of the facts was simply his way of trying to get to the bottom of the mystery of who could have done such a thing, and then to make sure they were thoroughly punished.

"He graduated at the top of our class." Mike was almost talking to himself, in a far-away world. "He was a great cop."

"Since you were so close to him," the Chief interrupted, "I don't want you working on this case. You're too close to it."

"Can I at least be the one to tell his wife?"

The Chief thought about it for a moment, wondering who better to inform the family than someone close to them and able to comfort them. "Permission granted," he finally said. "Why don't you get out of here, away from this mess, and go talk to his wife."

Mike got to his feet, his legs wobbling and unsteady, and strode off to his car, which was sitting just beyond the police barricade. But instead of starting the engine right away, he found himself staring at nothing for the second time in the past half hour. He reflected on the years of friendship he and Sam had shared, from the Police Academy to picnicking and going on vacations with each other's family to their simple meetings for coffee, like they had done—or the last time—just a short while earlier. And he reflected on what could very well become yet another unsolved, violent murder of someone close to him. First his sister, then his parents, and now his best friend.

He went numb when he realized that he had not only one family to inform of the terrible tragedy, but two. Sam's wife, Rachel, of course would need to be told. But it might turn out to be even more difficult to tell Jane, his own wife.

* * *

Chief Duncan looked around, trying to find Detective Rojas, who should have been in charge of the crime scene, and who would be in charge of the following investigation.

"Rojas!" He barked, trying to get the attention of that individual.

The rail-thin detective who was still talking to John excused himself and jogged back over to the original crime scene where the Chief was waiting.

"And just where the hell have you been?"

"I was dealing with the other victim."

"What other victim?"

"Chief, there's more than one victim."

"What do you mean 'more than one'?" The color began to drain from the Chief's face at the thought that two of his police officers had been murdered.

Rojas led him toward the ramp where Sarah's body was being photographed, and where John was still huddled in shock, staring at what had been his fiancée.

"What do we know about this one?" the Chief said with just a touch of relief that it was not another of his men. It was a tragedy nonetheless, but at least he hadn't lost another cop.

Rojas repeated the story he'd been told while the Chief watched John, who was clearly still in shock.

The Chief left Rojas with the body of Sarah, and quickly returned to the scene around Detective Sam Sloane's inert form. The members of the forensics team going about their business reminded Chief Duncan of flies swarming around garbage.

Never in his twenty five years on the force had he seen such disregard for human life. Truly he must be dealing with a psychopath. Chief Duncan had a long night ahead of him. He swore softly as he realized that he had only two cigarettes left in his pack.

* * *

Detective Mike Green decided to drive to his own house and break the news to his wife before going to the home of his good friend Sam. He had to let Rachel know that an unknown assailant had killed her husband in the line of duty, but he would tell his own wife first that one of their best friends was gone.

He pulled into the unlit driveway of his two-story home in Park Ridge. It was a modest two-story home, on a quiet, ordinary street. The money from his parents' estate had been more than enough for a down payment on the property, but with family finances being tight, he was having a hard time covering the monthly mortgage payments.

He parked his car next to his wife's Mazda in the two-car garage and entered the house through the connecting door into the kitchen. The house was dark; it was already nearing midnight, and his wife and their daughter were already in bed, fast asleep. But Mike managed to navigate in the dark, only tripping occasionally over a toy or other child's object that had not been put away.

Mike crept up the carpeted stairs and stopped at the first door in the short hallway, the door to his daughter's bedroom. Opening it slowly so as not to wake her, he entered the room and took a moment to gaze lovingly at Meagan. The four-year-old looked like an angel with her blonde curly hair spread across her pillow forming a halo around her head, and her thumb still in her mouth. Meagan never sucked her thumb when she was awake, not even as a tiny baby. But every night in bed, it was the only way she would go to sleep.

As gently as possible, Mike pulled the blanket up around her shoulders, and bent down to kiss Meagan on the forehead. She stirred, but did not wake.

Mike backed out of the room and closed the door as quietly as he had opened it. He'd begun to walk down the hallway toward his own bedroom door when he was stopped by a familiar pair of paws on his knees. He bent down and patted the head of the family beagle.

"Say, Digger, you watching the ladies for me while I work?"

Digger's whole body began to shake with excitement.

"Down, boy, I'm home on business, not to play."

Digger sensed that something was wrong. He backed down and trotted toward Meagan's room, where he lay down in front of the toddler's door, protecting her from whatever evil it was that his owner had to deal with.

Mike quietly opened the door to the bedroom he had shared with his wife of six years. Jane had seen him through a lot, stuck by his side through his Academy days, finally marrying him once he graduated, and supported him in every decision he made. She even helped him to kick the drinking habit that had almost ended his career before it began.

Quietly, Mike sat in the chair on Jane's side of the bed and put his head in his hands. He didn't know if he had enough strength left to wake her and tell her about Sam. The only thing he was certain of was that he had no more tears left to shed.

Mike got up from the chair and sat on his wife's side of the bed. He placed a hand on her shoulder and shook her. Jane awoke with a start and sat up immediately.

"Mike! What's wrong?" She knew that being awakened in the middle of the night almost always meant something serious had happened.

Mike grabbed his wife and held her tightly. Although he had been sure his tears had run dry, he began to cry again.

"Mike? Mike, what's wrong?"

"Oh, Jane, something terrible has happened tonight. Sam's gone."

"Gone? What do you mean gone?"

Mike began to cry harder. "He was lost in the line of duty. Someone killed him tonight in Grant Park."

Jane didn't know what to say, so she just held her husband, offering silent comfort against something that couldn't be comforted. A part of her gave thanks that it wasn't Mike who'd been killed. She knew he had a dangerous job, and every day could be the day she'd get a visit from a sad-faced, solemn police officer coming to break the news. Her husband and their daughter were her entire life. She didn't know what she would do if she lost either one.

Husband and wife sat intertwined and cried together over the senseless loss of a good cop, a great man, and a dear friend.

SEVEN

The night sky began to turn purple, signaling the rising of the morning sun over Lake Michigan. Elizabeth had to get back to her coffin in the top of the old Water Tower or she would—quite literally—be toast.

Rising from the rose garden where she'd spent the entire night, brushing the dirt from her clothes, she looked around the garden. She was pleased not to see anyone out for an early morning stroll. She made her way across Jackson Street, through Grant Park, and began retracing her steps back to her "home".

She moved much slower than when she had come the opposite way earlier in the night, still trying to make sense of the events of the last hours. For the first time in three hundred years, Elizabeth felt alone. Very alone, and scared, with no one to turn to.

She made her way north on Michigan Avenue, walking among the early risers and the overworked people who had to be on their way to their daily jobs well before the sun rose.

Near the north end of Michigan Avenue, near the world-famous John Hancock Center, she came to Chicago's Water Tower. Designed in 1869, it had become one of Chicago's most cherished landmarks. Originally designed to house a 138-foot tall three-foot diameter standpipe, the Water Tower, along with the pumping station located across the avenue, controlled the flow of fresh water for most of downtown Chicago. It was the limestone shipped in from Joliet and used in the construction of both buildings that saved the structures on October 9, 1871, when the Great Chicago Fire leveled almost every other building in the area.

The standpipe was removed in 1911 and the tower temporarily abandoned. A year later, Elizabeth arrived in Chicago and was instantly attracted to the tower's Gothic architectural elements, originally designed to recapture the romance of medieval castles. She moved into the cupola and sealed off her new home from the four lower sections of the building.

She had a minor discovery scare in 1972 when the building was nationally recognized and the Chicago Landmarks Commission turned the lower levels of the tower into an art gallery where tourists could get a glimpse of Chicago history. Luckily for Elizabeth, the CLC only used the ground floor. The top level was simply forgotten, and Elizabeth was able to remain in her Chicago home.

Before opening her coffin and going to sleep for the day, Elizabeth stood for a moment in front of the windows just inside the balcony atop her Water Tower and looked out at the gardens and fountain to the west where dozens of mortals would sit and relax throughout the day, completely unaware that just 150 feet above their heads slept an immortal with the ability to take their lives in an instant.

Elizabeth turned to her coffin and raised the lid. What a terrible night, she thought as she lowered herself onto the rose-colored satin lining and closed the lid. It took almost no time for her to drift into a fitful sleep.

As she slept, Elizabeth dreamt again of Dominick. She couldn't believe that it had been nearly four hundred years since she last saw him. Her dreams took her back to one of the last times they spent together.

* * *

In the early 1600's, Venice was not yet entirely flooded. The Venetians had no qualms about simply throwing their trash out the window and into the street, leaving a continuing stench of rotting garbage throughout the city. But the lagoon did spill over into the polluted streets on a fairly regular basis, flushing the offal out to sea, and turning the swelled canals into a popular form of travel.

Elizabeth was with Dominick, floating in a gondolier through one of those canals. She heard his thick French accent and felt his flowing black locks as she lay beneath him. His hair seemed to surround her in a curtain and, although she missed the sun, she couldn't have been happier.

She reached up to him to pull him down for a kiss, but he grabbed her hand and shook his head no.

"Don't you understand dear child, it is not for us to experience the same type of love that mortals experience."

"But I feel a hunger for you that no amount of blood could satisfy."

Dominick threw his head back and with a cruel laugh said, "Yes, I know that hunger all too well. But you and I must never give in to it. The Code does not permit it. Other hungers, yes, but not the hunger of physical love, whether it be with mortal or immortal."

"I don't understand," she whined. "Why can't I make love to you like a mortal woman makes love to a mortal man?"

"We do not live by the same rules of nature, Elizabeth. Do you remember the night you became immortal? And the instructions I have given you about the Code? You must keep the Code foremost in your mind at all times."

Elizabeth refused to answer him, giving him the petulant look of a young child who wasn't getting her way.

"You died from your mortal life and became something more. You are able to sense more than any mortal could sense. You see in the dark like the owl. You have strength that no mortal could ever match. And your speed is faster than that of a cheetah. Elizabeth, darling, you are something that only another immortal could understand."

"But there are times when you don't seem to understand me. Yet you are the one that made me!" exclaimed Elizabeth, growing more and more annoyed with her companion.

He laughed at her as a parent laughs at a curious child asking questions about things they are far too young to understand. "I understand you more than you know. It is you who still does not understand."

"What is it that I do not understand?"

"Your immortality comes with a price. You must live according to the Code, and refuse to give in to certain hungers."

Jerking her chin away from him, she said, "If I have all the power you say I have, I shouldn't have to follow those rules. And I certainly don't need you, do I?"

With that, she flew out of the gondolier and disappeared into the night sky over the rooftops of Venice, leaving Dominick alone. He knew it was a mistake to let her go. She had not learned the lessons of the Code. Yet he also knew she needed time away from him to think. What he didn't realize was that she would take nearly forty years before she would see him again.

Those forty years were lonely ones for Elizabeth. She traveled all over Europe and met many other immortals, some of them as young as she, and some older than Dominick. Many of them taught her the lessons of the Code, lessons she would have learned from Dominick had she not gotten angry and flown away from him.

One of the lessons she learned was that some small traits from her mortal life would always remain with her. It was true of any mortal turned immortal. In her case, the traits she retained were her pride and her boldness. She sated her pride and fed her boldness by feasting on the blood of mortals that she considered a "challenge". She fed on those that other mortals considered "famous". Her victims included the Marquis De Sade and Countess Elizabeth Bathory; the murders of both remained unsolved in the years that followed. The ongoing mysteries surrounding many of her victims and the fact that the mortals had not the slightest idea that it was the work of a vampire was what fed the great pride she retained.

Over time she became bored with simply feeding on mortals. She needed to keep herself entertained, so she began to feed in unusual ways. She didn't care whether or not it was considered "normal" according to vampiric law, or acceptable under the Code. She was impetuous and unorthodox. She would find the line dividing what the Code allowed and what it did not, stand with her toes on that line, and lean as far over as she could. It was dangerous to her, and to all other immortals, but it would be years before she learned the importance of living according to the immortal laws.

While in London in the late 1800's, she fell in with a group of immortals who had taken a liking to eating the body parts of their victims. She tried to join in their feasts, but the taste of human flesh repulsed her. She didn't realize that these immortals were not vampires, like her, but ghouls. She would simply carve up her victims, feeding the removed organs to her new friends. She never allowed them to touch her victims. They would have left nothing but bones. It was much more entertaining for her to watch in the days that followed each attack, and laugh at the mortals who searched every crack and crevice looking for the person they thought was responsible: Jack the Ripper.

Through the years she joined countless bands of vampires as they searched for victims. Although the others enjoyed these hunts, and Elizabeth knew it was necessary to survive, something inside her told her it was wrong.

EIGHT

Mike and Jane made breakfast for their small family, then finished their normal morning routine of taking Digger for a walk, washing the dishes together, and taking out the trash. They tried not to let their grief show in front of Meagan. She was still too young to understand the complexities of life and death. Plus she adored Sam, and would be crushed when she was told that she wouldn't get to see him anymore. They'd decided it would be best to get through their own grieving process first, so that they could better support their young daughter through hers.

But no matter how hard they tried, they were simply going through the motions of their routine, not really thinking about anything other than the events of the night before.

After the kitchen was cleaned up, Mike decided that it was finally time to go and talk to Rachel. He really should have gone the previous night and told her about what happened before she had a chance to hear about it on the news, but once he started talking to his wife, he just couldn't get himself to go. He needed to be with her for a while so they could lean on each other's shoulders. He'd need all the strength he could muster to tell his best friend's wife that her husband was dead, and being with Jane helped him build up that strength.

Jane offered to tag along to lend a little extra support. She suggested it might make things easier.

Mike put his hand on her cheek and said "No, babe. This is part of my job, and it's something I have to do myself."

"Well, if you're sure." Jane didn't sound convinced.

"Besides, Meagan would have to tag along, too. And that may not be the best way to tell her what's happened to Sam"

"Sam?" The little girl's face lit up at the mention of his name. "Is Sam coming over today?"

"No, sweetie," Jane said, crouching down and taking the toddler by the shoulders. "Sam's not coming today. In fact," she looked to Mike for support. He merely nodded. "Sam won't be coming over any more."

"Did Sam and Daddy have a fight?" It was more a statement than a question, the kind only a child can make. She crossed her arms and gave her father a stern look that said, "You go make up with my friend Sam right now, so he can come over again."

"No, honey, they didn't have a fight."

"Sam is, well …." Mike tried to find a way to explain it to the little girl. "Sam died last night."

"Died?" The toddler had a look of confusion mixed with

concentration on her face.

"Yes, honey."

"Like when Digger's Mommy died and we buried her?"

"Yes, honey." Mike thought maybe the youngster had a better grasp of life and death than he had originally believed.

"Do we have to bury Sam now, too?"

That question was too much for Jane. She wrapped her arms around the little girl and began to cry. "Yes, sweetie. We have to bury Sam now, too. That's why he can't come over any more."

"The Night People did it, didn't they." Again, a pronouncement, not a question.

The words were so sudden and unexpected that both Mike and Jane just looked at their daughter for a moment, Jane leaning back and holding her daughter at arm's length. "What Night People, sweetie?"

"You know, the people that fly around at night."

"Have you seen these people?" Mike was starting to worry about the seriousness of his daughter's comments. She seemed so certain they were real. It wasn't as if she were talking about the boogieman or an invisible friend. She seemed to be talking about something she had actually experienced.

"No, Daddy. I haven't seen them." Mike breathed an inward sigh of relief. "But I've heard them. They fly through the air at night. They sound like big birds, and they're really mean."

Mike was certain that what his daughter had heard were, in fact, large birds. What other explanation could there be? There couldn't be people flying around the house at night. But he asked his daughter another question, the investigator in him curious. "If you haven't seen them, how do you know they're mean, honey?"

"Because they don't like roses," she said matter-of-factly. "If they were nice people, they would like roses." The simple logic of the four-year-old was astounding.

"How do you know they don't like roses?"

"They cry when they come near our house. They can't go past the rose bushes Mommy planted outside."

Mike tried to tell himself that it was just part of the active imagination of a four-year-old mind. He decided to leave it at that, at least for the time being. But it was strange that she would instantly and so certainly associate these "night people" with Sam's death. The detective in Mike told him not to let that episode fall too far into the recesses of his mind. Something told him it was important.

"Mommy likes roses, don't you Mommy?" she continued, unaware that her parents were concerned about the things she had been saying. "I like roses, too. I think they're pretty."

"Yes, they are," Jane said, scooping the toddler from the floor, eager to change the subject from death and "night people" to something more pleasant and safe, like flowers.

Mike left his wife and daughter in their kitchen and climbed into the family's Mazda, the vehicle Jane normally drove, the vehicle he and Sam had taken on numerous trips in the past, and drove over to Sam and Rachel's house.

No, not 'Sam and Rachel's' anymore, he thought sadly. Just Rachel's now.

The drive was a short one. Mike only had to go from one neighborhood to the next. It was practically within walking distance, but he wasn't sure how far his legs would carry him if he tried to make the trip on foot. He drove past all the familiar manicured lawns, down the same streets he traveled every day, and even thought about stopping at the coffee shop on the corner where he would get his first "strong" cup each day. Jane didn't like coffee that was thick and strong, so she always made their coffee so light that Mike swore he could see right through it. Once he left the house, he would stop at this coffee shop and get a cup of coffee so thick he could practically eat it with a spoon.

The thought of the coffee shop reminded him of Sam. It was one of the places they had stopped together regularly. And that thought refocused his mind on the task at hand. He couldn't delay any longer. He had to talk to Rachel.

When he finally crossed the upper-middle income neighborhoods that he and Sam called home, he pulled into the driveway of the house he had visited so many times on much happier occasions. He was immediately greeted by one of the biggest Dobermans he'd ever known. The giant canine could have easily swallowed his poor little Digger in one bite. But even though the dog's massive size was scary, Drake was the biggest cream puff in the entire dog world.

"Hey, Drake! Who's a good dog?" Mike greeted the dog, reaching out to pat its colossal head, having to fight the monster's brute strength just to get his car door open and get out. Once Mike was free of the Mazda, the dog began to bark playfully and jump up and down, almost knocking Mike to the ground. He's certainly in a playful mood today, Mike thought.

Rachel saw Mike drive up as she looked through her kitchen window, and came out to greet him.

"Sam's not home yet," she called out, assuming this was the reason Mike was visiting. "He had a late shift last night, and shouldn't be back for another couple of hours. But come on in. I've got breakfast cooking."

She motioned him up to the door of their pristine brownstone. It was a much larger house than they needed for a family of two. Rachel had found it for them when they first got married. She knew a thing or two about realty and property. It was what she did for a living.

The main floor held a large living room that they used for entertaining, a full formal dining room decorated with antique furniture, and a kitchen that was spacious enough to be the envy of the neighborhood. It was much more refined and "adult" than the unsophisticated look that Mike and Jane's house had taken on, the result of decorating specifically with a four-year-old's temperament and little fingers in mind. Upstairs were three bedrooms: one that had been shared by Sam and Rachel, one that was used as an office for Rachel's work, and a spare room that was set up much like a hotel room for friends or family who wanted to spend the night over a long weekend or an extended visit. It had long been Sam and Rachel's hope to move the office to the finished space in the basement, take apart the "hotel room", and fill those two extra bedrooms with children of their own.

When Mike reached the door, they exchanged hugs before Mike said "Rachel, come inside. There is something I have to tell you."

"Jane's pregnant!" she exploded with a vibrant gleam in her eye.

"No, Rach, this is something important."

She could tell from Mike's tone of voice, and the serious look on his face that the news was not good. Even Drake stopped jumping and barking, and quietly lay down on the ground. She allowed Mike to lead her inside to the couch in the living room, where they both sat down.

Mike looked around the room at the pictures of Rachel and Sam on their wedding day, at Mike and Jane's wedding, and on the many other happy occasions they had shared. There were also numerous photos of Sam with Mike, and photos of Mike, Jane, and Meagan. It was the first time that Mike realized there were more pictures of his own family than of either Rachel or Sam's families. It didn't surprise him. His home was filled with pictures of Sam and Rachel as well. It was a sign of how close the two couples had become.

He took Rachel's hand into his and looked her in the eyes, seeing that she now feared the worst. He knew there was no simple way to tell her what had happened, and he couldn't sugarcoat it. He had to tell her what had happened to her husband.

"Last night something bad happened to Sam while he was on duty in the park. There's no easy way to say this Rachel, so I'll just say it. He's gone. Lost in the line of duty."

"What?" She didn't seem to believe him at first, thinking that maybe this was one of the practical jokes that her husband and his best friend liked to play on her and Jane, albeit not a funny one. But when no punch line came, and the look on Mike's face remained somber, she knew. He was telling the truth. Tears began to flow down her face. She had suddenly lost everything in one moment. Mike took her into his arms and held her while she cried.

"Rachel, Jane and I will be with you every step of the way through this. You're not alone."

He said nothing more, just sat for what seemed like hours while the front of his shirt became soaked with Rachel's tears. Mike tried to recall all of his past experiences comforting the innocent families of violent crime victims, but he didn't know what else he could say to the wife of his best friend. What could he say to this woman who'd just lost her husband, this woman who'd been trying for years to have a child, but couldn't for a myriad of medical reasons, this woman who he knew felt as he did, like he'd been punched hard in the gut and couldn't breathe?

A light rap on the door startled Mike and Rachel out of their own thoughts, and back to the present. Mike stayed on the couch while Rachel stood, took a second to compose herself, and went to the door. She opened it to find Jane standing on the front stoop, her face wet with tears. Next to her, Meagan stood, holding her mother's hand.

The two women embraced, Rachel letting go of her composure once again, and sobbing. As they stepped into the house, Meagan hesitated, looking through the doorway as if into a dark and scary place.

"Come inside, Meagan," her mother told her. The child stood still in the doorway, her tiny body silhouetted by the morning sun. "Meagan," Jane's tone became firmer, "come inside."

Reluctantly, the little girl entered the house, looking from floor to ceiling and wall to wall, as if she were seeing the familiar surroundings for the first time.

"Is this where the Night People hurt him?"

"No, honey," Jane said, understanding why Meagan had been hesitant to enter. She thought Sam had been killed right there in the house. "The Night People have never been here."

Meagan relaxed a little, and walked into the living room to sit on the couch next to Mike. "You should plant some rose bushes outside," she said. Rachel gave Jane a quizzical look.

"I think the 'Night People' is her way of dealing with Sam's ...." She didn't want to say the word "death" out loud, as if by avoiding the verbalization she could make it not be true. "Anyway, apparently they don't like roses."

Rachel took Jane's hand and the two women went to the couch to join Mike and Meagan.

Mike gently chided his wife. "I thought I said not to tag along."

"I just wanted to be here to comfort Rachel."

Mike had known she'd come eventually. He just hadn't known how soon. Inside, he was glad she was there. He'd need to get back to work soon, and he didn't want to leave Rachel alone in that big house.

"And besides," Jane continued, "you left your cell phone. Chief Duncan has been calling for you."

Just as Mike suspected. He needed to get to the office. He stood up, and kissed all three of "his girls": his wife on the lips, his friend's wife on the cheek, and his daughter on the top of her curly head. He handed Jane the keys to the Mazda. She gave him the keys to his unmarked cruiser, which she had driven to Rachel's house. It was parked in the driveway next to the Mazda, with Drake watching guard over both vehicles. The huge dog stood up on his powerful legs as Mike approached and trotted toward him. But still sensing the somber mood of the people in the house, he didn't bother trying to play. He simply walked Mike to his car and watched him drive off.

NINE

The city was dotted with evenly spaced police precinct headquarters, each with domain over the crimes that occurred in its territory, and each charged with keeping the peace within its boundaries. Citizens could feel safe in the knowledge that no matter where they went, a police station was not far away. In the same respect, criminals had to be wary, for the same reason. Each precinct had its own captain who oversaw the officers assigned to his station, and who presided, to some degree, by their own personal style and set of rules. When criminals moved from one precinct to another, as they almost always did, the precinct captains had to work together, as did the officers involved in the investigation.

Overseeing all of the action was Chicago's Chief of Police.

David Duncan's office wasn't located in any of the headquarters that stood throughout the city. He didn't want to appear to be based in one specific precinct, or to give certain preference for one area. He also didn't want to get in the way of the everyday operations of any individual station, and he felt his presence would do just that. It would hinder the precinct captain's management and authority.

Instead, he wanted to be close to the rest of the city government and city officials. He had set up his own office, along with the rest of the Chicago Police general administration and the many detectives that were not assigned to a particular precinct, in a building located at the corner of Clark and Randolph Streets. It was an old building, made of solid brick painted a dull and faded yellow, and took up an entire city block. It was twelve stories high, large when compared to the office buildings of some cities, but dwarfed by the towers and skyscrapers that surrounded it. The building also housed the State Treasurer's Office, the County Clerk of Courts, and many of the city and county records departments. Across Clark Street to the east was the Daley Center, the glass-walled tower that served as the center of Chicago's city government. And across Randolph Street to the north was the squat, rounded shape of the State of Illinois building, where the State Administrative offices and the Secretary of State could be found.

It was to this government district that Detective Mike Green had been summoned, arriving half an hour after leaving his wife and daughter at Rachel's side. He drove to the underground parking lot, taking a valet ticket from the automated machine at the entrance. Everything is automated these days, he thought to himself. He found an open spot in the area reserved for authorized police vehicles and pulled in, hoping his unmarked cruiser qualified as "authorized".

The elevator from the parking garage reached only to the building's spacious rotunda, with its variety of hallways and stenciled doors leading off in every direction. The numerous entrances from street level all led to different areas of the building, some meant for public access, some private, and some under heavy security. Although each entrance and walkway was clearly marked as to what departments were contained within, a first-time visitor could easily take a wrong turn and become hopelessly lost in the myriad of halls and checkpoints.

Mike had been here many times before, being one of the detectives who was regularly called upon to investigate cases that crossed precinct lines. But the formality of signing in at the security desk that led to the central police offices still surprised him. Good thing the individual precinct headquarters are easily accessible, Mike thought. The average citizen would sure have a hard time getting through all of the security just to talk to the cops here.

Showing his badge at the security doors, he signed the security log and was admitted quickly through to the bank of elevators that led to the Chief's floor.

After navigating the seemingly endless labyrinth of hallways, he reached Chief Duncan's office and was quickly ushered in by the receptionist.

"You wanted to see me?" he said.

"Yes, come in. Shut the door and sit down a minute."

Mike did as the Chief asked and took a seat in one of the beat up, government issued chairs parked by the Chief's steel grey, government issued desk. The Chief began to speak like a professor giving a private tutorial lesson to a favorite grad student.

"Look, Mike, I know that you and Sam and your families were close, but I want you to stay off this case and let someone who's not so involved handle the situation."

"Yes, sir," Mike replied, not sure why this was such an important topic that the Chief had needed him to rush to the office to talk about it.

The Chief strongly suggested that Mike take off for two weeks to get his head together. Losing a close friend was serious business, and it wouldn't do to have him on the streets working cases if he wouldn't be able to concentrate. His only current case was the new one he had gotten the previous night, the guy found burned up in the dumpster, and that case could easily be assigned to someone else. Mike had the distinct feeling something was up with that case, and someone didn't want him looking into it. He had no evidence, of course, but he couldn't help feeling there was more going on than Chief Duncan was telling him.

However, there was little he could do at the moment other than agree to take some time off, and leave.

Mike walked out of the Chief's office and went straight to the parking garage. He got into his car, still trying to shake the uneasy feeling that something was going on, something big. He wondered what to do next.

His wife and daughter would still be at Rachel's. He had only left them a short time ago, and he thought the women could use some time alone.

He certainly didn't want to go home. The house would be empty, and he couldn't bear the thought of being alone there.

He had just lost his best friend, and then had been asked to take a couple weeks off from his job, the one thing that would have allowed him to keep his thoughts organized. He had nowhere to go. And to top it all off, his daughter was talking about hearing "night people". Was she just an overly imaginative toddler, or was she showing signs of being crazy?

As he drove aimlessly through the city, he came across a bar that he had seen several times but had always avoided. In fact, he had avoided all bars. It had been nearly six years since he had hopped on the wagon, and he had hardly been tempted by the evils of drink since then. But now the liquor seemed to call to him. With Sam gone, the temptation was stronger than ever. He decided that the one thing he needed at this point was a good stiff drink. Finding a parking spot on the street in front of the bar, he walked in.

* * *

Denny's Well was a dingy little place, typical of the hundreds of small neighborhood bars that populated Chicago, with low lighting, bar stools that didn't match, and seating for no more than twenty people at best. The electronic dartboard in the back was broken, and the ancient billiard table had been shoved against a wall and covered with a sheet of plywood, transforming it from a form of entertainment into a storage space for stacking extra chairs and anything else that lost in the competition for floor space. The plank wood slats that served as a floor were warped and covered in peanut shells, the owner of the bar apparently having either misplaced his broom years earlier, or else forgotten how to use it. But although the place was run down, it had one very attractive feature. It was open, even though it was still early in the morning.

Mike sat down and ordered a shot of Jack Daniel's. The bartender eyed him suspiciously, wondering why this stranger would be doing shots so early in the day. When Mike took out his wallet and set a fifty dollar bill on the bar, all hesitation was gone. The bartender's mind immediately pictured the large tip this apparent big-spender would undoubtedly leave, and sprang into as much action as his beefy body would allow. The shelves behind the bar were backed with mirrors, effectively doubling the limited selection of liquor lining the shelves. The bartender reached up and selected a half full bottle of Jack Daniel's Old Time No. 7 Tennessee Whiskey and poured the shot, spilling as much onto the bar itself as into the shot glass. Mike quickly slammed the drink and set his shot glass on the bar. He felt the slow burn going down his throat, warming his stomach, and he prepared himself for the violent fall from the wagon that he was about to experience.

As his eyes adjusted to the low lighting, he realized that although there were five other people seated at the bar, he was the only one drinking liquor so early in the day. The others were all drinking coffee. They looked like the "pub regular" types, folks who spent their days in the local bars, drinking or not. They were either retired or unemployed, many with no family at home, so they had nothing else to do during the day. The bar became their home away from home, and the other regulars became the only family they knew.

The bartender reclined against the back bar, his big meaty arms crossed in front of his barrel chest. The man sported the tattoo of an eagle with its wings rising up his left shoulder, and a symbol of some sort on the right bicep. While the symbol was indistinguishable in the dark of the bar, those that had seen it in the light knew it to be a tattoo that the bartender had gotten while in the military, along with all the other brave men in his platoon. The sleeveless T-shirt he wore revealed not only the tattoos adorning his arms, but showed off the muscles that were clearly the result of a daily workout regimen. When the bartender wasn't behind the bar, he was in a gym lifting weights.

Mike motioned for him to come back and ordered another shot of Jack with a Budweiser chaser. The bartender poured the shot and popped the longneck bottle open on the bottle opener mounted just below the bar. Mike slammed the shot as soon as it was poured, and left the beer sitting untouched on the slick bar. It became clear to those observing that this was a man that could hold his liquor.

The bartender leaned over the bar and said, "Rough day, Buddy?"

"You have no idea," replied Mike. "How much for the bottle of Jack?"

"The entire bottle?"

"Yes, the entire bottle."

"I'll sell it to ya for forty-five bucks."

"Deal."

The bartender pulled a full, unopened bottle from a storage cabinet below the bar, and set it in front of Mike. As Mike twisted the cap off the dusty bottle, he knew he had been ripped off on the price, but was in no mood to haggle. He'd seen his best friend lying in a bush with his head turned backwards, and then had to break the news to that best friend's wife that her husband was never going to return home. It was one of the hardest things he'd ever had to do. He needed to do something to get the image out of his head before it made him put his own revolver in his mouth.

* * *

Chief Duncan kept calling the morgue to find out if the autopsies had been completed on the two victims from what was already being referred to as 'The Grant Park Incident.' He was trying to get through to them again when his secretary walked in.

"Chief, there's a call holding for you on line three."

"Whoever it is, tell 'em I'll call 'em back."

"But it's Captain Mullins from homicide in district 14."

Duncan barked into the phone for the morgue to get him his reports ASAP, and then switched over to line three.

"Duncan here. What'cha got for me?"

"Chief, we have a body that was found in the alley way off of Chicago and Pearson."

"We have lots of bodies in this city. Why are you bothering me with this one?"

"Just thought you'd like to know, we just got the autopsy report back."

"Well, what about it?" The Chief was beginning to lose his patience with what he took to be a routine investigation, and one that certainly didn't require his attention.

"Well, sir, it seems a bit odd. According to the report, there are puncture marks on the neck and the body has been drained of blood"

"What? What does that mean?"

"Well, if I didn't know better, I'd say the guy was killed by a vampire."

"Whaddaya mean 'if you didn't know better'?"

"Well, sir, I don't really believe in vampires and all that hocus pocus stuff. I know they don't really exist."

"So how do you explain this guy?"

"I'd say that whoever killed him, for whatever reason wanted to make it look like a vampire did it. Could be some new cult, or weird new gang activity. Who knows? We're just starting the investigation"

There was no response from the Chief.

"There is one other odd thing, though."

"It gets more odd?"

"If it was some sort of ritualistic killing, some cult activity, we're not sure how they killed him."

"What do you mean?"

"There's no other cause of death. From what the report says, the victim died of blood loss, plain and simple. But they didn't find any other wound, or place for the blood to have left the body. Seems kind of strange to me."

"Who did the autopsy?"

"It has Westwood's signature, but I dunno if he did it himself, or if his assistant Max did it."

"All right. I'll call them to find out what they think. Who's assigned to this one?"

"Uh," Mullins hesitated long enough to look up the officer assignment sheet, "Mike Green. It's his case."

"Great. I just gave him two weeks off."

"I didn't know he was taking a vacation."

"He's not. His best friend had his head pretty much removed last night. I thought he could use some time to get over it."

"Man, that's rough."

"Yeah, it is. Well, just fax me over a copy of the report." The Chief wanted to get the report in his hands as soon as possible. He knew he'd seen similar reports in the past, with the same puncture marks and the same lack of blood. The strange thing was that the incidents were never investigated further. The cases were quickly closed and left unsolved, or key evidence and documents, including the reports themselves, disappeared altogether. It was as if someone was intentionally covering up whatever was going on, and he was determined to get a copy of this report before it vanished like the others.

Minutes after hanging up with the captain, the Chief had a faxed copy of the autopsy report from District 14 sitting in front of him. As he read, he felt himself turn pale and his stomach began to do flip-flops. It was just like the ones in the past.

He swiveled his chair around and opened the window behind his desk just a crack. These windows weren't supposed to open, having been sealed many years earlier because of government employees who committed suicide by jumping from their own office windows. After lawsuits from the families of the dead claimed it was the city that drove its employees to such behavior, the city decided to curtail that particular avenue of "escape" by sealing the windows of all private offices. Instead of changing the way city employees were treated, they simply cut off the opportunity to jump.

But the Chief had talked one of the late night custodians into bringing a few tools along on his rounds one night so he could break the seal and allow the window to open. He needed it to open. He had to have some way to ventilate his office to get rid of the smell of the other city policy he ignored. All city offices had been deemed "No Smoking" areas, including those of the police. But the Chief didn't see why he couldn't smoke in his own office, so he opened the window, sat on the windowsill, and blew his second-hand smoke out the window. At that moment, he didn't care if the Mayor himself walked in and caught him. He needed that cigarette.

His secretary came in carrying the two reports from the morgue that he had been waiting for. She didn't like that he smoked in his office, but she'd come to accept it. If anyone else had been about to enter, she would have made sure to call him on the intercom, giving him a chance to hide the damning evidence of his activities. But since she was alone, there was no need to forewarn him.

Scrutinizing the newly delivered reports, the Chief saw a distinct resemblance between the report from District 14 and the autopsy report on Sarah. Two victims, puncture wounds to the neck, almost all blood drained out of the bodies. The report from District 14 said the body was highly decomposed, as if the victim had been dead for several days. The report on Sarah also indicated a state of rapid decomposition, surprisingly rapid given the short amount of time she'd been dead. A shiver went up his spine. These were looking more and more like the reports he remembered from the past. The reports that almost always went missing. He stared out the window, barely seeing the panoramic view of Lake Michigan, and wondered if history was about to repeat itself.

TEN

St. Andrew's Cathedral is one of the oldest churches on the south side of Chicago. Underneath its Roman Catholic exterior lie a series of catacombs and hidden passageways completely unknown to those that led the current congregation and occupied the rectory of the church. This subterranean level had been created in secret in the late 1800's as a place to hide those being persecuted and sought out for their religious fervor and overwhelming support of the Catholic Church. It was a time that saw an increase in the violence between the supporters of organized religion and the secret societies that aimed at a single, scientifically enlightened world order.

But now the catacombs were sealed off, having lost their usefulness decades earlier with the fall of the secret societies that opposed the church. Their only remaining access to the world above was a single nearly vertical shaft that reached from the bowels of the hidden passageways to an unused balcony near the roof at the back of the church. This hidden access route contained a spiraled stairway made of stone, and had been originally created as a means of escape, a 'back door' exit should the catacombs ever be discovered.

Inside one of the many hidden chambers below ground, a coffin creaked open and a pair of long, thin arms stretched up and out. Raising her arms over her head and stretching out her back, the occupant slowly stepped from the coffin and began to sniff the air.

She looked into a far corner of the rock-walled room and looked at the body chained to the wall, hanging upside down. It was the body of a 22-year-old virgin, a young man who had disappeared without a trace. He was stripped to the waist, his throat slashed, his blood having poured across his face, through his light colored hair, and into the crystal punch bowl below.

With a sly smile on her face, the vampire sensuously slinked over to the corner where the young man hung and squeezed various parts of his body, wringing the last of the blood from his pale flesh. While she had slept, the rivers of blood had dried on his skin, giving his face a grotesque appearance.

When she was certain the body had no more blood to give, she walked to the second coffin in the chamber, one that had been placed near her own, and knocked lightly on the lid.

"The time has come, my love."

She opened the lid, its eerie creak filling the chamber with sound, and peered into its darkness. Dark emerald eyes opened to meet hers of royal blue. Raven colored hair splashed across the black satin pillow like the dark wings of a bird in flight. It mingled with her long blonde hair as she leaned down for a deep passionate kiss.

Virginia straightened and reached into the coffin, taking Nicolette's hand and helping her out of her resting place. The pair stood and admired the sacrifice they had left hanging on the wall, Nicolette's eyes gleaming with delight.

She dipped her fingers lightly into the crystal bowl, letting the fresh blood swirl around her fingertips. Virginia took her hand and brought it to her lips, licking and sensuously sucking the blood from the slender fingers. She wrapped her other arm around Nicolette's back, and pulled her naked body close to her own, releasing her lover's fingers from her mouth only to kiss her passionately on the lips, so deeply that she could nearly taste the blood of Nicolette's last meal.

When they finally broke the kiss, Nicolette leaned her head back, lolling weakly from the passion she was feeling.

Before Virginia realized what had happened, Nicolette had turned her onto her back, grabbed the punchbowl, and began to slowly pour the remaining contents all across Virginia's equally naked body, all the while with a wicked gleam in her eye, a gleam that said she was going to enjoy what came next.

Virginia leaned back and closed her eyes, reveling in anticipation of the pleasure that Nicolette was about to give her. She had never had anyone take control as Nicolette often did. Others were too intimidated, and let Virginia be the aggressor.

Nicolette's skilled tongue and lips made the whole universe spin. Virginia's entire body writhed in ecstasy as she reached the apex of her orgasm, and she couldn't help but cry out loud.

When the spasms of delight ceased, Nicolette raised her head from between Virginia's thighs, and slithered up the elder vampire's body, rubbing skin on skin with the thin layer of blood still between them. They kissed again, their tongues playing a secret game of tag inside their mouths. And then Virginia broke the contact. It was as if her mind had suddenly gone somewhere else.

Nicolette, spent after the moments of passion, climbed back into her coffin to rest, while Virginia wiped the remaining blood from her flesh.

She slinked over to a chaise lounge across the room and wrapped herself in a silk purple robe, the color that was at one time reserved only for royalty. She slowly followed the stone steps up the vertical passageway to the top of the Cathedral, swung open the window, and stepped out onto the balcony and into the soft light of the moon. Virginia's flesh soaked up the crisp night air with a thirst that could only be matched by her beauty.

She was an ancient, one of the oldest of vampires. Her life had spanned not only years or decades, but millennia. She had been born a vampire, had never known life as a mortal being, never known what it was like to live in the warmth of the sun. But a life in shadow, a life of cold was easy for her to accept, for it was all she had ever known.

The vampire who was still lying deep inside the catacombs was different. She was not an ancient, but had been born mortal. She was a made vampire, made by Virginia. Although she had been a vampire for a number of centuries, she still maintained a modicum of mortal feeling, as did most made vampires. Their humanity, although long since dead, would always be a small part of them.

Virginia stood on the balcony, her blue eyes looking across the skyline formed by the buildings to the south, long blonde hair blowing back from her face in the light breeze, and thought about hunting for her next meal. The activity she'd just indulged in had aroused her hunger and worked it to a frenzy. But first she had to contemplate a very serious problem. A problem that would soon rise from where it lay, spent and sated inside the catacombs, and join her high up on the balcony.

Nicolette was becoming uncontrollable and very dangerous to the Vampire world in which they lived. She had proven time and time again that she had little or no regard for the Code, the unwritten rules that Vampires had strictly followed and revered since the beginning of their time. The Code ensured the relatively peaceful coexistence of vampires and mortals, and kept the vampire community from being discovered and sought out by those who would destroy them out of pure fear.

Nicolette had only been seventeen years old when Virginia had made her, far too young to be able to understand and respect the Code. Or perhaps simply too young and impetuous to want to. But Nicolette's charms had belied her true age, and Virginia had convinced herself that she could make the young girl understand and abide by the centuries old way of life.

* * *

In 1561, during the reign of Elizabeth I, Virginia held the title of Comatose de Conde. She had passed herself off as a mortal and married the Comte de Conde, whose family had very close ties to the royal family. She had discovered many ingenious lies over the years that gave her excuses to remain indoors during daylight. Or, if she were required to be outdoors, she had excuses to remain shielded entirely from the sun. In that way, she could walk with the mortals and still keep to the shadows as her kind had always done.

It was on a hunting expedition outside of Herefordshire with the family of the Comte and the royal family that Virginia first noticed

Nicolette, one of the Queen's handmaidens. She intentionally lagged behind the group, feigning difficulty with her horse and professing to not want to slow the group. She asked only to have the company of one of the Queen's handmaidens, in case she needed assistance, and was granted her request in the form of Nicolette.

Her ruse worked, and soon the pair was far enough from the group for Virginia to coax the young woman into the woods where they would be entirely alone and unseen. There, Virginia seduced the young woman, who thought it strange to be in the embrace of another woman, but didn't resist, and quickly got over her discomfort, giving in to the pleasures of the flesh. She was surprised to find that she quite enjoyed it, and in fact became somewhat the aggressor.

At the height of their lustful passion Virginia could no longer resist the primal urge of her hunger. She bared her fangs and bit suddenly into the cleft of the young woman's breast. She drank of the blood that flowed from the wound while Nicolette moaned softly, undecided as to whether the new sensation was agonizingly pleasurable or agonizingly painful.

But before Virginia finished the young woman off, she began to feel pangs of loneliness. She had been walking among mortals for so long, and she missed the company of a fellow immortal. She decided it was time to make a companion, someone with whom she could spend eternity. This young woman had not only been a great pleasure to be physically intimate with, but also seemed to enjoy it herself. She would make a fine choice for a companion.

Virginia sank her fangs into her own wrist, causing a small flow of her own blood, and put her wrist to the young woman's lips. Nicolette drank the warm fluid, trusting this strange woman unconditionally, and her new life began.

The next morning, the two slipped off before early morning light, while the rest of the hunting party remained in their peaceful slumber. When they finally discovered that the Comtesse had gone missing, the Comte de Conde became upset. His bride had become lost in the woods, and he swore he would do anything to find her. He formed a small search party and went into the woods to look for her.

Later that evening, when neither the Comte nor the Comtesse had returned, the rest of the hunting party began a new search. What they found was a scene of horrible death. The Comte, along with everyone in his search party, was found hanging in the woods. When the bodies were cut down, it was discovered that their necks had been severed and their heads nearly torn from their bodies. This was attributed to a violent hanging, the ropes cutting through the flesh and causing the grotesque injuries. The limited science of the times provided no other explanation. The person or persons responsible, assumed to also be responsible for the disappearance of the Comtesse and the Queen's handmaiden, were never discovered.

In the years that followed, Virginia and Nicolette lived happily together in the shadows. Virginia taught Nicolette the ways of the Code. She taught her how to hunt, and how to hide from mortals. She taught her how to use her newfound immortal powers. And she taught her everything she knew about physical love. They were together at all times. At dusk they would explore their sexual pleasures. At night they hunted together. And at dawn they would lay down together in the coffin they shared. Although the Code forbid the mating of an ancient vampire with a made vampire, the act of physical love between two females was not addressed. Neither participant could become impregnated, and no offspring could result, so they felt that the Code didn't really apply.

But after nearly three and a half centuries, Nicolette had become bored with Virginia, which saddened Virginia greatly. She loved Nicolette and adored the times they had together. They had traveled the world together, and had met interesting people. And the passion they shared was unmatched. But throughout the 1900's, Nicolette had grown more and more detached, more and more independent, and more and more dangerous. She began hunting on her own, committing gruesome acts, and, worst of all, she began to violate the Code.

Bored with human prey, and bored with turning humans into vampires, Nicolette had taken up the sport of hunting dogs and occasionally turning them into vampiric creatures. She didn't do it often, but occasionally turn them she did. This was forbidden by the Code, for dogs act entirely on instinct and don't have the mental capacity to know when to stop their actions, to hold back from the blood lust.

Lately, Virginia had been following Nicolette when she went off on her own at night, and was growing tired of having to destroy the monstrosities that Nicolette created. But no matter what she said, the grisly and unnatural actions continued. For over one hundred years it had gone on; it was time to put an end to the abominations. The only questions for Virginia were how and when.

ELEVEN

Bordered by Peterson Avenue on the north and sandwiched between the Brown Line train tracks on the east and Western Avenue on the west lay Greenstone cemetery, one of the largest cemeteries on the north side of Chicago. In a crypt in the middle of the cemetery, a coffin creaked open for the first time in almost two decades and a lean figure emerged, greeting the cool night air. All around him, he could hear the sounds of other coffins and crypts being opened throughout the cemetery. It was a sound that Carlos loved, the sound of his minions awaking. They had slept for many years, hiding from those who would persecute them. But now it was time for them to arise. The night belonged to them, the unloved undead.

Stepping away from the entrance to his own crypt, he strolled through the cemetery and greeted each vampire as they arose. Although they were his followers, none of them knew where Carlos had originally come from or how old he was. The only thing they did know was that his orders must be followed down to the finest detail or their punishment would be severe. Carlos had the capacity to be a just leader, rewarding those who served him well. But when crossed or disappointed, he could be deadlier than the fiercest of King Cobras.

Each of the relatively young vampires who lived under the reign of Carlos had heard the story of his wrath, and what happened when a rather foolish young vampire by the name of Rodrigo challenged the older vampire over eight hundred years earlier. The reason for the challenge had been lost in the telling, the story embellished as it passed through generations of undead, but the outcome remained vivid. It was difficult to forget, especially with the constant reminder of Rodrigo's fangs hanging on a gold chain around Carlos' neck.

Although Carlos was considered old in the vampire world, he looked no more than twenty five years old. He wore his auburn hair shoulder length, a style that seemed trendy no matter the decade. And he stayed in the height of fashion by robbing his recent victims of their clothes and jewelry and making them his own. The only piece of jewelry that never seemed to change was the signet ring that adorned his right ring finger. A serpent entwined with a dragon in a tortured struggle, surrounded by dazzling gems. His eyes were as hard and cold as two pieces of onyx. Quick to smile even when his ire was up, his evil grin could turn anyone or anything's blood to ice. Dogs whimpered when he walked by, birds stopped singing, and women would suddenly begin their menses, even if it weren't the proper time. Some likened his image to Rasputin, others to Ivan the Terrible. But he was older than either of those two evil men from the history of Russia. Much older. And the power he held was far beyond that of tyrannical rulers.

As he walked along the path that wound through the ageless oak trees, his ears picked up an unusual noise, a rustling in the shrubbery. Carlos assumed it was one of his followers, but didn't understand why they were in the bushes. They would be hungry after nearly twenty years of sleep, and anxious to feed, but there would be no food in the cemetery.

As Carlos stood contemplating the shrubbery, a huge pit bull dog rushed out and stood in front of him growling, its larger than normal canine teeth bared, and acting like it suffered from a malady worse than rabies. Carlos stared at the animal with a look that sent other dogs cowering, yelping in abject fear as they ran away into the night. This animal, however, refused to back down from Carlos' evil glare. Instead, the animal returned his stare with red-rimmed eyes of its own. It stood still, holding its ground, motionless. If it weren't for the mist coming out of the dog's nose, and the trembling of the dog's lips as it growled at him, Carlos would have mistaken it for a statue.

Could the creatures of the world changed so much in less than two decades? Had his power to instill fear in the most basic of animals been rendered useless? As Carlos took a hesitant step back from the vicious beast, he heard another noise behind him. He slowly turned, trying to keep the pit bull in his peripheral vision to the right. Directly across the pathway, he saw another dog emerging from the carefully manicured bushes. Instead of a pit bull, this dog was a mastiff, also growling fearlessly at Carlos. Like the pit-bull, this dog was also baring unusually large canine teeth, and seemed unafraid of Carlos.

With one beast on each side, Carlos knew he couldn't attack without being struck from behind. Instead, he snapped his fingers, calling his minions. As if by magic, seven different vampires appeared from the mists and quickly surveyed the scene in front of them. Clearly there was something wrong with these animals, or Carlos, their leader, would have scared them away with a simple glance. Moving almost as one being, the vampires split into two groups, each group attacking one of the dogs. The dogs fought back with a ferocity that the vampires never expected, but after a short struggle, the vampires managed to snap the necks of the other-worldly creatures.

On the underbellies of the dogs, they discovered the familiar puncture wounds that could be found somewhere on each of their own bodies. Even more curious was the way the dogs suddenly began to melt into matching black puddles of burnt-coffee scented sludge.

Carlos wondered where these mutants could have come from and why he was unable to scare them away. And what had made him think that other vampires had caused the rustling in the bushes? His senses certainly should have known the difference between a vampire and a dog. It was their scent he recognized, a familiar, unique scent.

Suddenly, his head snapped up. He knew that scent! But why was she here in Chicago, here in his city? He and his followers had been asleep since his last horrific act, so she couldn't possibly have traced him here. But what other explanation could there be?

Those near Carlos looked at him in puzzlement. They knew that something was wrong and that soon they would be given orders. And they knew that whatever followed would be potentially deadly—not only for mortals, but for themselves as well.

* * *

The echo of footsteps ascending the spiral stairs of their secret passageway broke Virginia's thoughts. Nicolette had risen, and was making her way upward toward the moonlight. Virginia knew that Nicolette was keyed up over something, her youthful energy at a high point. It always was when Nicolette quickly walked the stairs to the balcony. It was a way to get her dark, cold blood pumping, much like a mortal becomes spurred on by adrenalin. Had she been less energetic, she would have taken the easier way up, using her vampiric power of flight. Virginia also knew that when Nicolette's energy was high, she was at her most dangerous. She would have to keep a close eye on her young protégé this night.

She stood with her back to the passageway as she waited and listened to Nicolette's rapid footsteps. It didn't take long for Nicolette to traverse the tower, and she was soon standing beside her mentor on the rooftop, her raven hair flowing in the light night breeze, her dark amber eyes glowing in the moonlight. The two immortal women stood watching the last of the late night commuters exit the train and rush to their cars to finish their journeys home after a long day of work.

"Ah, suburbanites, what weak blood they have," exclaimed Nicolette.

Virginia ignored the remark as her mind played with scenes from the past, and her heart grew heavy with the knowledge of what she must do. If the other ancients discovered Nicolette's antics, they would surely take matters into their own hands. Virginia had made Nicolette and she knew that she must be the one who handled the matter.

Nicolette nudged Virginia. "I'm hungry. Let's grab a bite to eat."

"All right, mon cheri. I guess it is time to feed."

The two women stepped from the balcony and drifted noiselessly, and unnoticed, to ground level at the back of the church. With no windows from the rectory facing the back of the church, and no neighborhood homes facing it, either, this was a simple way to leave the balcony without fear of being seen, especially at the late hours when they generally left. When they returned at dawn, it was much the same: fly upward to their perch, and then drop down the stairwell to the catacombs where they would sleep the day away.

Nicolette walked ahead of Virginia, still with the bounce of youth even though she was more than four hundred years old. It was as if the vigor and youthful expectation of her mortal life had never left. She was always on the lookout for something fun and exciting. And if nothing presented itself, she could easily create something on her own.

Virginia watched her partner bound ahead and pondered just how to effectuate Nicolette's demise. After everything they had been through, she loved Nicolette, and knew she couldn't make her suffer. So death would have to be quick, and as painless as possible.

They walked along the street until they arrived at a Blue Line "El" station. The train that traveled this track would drop them off in the populated area near the ballpark. Tonight a late game was letting out; there would be plenty of fresh meat.

They could have flown to the ballpark, or walked with their immortal speed, arriving within minutes. But Virginia enjoyed riding the train and studying the mortals around her. It was a small opportunity to walk with people, something she had always enjoyed doing. She did everything she could to blend in. She had learned over the centuries to act just like those around her, and go almost entirely unnoticed.

Nicolette was not so adept at anonymity. She would play games with the mortals, catching the eye of a fellow passenger on the train, winking, smiling coquettishly, and oftentimes making obscene gestures at them once she had their attention. She would laugh hysterically when they got disgusted or upset and turned away, drawing unwanted attention to herself and Virginia. It was just another sign of how dangerous she could be for the vampire community. On many occasions, she had even been so bold as to look at a mortal with a sneering smile that displayed not only her perfect white teeth, but her sharp deadly fangs, as well. It was a game to her. If she could get them to stand and walk away while the train was still in motion, she won. If they ignored her, she lost. And she did not like to lose.

The train arrived and the pair boarded, along with the few mortals that stood on the platform. The doors slid closed as the pre-recorded voice crackled over the speakers announcing the next stop. The fluorescent lights were blinding to the vampires who were used to shadows, but their eyes quickly adjusted. This late at night, the train was fairly empty, and Virginia had no trouble finding an empty seat where she and Nicolette could sit together. It was best to stay close, so she could keep an eye on the young troublemaker.

The two homeless vagrants on the train were both passed out, oblivious to anything around them, lying across open seats, each taking up the space of two people. The tattered bags that contained their worldly possessions were on the floor beneath them. A young couple no more than twenty-five years old sat near the front of the car, engrossed in each other's company, their hands and arms entwined. They would certainly not be paying attention to any of Nicolette's games that night. The only other passenger was a man of about thirty with sandy blonde hair who was intently reading a book, trying to avoid eye contact with other passengers. Nicolette tried several times to catch his gaze, but to no avail. When she began to rise, determined to walk over to the young man and speak to him in order to get his attention, Virginia put her hand on her companion's leg, a gesture to stay put and leave the man alone. The young vampire dutifully, if reluctantly, obeyed.

When the train reached the 35th Street stop, Virginia nudged Nicolette, who was still trying to get the attention of the young man with the book, and wordlessly rose and exited the train. With Nicolette close behind her, she left the train station and walked toward the ballpark.

"I liked that guy on the train." Nicolette was still looking back toward the train. "Why couldn't I just have him for dinner?"

"What would you do, kill him right there under the lights?" Virginia was obviously concerned by the young vampire's suggestion. "And then what would you do with the body?"

"Well, I ... I don't know. I just thought he looked yummy."

"How many times have I told you," Virginia lectured, "that we must not kill in the open? If one of us is discovered, it could mean the end of all of our kind."

"Well, then, let's find someone not in the open to have some fun with."

A block before reaching the outer parking lots of the ballpark, they glanced down an alley and saw two very drunken men relieving their bladders against the wall. Nicolette knew they would be easy prey, and walked down the alley, stopping directly in front of the larger of the two.

"Hey, baby, whatcha up to?"

He was unable to speak at first, unsure what to say to this woman who had appeared from nowhere. His baseball cap was perched on his head backward, concealing a thinning, receding hairline. His team jersey was worn loose, masking the slight paunch that drooped over his belt. The sudden approach of Nicolette had made him lose all sense of purpose and self, and he was unaware that the zipper of his denim jeans was still lowered, leaving him entirely exposed.

"Are you going to put that away," Nicolette said, glancing toward the man's crotch, "or do you intend to use it?"

He looked down at his hand still holding his flaccid member, and, suddenly embarrassed, slipped it back into his pants and raised his zipper. He looked to his friend to see if he had noticed the woman approach. The taller man, much thinner than his companion, had indeed been watching the scene, and tried desperately to finish what he had begun. He was only now done making his contribution to the alley's heavy urine smell, and was returning his own unit to its home.

Virginia waited near the end of the alley, allowing her girl to have her fun, and prime the prey. She had long since grown tired of playing with her meals before feeding, but she knew Nicolette was still young, and enjoyed the game as if it were her own form of foreplay. Her playfulness and cunning ways of taunting her victims were things that Virginia could never have taught her. They were abilities that were innate.

And although it gave Virginia great pleasure to watch her young friend put those skills to use, she knew they were also the same abilities that made her so dangerous. Her thirst for blood came in a close second to her thirst for fun, for taunting and playing with mortals. Many times she had nearly gone too far, almost making mistakes that would result in the discovery of the vampire world. It was then that Virginia would step in and finish off the poor souls, putting an end to it.

Nicolette stepped closer to the drunken man standing in the alley. "So, why would a big cuddly guy like you be hiding down these dark alleys?"

The man could only stutter and stammer, still unable to force his mouth to form a proper response.

"It's a shame you put that big tool of yours away so quickly," she said, glancing again at his recently zipped jeans and moving steadily closer. "We could have had some fun." She was inches from the man's face, able to smell the heavy scent of the beer he had consumed.

She took his hand in hers and began sucking lightly on his fingertips. "I've even got a friend for your silent buddy over there," she said, nodding toward his dumbstruck friend standing against the wall a few feet away. "Do you think he'd like that?"

Both men nodded enthusiastically, still rendered mute by Nicolette's charm.

"Right over there," she said, turning toward the end of the alley where Virginia was no more than a silhouette against the streetlights behind her.

Nicolette's eyes flashed through the darkness, the signal for Virginia to join her. She glided into the alley, her hair flowing freely in the breeze; the drunken men thought the apparition had to be either a figment of their alcoholic imaginations, or an angel.

She stepped toward the taller of the two men, who looked her up and down admiring her great beauty with the lecherous look of a caged animal eying a piece of raw steak. Virginia could feel loathing creeping up her spine; she was repulsed by the way the stranger looked at her. But she tried to ignore it, using it instead to play into the man's lustful thoughts. With her own gleaming eyes, she beckoned the man closer.

She was less interested in playing with her meal, wanting to end the lives of these vile creatures so she could feed and be on her way. There was no hesitation in her movements. Quickly wrapping her arms around him, she sank her fangs into his neck and began to feed. The liquor in the man's blood was almost overwhelming, making Virginia begin to feel intoxicated. She knew she shouldn't drink him dry, but she didn't stop. This would be her only mortal meal of the night.

Seeing Virginia draining the blood from her victim, Nicolette knew it was time for her to do the same. She looked deep into his eyes, holding him entranced, and opened her lips in a Cheshire-cat grin. With her fangs revealed, the look on the man's face suddenly changed from lustful anticipation to abject fear, which only made Nicolette's smile widen further; the final master stroke in her game had been achieved. She quickly pulled the man's head to the side and bit deep into his neck, puncturing his jugular vein with ease.

He tried to cry out, but her powerful fingers had grasped his throat and crushed his larynx, making it impossible for him to utter a sound. In fact, he could scarcely breathe through his ruined throat. He tried to fight back, but he was far weaker than his attacker. His feet and hands grew suddenly cold, and then completely numb, as the blood that normally flowed through and warmed them rushed from his body at an incredible rate. He lost all sensation in his arms and legs before he felt his internal organs begin to spasm and die their own agonizing deaths. Although there was no longer circulation to feed his brain, it was the last part of him to die, leaving him in a semi-conscious state, able to feel each and every part of him drained of the life-giving blood. When his heart realized there was no more blood left to pump, it ceased to function, and the light of life dimmed from his eyes. His horrible nightmare of a death had finally come.

Nicolette finished and dropped her man to the ground to join the discarded food wrappers and beer cans strewn around the alley. Wiping the blood from her lips with the back of her hand, she looked to Virginia, who had already dropped her victim into the puddle of his own urine created only moments earlier. Nicolette's eyes shone like two pieces of dark glass as she searched for approval in the eyes of her elder. But for some unknown reason, she sensed only sadness

Virginia's sadness was the result of having made up her mind, a decision that had tormented her, but one she knew had to be made.

Carlos would soon awake; she could sense it.

He had slept for nearly two decades, mistakenly thinking it was enough time for the others to forget his crimes, or at least forgive him for them. Virginia knew he was here in Chicago. She could feel his presence, and knew that he would soon return to the night.

But it was Nicolette who had found his actual location. It had been one of those nights when she'd snuck away to hunt on her own. Out of boredom, she had created a pair of monstrosities: immortal dogs that would feast on blood out of instinct. Virginia tried to capture and destroy these beasts before they could be discovered, but, instead, they led her to a crypt where she found Carlos, hiding from his punishment and his treachery.

He and his followers would soon arise, confident that they could walk again in the night. But the others were already on their way.

Before they arrived, and before Carlos awoke, Virginia knew she would have to take care of Nicolette. If she didn't, Carlos most certainly would. He would make her death painful and agonizing, drawing it out as long as possible just to please his own black heart. Virginia couldn't allow that to happen. She would do it herself.. And she had to do it now, before she lost her nerve.

"Come here, mon cheri. Come here and kiss me as you've never kissed me before."

Nicolette rushed into Virginia's arms and the two women began a deep, passionate kiss. Nicolette's arms wrapped around Virginia's neck and Virginia began to stroke Nicolette's back, her hands moving from her shoulders to the small of her back.

Before Nicolette knew, or even sensed, what was happening, Virginia dipped her like a dancer at the end of a tango, exposing her entire chest to the stars that watched their immortal dance. She felt her passion and desire grow at the rough handling by her mentor.

But passion was not to be fulfilled. With lightening speed, and strength unknown to mortal man, Virginia struck, forcing her bare fist into Nicolette's chest, and ripped out Nicolette's cold dead heart. She took a bite, piercing it with her fangs, instantly killing the young vampire she still held. She dropped the girl to the ground, knelt down beside her, and removed the chain that held the heart-shaped locket Virginia had given her young lover on their one hundredth anniversary. With blood tears flowing down her face, Virginia slipped a small piece of Nicolette's black heart into the locket, and kissed her cheek.

"Sleep well, my love," she nearly whispered.

She slipped the locket around her own neck, and stepped back as the dissolution of her beloved began, the body quickly melting into an oily black goo, the same substance she'd seen other immortals become upon their own deaths. The pungent aroma of burnt coffee that accompanied the death of an immortal assailed her nostrils as she completed the grisly task of disposing of the two bodies she and her former companion had feasted upon only moments earlier.

She picked them up, and easily snapped their necks. One she drove head first into the ground. The other she threw up against the brick wall. Once the flesh rotted away, the broken bones would appear to have been caused by an attack, and no one would ever suspect the real way the men died. She easily hefted them into one of the nearby dumpsters so thoughtfully provided by the city for disposal of victims. As long as no one dug through the trash before it was emptied into a truck headed for the city dump, the bodies would decompose long before they were found. If they were ever found.

With a last look at the oily black puddle left on the pavement, Virginia turned and sped off into the night, back toward her church and the empty catacombs beneath.

TWELVE

Elizabeth strolled down Michigan Avenue among tourists and young lovers walking arm in arm. The moon was hiding behind the clouds, leaving only the streetlights and the neon signs in the store windows to light her way. The day had been warm, but she had slept through the short-lived heat wave. A cool breeze blew in from the lake, a refreshing break from the earlier warmth, but it wasn't the breeze that gave Elizabeth chills. She had seen the newspaper stories about the incident in Grant Park, stories about her incidents. So far the authorities had no clues or leads, and the killings were listed as "under investigation". Elizabeth was hopeful that they would fall into the "unsolved" files, so that the existence of her kind would not be revealed.

When she reached the end of Michigan Avenue, she continued north on Rush Street until she turned the corner onto Division and began mingling with the young partiers who frequented the bars lining both sides of the street.

Suddenly she felt the hairs on the back of her neck stand up as she sensed another vampire in her midst. She looked around, trying to find the source of the feeling, and collided with a form that had materialized from the mist in front of her.

"Liz! What are you doing still in Chicago?" he said with all the sincerity of a telemarketer who claims to be interested in helping only you.

"This is my home, Victor." She recognized him as one of the mindless drones who followed Carlos, answering his every beck and call. "And I don't intend to leave it simply because you're here."

"Well, Liz, you're not alone here anymore." Victor had the cockiness and self-assuredness of a successful and highly sought-after movie star. His square jaw and rugged face gave him the looks to match.

"And where is your Lord and Master? I'm sure with one of his lapdogs present, he must be near. After all, he never lets you stray far, does he?" She looked deep into the black pits of his eyes, searching for any clue why he was in Chicago. She wanted to know if they were there for her because of the mistakes she had been making, or if it was simple coincidence. Many in the vampire world knew she had lived in Chicago, but few knew she still lived there. If the story of the Grant Park murders and the journalist in the dumpster made national headlines, they would all know she—or at least one like her—was still actively hunting in Chicago.

What stared back at her was the cold of a bottomless well, a soulless gaze that gave away nothing. He sneered at her, the corners of his narrow lips rising in a cruel smile, his strong face wrinkling around his perfectly straight nose.

"When are you going to come to your senses and join us? Carlos has always wanted you for himself, you know."

She didn't know if Carlos wanted her simply as an addition to his list of servants, or as a personal trophy to be displayed by his side, his own personal concubine. Either way, Elizabeth was repulsed by the thought. "When heaven and hell become one," she shot back.

"Wake up, Liz. That time is coming sooner than you think." The sneer turned into a Hollywood grin, but the empty eyes did nothing more than reflect the light from the street lamp.

She shoved Victor with all her might, sending him crashing against the solid brick wall of the building next to them, and sped through a maze of back alleys and side streets. She took every corner she could, hoping to lose Victor, if he had even followed her. She came to the backdoor of a club that she knew had been shut down for quite some time. Using her immense strength, Elizabeth wrenched the door open and slipped inside.

When did they get back into town? And what are they doing here? And why does he insist on calling me 'Liz'? She hated to be called Liz. But even more, she hated Carlos, those that followed him, and all they stood for.

Standing with her back to the door, leaning against the bent and torn frame, her mind played back to her first meeting with Carlos. It was at the wedding reception of Ekaterina Alekseevna—Catherine the Great—to Grand Duke Peter Fedorovich of Russia, who would later become Emperor Peter III.

* * *

Elizabeth and Dominick passed themselves off as dignitaries from Siberia, and entered the ornate grand ball room in the center of Petersburg, named for Peter the Great, the grandfather of the groom. An orchestra on the small stage played chamber music, and couples danced around the polished mahogany dance floor. The remains of the feast that preceded the reception ball had been cleared away, but plenty of good food and wine remained in a side room where guests could retire and continue to gorge themselves if they so desired.

They walked slowly through the mass of wealthy aristocrats, the upper echelon of Russian high society, debating whether or not to partake in a feast of their own this evening.

As they circled the ballroom, Elizabeth sensed a presence. It was a presence she felt whenever Dominick returned, whether from a trip or just a short time away. She had felt it when he finally found her again, nearly four decades after she had left him in the gondola in Venice. But now she felt the presence even though he was already standing by her side, which had never happened before.

The Crown Prince of Spain stepped in front of the couple and greeted them as if they were old acquaintances. His jet black hair was slicked back in a ponytail that reached just below his collar, and his dark eyes reminded Elizabeth of the way Dominick had first looked at her. The laugh lines at their edges gave the impression of a jovial soul, but the eyes themselves looked soulless and dangerous. The prince's sharp nose led to a sinister looking pencil-thin moustache, below which was a wicked grin that matched the expression of his evil eyes.

"It's been a long time, Dominick. Where do these fine mortals think you are from this time?"

"Siberia. We are simply visiting dignitaries at the wedding."

"Ah, how quaint," replied the younger man. "And who is this beauty," he asked with a lustful sneer, taking in Elizabeth's body from head to toe with those lecherous eyes.

She felt the presence grow in intensity, and knew that it was coming from the vulgar man standing in front of her. She just couldn't understand why.

"Her name is Elizabeth," Dominick answered through gritted teeth, obviously trying to be civil in front of the throng of party guests, but failing. It was obvious that he bore a strong distaste, if not hatred, for the man in front of him.

"How lovely." The look on the stranger's face made Elizabeth quite uncomfortable. He reached out with slender fingers, taking her hand in his own, and bent down to kiss it.

Dominick snatched Elizabeth's hand. "Back off, blood sucker. She's mine!" It was barely a perceptible hiss, just loud enough to be heard by both Elizabeth and the prince. None of the other guests seemed to be paying any attention to the exchange, content to eat, drink, and dance.

The prince stood up to the challenge. Toe to toe and eye to eye with Dominick, he sneered. "Shall we take this outside?"

"After you, my good sir," Dominick said with as much contempt as he could muster, and the prince slipped from the room as quickly as he had appeared.

Elizabeth became frightened and held fast to Dominick's arm. "Please don't do this," she pleaded. "I felt an odd presence from that man. I don't understand what it was, but I do not have a good feeling about this."

"Not to worry, my pet," he lectured her as if she were a young schoolgirl. "The presence you felt, the same one that you feel when I am near but not with you, is the presence of another like myself. Another ancient immortal."

It was the first time Elizabeth realized that there were others like Dominick in the world. Until that moment, she had thought all other immortals had been made, like her. She could sense when they were near, but not in the same way as she could feel Dominick's presence. Now she knew that there were other ancients as well, and the evil stranger waiting outside was one of them.

"Carlos is a clown," he reassured her. "I'll put him in his place and be back before the next waltz begins."

Elizabeth watched him head off in the direction the Crown Prince had taken. She waited impatiently for the return of her escort for what seemed an eternity, never taking her eyes off of the door. She was shocked when the figure that stepped through was not Dominick, but Carlos, the stranger with the evil presence.

"Where is he? What have you done to him?" she nearly screamed as she rushed toward him and out of the door. Party guests watched the woman rushing from the room, but Carlos gave them all a smile, a shrug of the shoulders, and a reassuring look that said, "She'll be all right. I'll just go after her." They all returned to their celebrations.

Carlos swiftly left the room and caught up to her, taking her by the arm and leading her to the unoccupied stables in a distant corner of the estate. He turned to her with his evil eyes, gave her another wicked smile and said, "We should be just in time for the main event," before pulling open the door to the stable.

The scene revealed made Elizabeth nearly faint. Dominick hung from a wall, held in place by stakes driven through his shoulders and into the wood behind him. His clothes had been torn from his body, leaving him entirely exposed, accentuating his defeat at the hands of Carlos. His lifeless head slumped, his silky hair hanging down, covering his face. The entire midsection of his body had been ripped out, gutted, his black heart pierced and perched neatly atop the pile of discarded entrails on the ground below his dangling feet.

"Ah," Carlos said, "perfect timing. I was hoping you'd get to see him before the dissolution began." He laughed at the bloody tears that began to flow from Elizabeth's eyes as the body of her maker began to melt from the wall and became a puddle in the straw below, the stench burning her nostrils, making her feel as though she would retch.

* * *

"What are you doing in my home?" a voice rough as sandpaper came out of the darkness and snapped Elizabeth out of her past.

She turned toward the shadow that was slowly clambering through a broken and splintered windowpane. The movements of the hunched figure were unmistakably those of someone who had spent a good deal of time in this abandoned space and could find their way through the darkened recesses with little trouble. The pungent stench of Dominick's decaying body in Elizabeth's reverie transformed into an equally repulsive aroma, this one emanating from the approaching figure. The smell of urine and dirt told her that this was one of the many who made up the city's homeless population.

"I'm just waiting for you, my love," Elizabeth replied, waiting for the figure to emerge from the shadows. When it did, the picture of homelessness was complete: tattered clothes hanging loosely from the woman's shriveled, malnourished frame, stringy unwashed hair hanging from beneath a torn felt cap, and a care-beaten face.

"You shouldn't be here. This is my home. Get out."

Some home, Elizabeth thought as she looked around at the broken beams, rat-infested piles of trash, and dirty, broken floorboards. "But I came to give you something," she smoothly lied to the approaching figure.

The gruff voice was filled with apprehension and suspicion. "What is it? Give it to me and get out."

"I can't just hand it to you."

"What is it, then?"

"It's relief. Relief from your hunger. Relief from your pain. Relief from your misery."

Deep down, Elizabeth was repulsed at the idea of feeding on this vile creature, but it was either this or rats for dinner. And rat tartare just doesn't sound appetizing, she thought.

Elizabeth beckoned the woman closer to her with another offer of release from her hellish nightmare of a life. The woman was hypnotized not only by Elizabeth's voice, but by the intoxicating violet eyes that could be seen clearly, even in the darkness of the abandoned room. She never saw the fangs as they flashed through the shadows toward her throat, and she didn't resist as Elizabeth bit through months of grime to get to her prize. It was as if she were immune to the pain, seemingly willing to be taken from this god-forsaken place, cherishing the long awaited relief that came with death.

With her last breath, she gurgled three simple words: "Thank you, dear."

THIRTEEN

Virginia walked slowly through the streets, mourning the loss of Nicolette. There were hundreds of other vampires who would come to her in an instant, the ones she had made over the centuries. She allowed them to roam free, hunting and feeding on their own, as long as they adhered to the rules of the Code. But whenever she summoned one for anything, from the smallest request to the largest of troubles, they were all there. She was their leader, their mentor, and their master. She could have had any one of them to share her coffin.

But Nicolette had been special. And her absence would be felt for a long long time.

She knew she should have fed more. One victim a night was not nearly enough for an ancient, especially when that one was tainted with a large amount of alcohol. But she just wasn't up to the hunt. First she had to grieve.

As she walked along, slowly making her way toward the catacombs, she ignored everything around her until she heard the flapping sound of bird's wings. There were many species of bird in Chicago in the spring and summer, and to most of the city's inhabitants, this would have been nothing more than the sound of one of the larger species. But this was different, and Virginia knew it. It was accompanied by feeling the familiar presence of fellow immortals.

As Virginia continued walking, she was enveloped in a light mist. As it slowly dissipated, three of the nastiest looking vampires she had ever seen emerged. They were not hers, and she knew that the only other Vampire in Chicago was Elizabeth, who had no children because she was a made Vampire, not an ancient. These savage beasts could only belong to Carlos, which meant that he had awakened.

"Get away from me, scum," Virginia said. "Go back to whatever rock you crawled out from under."

"Do you know why we are here?" said the one in the middle, the one she knew was called Grayson. He had a cocksure in-charge attitude. His grey, colorless skin set off the bright red of his lips and eyes; his mangy black hair cascaded down to the black overcoat he wore over his skinny body. A gaudy gold chain sparkled beneath the coat, a prize taken from a victim sometime in the past.

Virginia turned her blue eyes to him. "Frankly, I don't give two shits why you're here. But if you don't leave soon and stay out of my way, you'll be my next meal."

"Three against one? I think I like our chances," said the one on the left. Virginia was familiar with this one as well, a weasel of a vampire named Davidson. The way he stood back and to the side made it obvious that he was an underling of Greyson's. The ranking was confirmed in the way Davidson looked to Greyson for approval after his comment with the eager look of a lapdog anticipating praise from his master.

Virginia never understood why Carlos chose to form ranks among his followers. To her, they were all equal. But in Carlos' regime, there was a militaristic ranking of power. And the only way to move up the ranks was to destroy the vampire one tier above you. Of course, that vampire would be above you for a reason, and destroying him or her wouldn't be an easy thing to do. In addition, if Carlos felt someone wasn't deserving of the higher position, he would simply destroy that person, as well, and promote a different vampire to the position. Because of the danger of Carlos' anger, challenges of rank didn't happen very often.

"Try me, bitch, and see." Virginia directed her words at Davidson, causing him to shrink back a step, losing a bit of his bravado. "You have no idea who I am."

She looked into the eyes of Greyson for only a moment before the three attacked as one, flying directly at her. Unfortunately for Grayson, Davidson and Emile, the third of the trio, they had severely underestimated her strength and power. With movements faster than sight could track, she decapitated all three. The contest was so mismatched, it was over in a matter of seconds, with the three headless bodies falling to her left, and their heads rolling to a stop on the right. She laughed at the look of shock forever frozen on the faces of Davidson and Emile. They could not have possibly known who or what she was. The face of Greyson showed only acceptance. He must have realized what would happen only at the last instant.

Knowing that their bodies would not last long, Virginia began feasting on their blood before the dissipation could begin, and their bodies melted away to black sludge. She drank to the point of gluttony, realizing just how hungry she had become, all the while thinking, Oh, Nicolette, how you would have enjoyed this.

Since the heads of the three brutes were separated from their bodies, Virginia knew they would not dissipate. She decided to leave them for their former master. It had been her calling card in the past, so he would know exactly who the "gift" was from now. After all, she thought, it's rude not to let an old friend know I'm still in one piece.

She picked up the three heads, tied them together by their long hair, and flew north. She had already discovered Carlos' current resting place, and she knew they would all be out hunting at this time of night. Unlike Virginia, who let her children roam free, Carlos kept his close by him at all times, only letting them go off on their own when he sent them on a specific mission. These three, separated from the pack, must have been sent to find and destroy her. Too bad their master hadn't seen fit to warn them that she was an ancient.

She reached the north side graveyard and found it deserted as expected. Carlos was too conceited and arrogant to think anyone would come in search of him, so didn't bother leaving a guard. Virginia landed at the entrance to his crypt and left the heads, still tied together, lying on the stone steps leading inside.

As she stepped back, she looked up and saw the heads of two fierce dogs mounted like trophies on the top of the crypt. Their sharp fangs were bared in an eternal snarl, and their sightless eyes gleamed in the moonlight. She instantly recognized them as the last dogs Nicolette had turned, the ones she hadn't been able to find and destroy.

"So that's how he knew I was here," she said to the empty crypt.

With that, she turned and flew off to her own home deep in the catacombs.

* * *

Mike sat at the bar, pounding down drink after drink, shot after shot, as if the fate of the world rested on his shoulders and his ability to get, and stay, drunk. Once he started, he couldn't stop himself from wasting the entire afternoon and better part of the evening. It was as if he had been transported back six years, before he had kicked the habit, and before he had taken the first of his twelve steps. The bottle of Jack Daniels Tennessee Whiskey had long since perished, now sitting among the other bottles Mike had emptied. He was well on his way to total drunken oblivion; it was a rock-solid fall off the wagon.

His pager went off, unnoticed for a few moments. It took some time for the incessant beeping to fight its way through his alcohol-induced haze, and recognition to sweep over him. He removed it from its cradle and, without bothering to look at the number on the illuminated display, dropped it to the floor where it landed with a light thud. He raised his leg, almost falling off the stool where he was perched, and brought it down with enough force to smash the offending pager into the great pager afterlife. He missed by a wide margin due to his drunken state, accomplishing nothing more than causing a loud bang to reverberate throughout the slowly filling tavern, and nearly knocking himself to the floor. Of course, this brought out more than a few chuckles from Mike's fellow barflies, but it didn't stop him from repeating his pager stomping dance until he got it right, hit his mark, and ended the pathetic life of the little plastic device.

Somehow, the violence made him feel just a little bit better. Now if only the bartender would be content to just serve the drinks, and stop bugging him.

"Wanna talk about it yet?"

Mike glared at him and replied, "You wouldn't understand."

"Try me."

"Okay, then. My best friend and I are cops."

The bartender instinctively took a step back. An angry cop was bad enough, but a drunk one was downright frightening. He would have stopped serving the guy earlier if he had known. The man was probably carrying a gun. Now he had to figure a way to either get the gun away from the drunk, or make sure someone else could make sure he didn't start shooting it at innocent people.

"He was killed in the line of duty last night," Mike continued, "when someone damn near ripped his head off."

"Off?" The bartender was sure it was an exaggeration.

"You heard me. Off. Don't you read the papers? There were hundreds of witnesses."

One of the regulars who had been sitting at the bar most of the day spoke up for the first time. "Yeah, I heard about that. You must be talkin' 'bout the cop what got himself killed in Grant Park. Had his head torn off."

"That's him," Mike said, his head dropping toward the bar.

The bartender didn't know if he was about to pass out on the bar or if he was just hanging his head in sorrow. He almost hoped Mike would pass out, so he wouldn't have to worry about the gun. He reached across the bar and laid a hand on Mike's arm and said, "Oh, man, I'm so sorry. Here, have a double on the house." As soon as he said the words, he regretted them. Just what a drunk with a gun needs, another drink.

Mike gave him a look of thanks and downed the double shot that was set in front of him. He thought about asking what it was, but he really didn't care, as long as it contained alcohol. If he had asked, the bartender would have lied to him anyway. Mike had gotten so drunk that he didn't even realize the bartender was slipping him coffee and water every once in a while.

A cell phone went off and Mike knew it was his. He pulled it from the inside pocket of his sport coat, which he had laid across the beer-soaked bar, and tried to focus on the lighted display on the face of the phone. Through a difficult series of callisthenic squints, he managed to make out that the call was coming from Jane's cell phone.

He flipped open the phone, and put it to the side of his head. "Hello?" he slurred into the mouthpiece.

"Mike! Where are you? Are you okay?" Jane was frantic.

"Yeah, I'm fine. Just fine."

"Have you been drinking?" She could hear his slurred speech, and knew right away what was happening.

He slammed the phone's lid shut, breaking the connection, and grabbed his coat from the bar. He slid from the bar stool, taking a long moment to balance on wobbly legs, and stumbled toward the door.

"Hey, man, let me call you a taxi." It was that damned bartender butting into his business again. "Or maybe one of your cop buddies."

"There's no need. I'll just take the train home."

Mike stepped out into the night air and cringed as his cell phone started chirping again. Without looking at the display, he knew it was probably his wife calling back, furious at him not only for drinking, but for hanging up on her as well. He was in no mood for a lecture about getting drunk, so there was no way he was going to answer the call. It didn't matter if it was someone else entirely, because there was no one else he wanted to talk to about anything, either. The one person in the world he wished he could talk to was Sam, and Sam wasn't going to be calling his cell phone any time soon. Or ever.

With all the strength he could muster, he heaved the phone into the middle of the street, listening with a smile on his face as he heard the black plastic hit the pavement and break apart. Only then did he start to walk toward the train station a couple of blocks down the street.

Along the way, he realized his bladder was calling to him, which was no surprise after all the liquid he'd poured down his throat, and he needed to relieve himself before he involuntarily wet his pants. With no public restroom between the bar and the train station, he ducked into the next alley. Far too intoxicated to fear its darkness this late at night, the emergency signals from his bladder overrode any sense of caution. He stepped behind a dumpster and unzipped his fly.

Out of the corner of his eye, a small movement caught his attention. He turned to look further down the alley, and saw two bodies lying on the ground. He did a double take, squinting through the haze, not sure if it was the dark alley or the alcohol playing with his vision, making the bodies appear headless. He decided it wasn't blurred vision, since he could make out other details like the color and style of their clothing, and the direction the bodies were facing. Off to the side of the alley, he saw a tall blonde woman holding up yet a third body, this one also headless. It has to be a hallucination, he decided, mostly because the woman appeared to be sucking the blood from the body she held in her arms. When Mike glanced to the far side of the alley, he swore he could see eyes staring at him from a small mound that he imagined would be the decapitated heads. The eyes seemed to glow, reflecting the little light that penetrated the darkness of the alley, shining toward him, begging for help.

He stumbled and backed out of the alley, fumbling to raise his zipper, and trying to remember what had happened to his phone. Should he call 911? Should he call the Chief? Who would believe what he had just seen? And had he really even seen it?

Like a curtain, the alcoholic haze suddenly parted, and he remembered what had happened to his phone. He ran back to where he had launched it into the street, only to find that it had, in fact, exploded upon impact. The remaining pieces had been run over several times in the busy traffic, rendering the phone far beyond any hope of being repaired.

His mind, now clearer, recalled the scene he'd witnessed only moments before. The dead bodies came back in a flash, their lifeless heads separated from them by something; he couldn't even imagine what. And what was the blonde woman doing? It sure looked like she was drinking their blood, like a scene out of an old horror movie.

At that thought, Mike leaned against a blue Volvo parked in the street and threw up.

Once finished relieving his stomach of its liquid load, he thought again about who to call. Who would believe him? He still wasn't sure he believed it himself. He decided he better go back and take another look.

He slowly crept into the alley and saw that the woman was gone. He moved further down, looking from side to side, and chided himself for his overactive imagination. There was nothing there. The heads he thought he'd seen were gone, and where he thought the bodies had been lying, he found only a black oily substance. There was an awful stench in the alley, but that was normal. He thought nothing of it.

He turned around and left the alley, walking to the train station as fast as his unsteady legs would carry him. Although he was certain he had imagined the entire scene with the help of the abundance of alcohol he had consumed, he couldn't get the picture out of his head. When he reached the train station, he jumped the turnstile, ran up the stairs to the elevated platform, and slipped into the doors of the waiting train just as they began to close. He took an empty seat near the middle of the train, and stared at the passing scenery. Three stops later, he realized he had boarded the train going the wrong direction.

"Oh, well," he muttered, "ain't that just the icing on the cupcake of my week."

Mike settled back into the seat and tried to decide if he should get off at the next stop and board the correct train, or if he should just ride to the end of the line and take a taxi home. It didn't take long for the gentle rocking of the train to lull him to sleep.

FOURTEEN

"End of the line, pal!" A rough hand shook him awake. It took Mike a moment to realize where he was. This was the famed "South Side"; he was far from home. He took his time getting his bearings, and standing up, while the train operator stood over him with a disparaging look. Once on his feet, Mike exited the train and left the station, hoping to find a taxi outside on the street. He didn't hope too high, though; he knew taxis avoided this part of town as much as they could. It was illegal for the cab drivers to intentionally avoid certain neighborhoods, but it was a law that was next to impossible to enforce. Mike started walking toward what he assumed was the nearest "main" thoroughfare; maybe his luck would be in and there'd be a cab there.

Along the way, he looked at the run down housing complexes, the beat up buildings, and the shabby cars that lined the streets. He realized that this was similar to the neighborhood where Sam had grown up, and was exactly the kind of place Sam wanted to patrol. He also noticed that there were few people out at this time of night. In his neighborhood, there would still be people out and about, although it was starting to get dark. Kids would still be playing in the yards. But here, where the residents never knew what crimes were about to occur, people stayed indoors to avoid becoming an "innocent bystander".

Eventually, Mike reached a well-lit street, and saw a taxi headed his way. The driver seemed to be in a hurry to leave the neighborhood, but slowed just in time to see Mike's hail, then stopped just long enough for Mike to hop into the backseat. The driver was on his way before Mike even had the chance to give him a destination address.

At a red light, Mike looked out the window and noticed a liquor store that was still open. He threw a hundred dollar bill onto the front passenger seat. "That tip's yours if you'll pull over and wait for me right here."

The driver hesitated, wanting to get to a safer neighborhood, but did as requested, watching Mike disappear into the liquor store. He didn't like sitting and waiting for a fare, but it had been a slow night, and he could use the big tip.

Moments later, Mike came back out with large bottle of Jack Daniel's under his arm. Noticing the look on the driver's face, he promised not to drink in the cab. On the rest of the ride, Mike swore the warm honey-amber liquid was calling to him. The driver tried to engage Mike in small talk a few times, but Mike wasn't interested in talking. He'd done all the talking he wanted to do with the bartender, and now he just wanted to get home and continue his fall from sobriety. And he certainly didn't want to tell this man about his visions in the alley. The guy would turn around and take him straight to the psych ward of the nearest hospital.

Instead, Mike lay back his head, closed his eyes, and nearly fell asleep more than once during the long drive home.

* * *

When the cab arrived outside Mike's home, he dropped his fare into the front seat, along with the extra hundred bucks, plus a sizeable tip. He got out of the car, stumbled up the curb, and went through the garage, heading straight for the basement. Jane was either in bed early or wasn't home, but he locked the door just in case. She knew he'd been drinking, and would be pissed when she found him. He decided to postpone the inevitable as long as possible.

He dug through the piles of boxes that had been stored underneath the stairway, finally pulling out the ones he was looking for. When he had quit drinking, he had stored his home bar supplies in these boxes. There were glasses of varying sizes and shapes, openers, cutters, shakers, peelers, an ice pitcher, and an array of tools for creating specialized cocktails. Jane had wanted to toss it all in the trash and get it as far from Mike as possible, but he wanted to hold on to it with the excuse that it would come in handy whenever he and Jane decided to entertain guests. Of course, Jane never let him get anywhere near the stuff for fear that he would give in to temptation and fall back into his old, bad habits.

Inside one of the cardboard boxes, Mike found the tumbler that had been one of his favorite drinking glasses, an oversized job that held nearly twice the amount of liquor as a standard glass. He recalled many memories, good and bad, associated with that particular tumbler as he walked with it to the utility sink. It took him several minutes to scrape and wash away nearly six years' worth of dust and grime and restore the glass to its smooth, glassy shine.

Next to the utility sink stood the old refrigerator that Mike had used in his "bachelor pad" during the years in the academy. Now it was used by Jane to store extra food that didn't fit in the kitchen refrigerator. She liked to shop at warehouse clubs, getting better deals on food and supplies by buying them in large quantities. The fridge had a single, heavily insulated door with a stainless steel handle. With the door standing open, the upper third of the interior contained the freezer compartment, an off-white plastic door separating it from the rest of the refrigerator.

Mike opened the freezer compartment and was pleasantly surprised to find a plentiful supply of ice cubes. He dropped several into his freshly washed tumbler, listening with pleasure to the frozen cubes clinking against the glass. They brought back even more memories. He covered the ice with a generous splash of Jack Daniels, pouring until the amber liquid nearly reached the lip of the tumbler.

Pushing a few more boxes out of the way, Mike unearthed an old futon, another remnant of his single days that had been relegated to the basement because it didn't match the furniture currently occupying the living room. It seemed to Mike that quite a few of the things he possessed before meeting Jane had been sent to the obscure purgatory of the basement, not being thrown completely into the trash, but not meant to be used in any capacity, either.

He dropped his tired form into the pale green cushion, and sipped at his drink, picking up where he had left off at the bar. He continued drinking to try and erase the memory of the past two days. First Sam, with his grotesquely twisted head, and having to tell Rachel about it. Then the Chief telling him to take two weeks off. Then whatever it was that he had seen in the alley. He still wasn't sure if it had been real, his imagination, or something in between.

What he was sure of was what his mind kept telling him it was. Something supernatural. Something evil. And something out of a science fiction movie. But vampires didn't really exist ... did they?

* * *

Chief David Duncan was used to working long hours. It came with the job and responsibility of serving and protecting the third largest city in the United States. But tonight it wasn't work that kept him in his office. Tonight it was a memory from twenty-five years in the past, a memory that he thought he had suppressed forever.

Fresh from the academy, David Duncan was assigned, like all rookie cops, to foot patrol. He was one of the lucky few who actually got an assignment in a neighborhood he was familiar with. It was the neighborhood where he had grown up, and where his mother still lived. He had only been on the force for a few weeks, but he was already falling into a routine, stopping at the same shops, talking to the same businesspeople, and generally letting the neighborhood know that he was around, should they need help. It made the neighbors feel better to have one of "their own" working the beat, instead of some cop recruited from far away. Having grown up there, Duncan would be more invested in protecting the neighborhood instead of simply going through the motions.

He was walking down one of those familiar streets one evening, watching the lights come on in the apartments, imagining the families settling down for the night, when he heard the blood-curdling scream of a woman coming from an alley. David had pulled his revolver and held it up, ready to fire a warning shot at whoever was causing the disturbance, when he realized he had no backup in the immediate vicinity. If this were a major crime in progress, he would have to handle it alone. Rookie or not, he felt up to the task.

He ran toward the screaming and stopped when he came to the alleyway. Pressing his back against the brick wall, he peered around the corner, and saw the shadow of two figures locked in an embrace. It appeared to be a rape in progress, with the attacker forcing the victim to the ground right there in the alley. David turned into the alley and pointed his revolver at the scene. He knew he couldn't fire the weapon. He couldn't be certain which was the attacker and which was the victim. And even if he could distinguish which was which, he wasn't positive he could get a clear shot without injuring the person he was supposed to be saving.

As he moved down the alley, he saw that the apparent attacker had his face buried in the other person's neck, seemingly having the upper hand in the struggle that was occurring.

"Freeze! Police!" David shouted, expecting the standard order to make the attacker either stop and surrender or run away. What he didn't expect was for the attacker to stop, look up at David revealing a mouth covered in the victim's blood, and actually grin at him. The dark eyes that stared down the alley stunned David momentarily, causing him to nearly drop his guard. The black hair was pulled back slickly into a small ponytail slung across his shoulder. His mesmerizing eyes glinted and reflected the light of the moon like pure obsidian. His lower face, from the tip of his straight nose to the bottom of his square chin, was covered in blood, the only breach in the red void being the sparkle of immaculately white teeth. David started to run toward the attacker, seemingly in slow motion, and could see that the teeth included a set of deadly sharp fangs.

The man suddenly dropped the body of his victim, letting it crumple to the ground like a piece of old newspaper, before flying straight up into the air.

David was out of breath when he reached the spot. He circled the body, looking skyward for any sign. There was nothing but empty fire escapes and bricked-over windows. He couldn't understand where the attacker had gone, or how.

David turned his attention to the victim lying at his feet. He could immediately tell he was looking at an older woman, and dreaded the worst. The neighborhood would be up in arms about the attack, but the fervor would be increased exponentially if the victim were one of the elderly residents.

He gently rolled the body over, careful not to touch the severe wound in the woman's neck. He knew the investigators would want a clean look. When he turned the victim enough to see her face, his lungs seemed to collapse inward, and David lost the ability to breathe. The face was that of his own mother.

He touched the fabric of her coat, and recognized it as the one she always wore. He looked at her shoes, her clothes, her hair, hoping for some sign that this body was not hers. But when he looked to the side of the alley and saw the wheeled cart that his mother always used to carry groceries from the corner store back to her apartment, he couldn't deny what he was seeing. He had just seen his own mother murdered, and had let the attacker get away. He looked helplessly into her eyes as the last signs of life faded away, before gently closing her eyelids with his fingertips and bowing his head in sorrow.

He turned her head to the side, where the attacker had been focused, expecting to see a giant gash, or at least enough torn flesh to have caused her death. Instead, he found two tiny, neat puncture marks on the side of her neck. There was hardly any blood.

David had read about the supernatural as a youngster, and had taken a keen interest in vampires and werewolves. But he never realized that the stories could have any basis in reality, or that something so horrible could strike so close to home. His mother's murderer was never found, and the case remained unsolved, officially listed as a "ritualistic slaying", some cult activity, probably some sort of satanic ritual sacrifice.

David was not convinced. He was certain of what he had seen, and insisted that the perpetrator was not of the natural world.

The current Chief, not wanting to lose one of his brightest and newest recruits to an insane asylum, paid for therapy out of the force's own funds, hoping to break David of his thoughts of the supernatural. David fought the therapy for a while, continually trying to convince others of what he was certain he witnessed. But no matter what he said, he still couldn't make anyone believe what he saw.

He eventually gave in, even going so far as to allow himself to be hypnotized and have the memory and his beliefs in the supernatural buried deep within his psyche. With those thoughts secreted safely away, he managed a long and successful career in the Chicago Police Department, escalating through the ranks to his current position as Chief of Police.

But now, having seen two autopsy reports nearly identical to that of his mother's, his subconscious mind began to break through the barriers that were set in place by the hypnosis of twenty-five years ago.

David's hands began to shake at the memory, and the thought of what might be out there, prowling the streets of his city. He pulled open the bottom drawer of his desk and reached into the very back, where a small bottle of Bacardi Rum had been hidden. Placing it on the desk, he walked out of his office into the deserted hallway. At the end was a small vending area, where David walked and deposited three quarters into a Coke machine. He returned to his desk, Coke can in hand, and mixed it with the smooth rum in a styrofoam cup meant for the stale coffee that was always prevalent in the department. After downing the first cup and mixing another, he lit up another cigarette.

Just how many of the 'unsolved' deaths in the city had puncture wounds somewhere on the body? How many satanic cult sacrifices are listed in the unsolved murder files? And how do I start a task force to research this?

It wasn't something he could make public. And it certainly wasn't something he could have circulating through the office. He'd be chased from the department. Vampires in Chicago? That theory would surely get him committed to an asylum for life, and cause his family to become outcasts from society.

So, who could he trust to help him solve this mystery?

FIFTEEN

Ever since Carlos had tracked his unsuspecting prey into a crowded concert hall where he first experienced Big Band Jazz, he had been addicted. Whether it was the high energy of Bebop, the sultry tones of Blues, or the massive sounds of a Big Band, his hunger for jazz nearly matched his hunger for human blood.

Soon after moving to Chicago, Carlos had discovered an out of the way jazz club, where the pickings for dinner were as exceptional as the music. It was a small club on the north side, little more than a hole in the wall, hardly visible from the outside. But despite its shabby exterior and nearly vacant look, the place was packed wall-to-wall almost every night. He had spent many nights there, enjoying the sounds, and choosing his victim of the evening.

After sleeping for almost two decades, Carlos was pleasantly surprised to see that the club was still open and entirely unchanged.

Nothing like good music to go with your dinner, thought Carlos as he fought his way through the dense crowd. To one side, in a far corner of the bar, was a table that featured a clear view of the stage, the entrance, and most important, the jazz aficionados that frequented the club. It had been his table in the past, and he headed toward it once again.

The club was filled well beyond capacity, the floor pulsing to the beat of the five-piece hard bop combo playing the music of John Coltrane and Dizzy Gillespie, nearly every foot in the place tapping in rhythm with the band. It would not be a simple task to take his victim out through this crowd without being noticed, but Carlos was patient, especially when he had some of his favorite music to listen to while he waited.

He reached his table to find it already occupied by a trio of lovely ladies. He glanced at the wall above their heads and was pleased to see that the image of a serpent intertwined with a dragon was still there. It was small, and somewhat obscured in the wall after several years of wear, but the symbol that matched the image on his signet ring still remained.

"Good evening ladies." He gave them his most charming smile. "Mind if I join you? There's not another seat in the house."

"Be our guest," said the buxom brunette. "We have room for one more."

Carlos smiled, tight-lipped, and squeezed into the soft cushion seat that surrounded the table. He noticed that the fabric covering the seat had changed in color and texture since his last visit, but the table itself appeared to be the very one he remembered so well.

The waitress worked her way through the throng with the adept movements of someone who had been slinking through packed crowds for years. When she reached Carlos and his three new companions, she asked him what he'd like to drink, her voice husky from a decade of breathing in the second hand smoke that filled the air inside the small, unventilated club.

Carlos ordered a glass of merlot and began to tap his foot to the music coming from the stage, falling into the same trancelike state that had overcome the rest of the audience. He leaned his head back against the wall, closed his eyes, and allowed the music to wash over him while he waited for his drink to arrive.

The trio of girls, whom Carlos estimated could be no older twenty-two, giggled and whispered amongst themselves. He knew that they were focused entirely on him, but didn't let on that he could hear them. Instead, he remained absorbed entirely in the fast paced jazz emanating from the stage, confident that one of the three girls would eventually come to him.

"So, what college do you go to?" asked the strawberry blonde, snapping him momentarily from the spell of the music.

"I'm not in college. I work at Greystone Cemetery." He could have added that he was far too old for college, having been born centuries ago. But then he would have had to explain that his mother and father were ancients, immortals who had mated in accordance with the Code. That wasn't exactly the kind of thing he wanted to discuss with these young ladies.

For some reason, the girls exploded in peals of laughter. Perhaps it was the thought of this elegant looking "young man" working in a cemetery, but Carlos wasn't sure. He played along with the joke anyway, and laughed with them.

"So, you ladies find a working man funny?"

"No," said the brunette, "we just took you to be one of those serious, studious types."

"Ah, I see." Carlos found himself looking into the dark green eyes of the auburn haired girl who hadn't said a thing except to giggle with her girlfriends. She was obviously the shy, reserved member of the group, yet he found himself speaking directly to her, practically ignoring her two more boisterous friends.

"And what's your name, my dear?"

"Jennifer," came the timid, almost inaudible reply.

"That's a pretty name, Jennifer. A pretty name for a pretty girl." She blushed, and looked down at her hands, folded in her lap. It was as if she were ashamed to have him speaking directly to her. "Do you go to college?"

"Yes, I'm a psych major." She still didn't look up.

Jennifer's friends found the conversation uninteresting, and certainly not headed in the direction they'd expected. It was normally one of them that a man in the bar would talk to, rarely, if ever, Jennifer. She was shy, mousy, and although potentially attractive, seemed to go out of her way to make herself appear plain.

It wasn't only Jennifer's insecure personality that kept most men at bay. She also had a prosthetic leg, which, once noticed, made men act as if she had suddenly developed the plague. They quickly lost interest in her, and find someone more "interesting" to talk to, such as Jennifer's friends. At evening's end, Jennifer would drive the smitten young couples home before returning to her own apartment, alone yet again.

But this time it was as if the world had melted away, leaving only Jennifer and Carlos in the club, talking, laughing, and enjoying the jazz music. Her friends quietly got up and excused themselves, leaving Jennifer and Carlos alone at the table, so that Jennifer could have a little fun—a little hope—before the stranger discovered her leg and suddenly remembered a "pressing engagement" elsewhere.

Jennifer, suddenly alone with the strange man, found herself telling him all about her life and childhood, her likes and dislikes, her hopes and dreams, and her fears. It was as if a cocoon had opened and a beautiful butterfly had emerged right in front of Carlos' eyes. He normally didn't get this involved with his meals, preferring that they remain nameless, unknown creatures, but he found himself drawn to this girl. He couldn't explain it, but he knew she would be more than a simple snack.

"Why don't we get out of here and go for a walk?" he finally asked.

"Um," she hesitated for the first time, "I don't walk very good, and I don't know if my friends would appreciate me leaving them."

"It's all right, my dear. I have a horse-drawn carriage waiting outside. Let's take a ride in the fresh night air and get to know each other better."

Carlos stood and moved easily across the crowded floor to the bar, where Jennifer's friends were still flirting, looking forward to a night of romance, passion, and lust. He informed them that he was taking Jennifer on a carriage ride, and that he would make sure she got home safely. They were immediately concerned about their friend. Had he not yet seen her prosthetic leg? Was he some kind of psycho who might harm her? They certainly didn't want anything bad to happen to her. On the other hand, she was a big girl, and could take care of herself. If she was comfortable leaving with this man, who were they to stop her? After all, they'd left with strangers many times before.

The girls offered to help Jennifer get through the crowd and out of the building, but Carlos waved them away. Their thoughts turned again to Jennifer's unnatural leg, and whether or not the stranger knew. They watched as he returned to their table, the crowd neatly parting for him, and, with an arm around her shoulders, easily lift the girl out of the padded seat. He helped her limp out of the bar, oblivious to the condition of her leg, with the crowd again parting and leaving a clear path. Jennifer's friends could only watch in amazement and wonder who the stranger was, and what Jennifer had said to create such interest.

Outside, Carlos assisted Jennifer into the waiting carriage before climbing in and sitting down beside her. A pull on a short rope rang a bell on the outside, telling the driver they were ready to begin their ride. He urged the horses forward with a snap of the reins and a sharp "Giddyap!" steering the carriage toward the lake and along the shimmering lakefront.

Jennifer felt simply giddy. Nothing like this had ever happened to her. She was always the one who ended up going home alone, but here she was, in a horse-drawn carriage, sitting beside what had to be the best looking man she had ever seen.

To punctuate the moment, Carlos reached under the seat and, seemingly from thin air, pulled out a white rose and presented it to Jennifer.

"For me?" she asked, tears forming in the corners of her eyes. She took it and touched the petals, realizing they were silk. She looked at him questioningly. "It's silk. I thought it was a real rose."

"You deserve pretty things. And you deserve things that will last forever. Real roses die. But you, my dear, should have eternal beauty." Carlos slipped his arm around the back of her neck and Jennifer felt a shiver go up her spine. She assumed it was from the chill night air, and drew her arms tight across her chest in an effort to keep warm, clutching the rose tightly in her fingers. Carlos recognized the shiver as the feeling all mortals get when in the presence of the undead, and he drew her closer to him.

"Don't be afraid," his soothing voice floated to her ears. "I don't bite … much." They both laughed at the comment as if it were the funniest ever uttered.

An idea was forming in Carlos' mind. He could simply have this girl as his evening meal, giving her a quick and painless death. But he was in need of a new companion. He had just awakened and longed to have someone by his side. He was getting tired of the mindless followers he had created who feared him and did his bidding, for they did not fulfill his desires. A new companion could join him night after night, and sleep beside him during the day. He had already sensed something special about this young girl, and felt she would be perfect.

"Did you ever wish that you had unlimited power? The power to do anything you wanted?" asked Carlos.

Jennifer ducked her head sheepishly, as if she were afraid to admit to such a selfish thought. It didn't occur to her that he had suddenly changed the subject and become very serious. She assumed he was just trying to get to know the "real" Jennifer, so she replied as honestly as she could.

"Yes, I have. I've thought about having power over all those who made fun of me over the years. And I've thought of making them pay for all the awful things they did to me and said about me."

Really?" Carlos was surprised at her complete frankness. He was also very pleased. Her feelings would make what he hoped to accomplish perhaps quite easy. "Because I can make that happen."

Jennifer looked up into his dark eyes, searching for some sign of a smile, a laugh, anything to give away the joke that she was sure was to follow at her expense. But she saw nothing but a solid mask of seriousness.

"What do you mean, Carlos?"

"I can make you my companion. You would become one of the most powerful people in the entire world, Jennifer. No one would laugh at you again, and no one would ever doubt your power."

Jennifer looked down at her hands, trembling in her lap, and considered the offer for a moment, wondering who this man really was. She remembered her mother once telling her that "anything too good to be true, probably is". She was afraid to find out that this simply was too good to be true. There had to be a catch. Finally, she looked back into his face, still set in its stony expression, and said, "What would I be giving up?"

Pleased at her willingness to remain and explore his offer, his lips curled into a smile as he said, "Just mortal life."

"What do you mean, mortal life?" Jennifer was beginning to feel frightened, but something about the look in his eyes was keeping her from asking to return to her friends. Something about him intrigued her; she found that she didn't want to leave him.

Carlos looked deeply into her eyes. "My dear, there is a world that co-exists with your mortal world. We have lived in the shadows for centuries, without discovery. We have walked among you, without your knowledge. We are the children of the night, the immortal, the vampires."

At the mention of vampires, Carlos had seen a variety of reactions. Fear was normal. Skepticism and disbelief were fairly regular reactions, as well. But instead of either of those reactions, Jennifer simply thought quietly for a moment. Carlos wanted to know what was going through her mind, but he relied on his patience and waited for her to respond.

He would have been pleased to know what it was she was actually thinking. She was still unsure about him. He seemed serious, but was talking about things that couldn't possibly be real. On the other hand, she wondered if it would be so bad becoming a vampire? She could take her revenge on people that made fun of her because of the accident that cost her leg. She had no family. She had few friends. Those that did act as friends only took her to the bars to ensure a designated driver, or to tease her with the fact that they could collect men like most women collect shoes, and she could not. And besides, she thought to herself with grin, I'm not exactly a morning person anyway.

She turned to Carlos, her decision made. He saw the smile on her lips before she said, "I've thought about it. I have nothing in this mortal world to hold me back. I'm ready."

Carlos looked at her, seeing her already begin to gain the self-assurance of a vampire. "Are you sure?"

"Yes," came the simple, yet firm, reply.

"You will be my companion for eternity."

"So I am to become your bride?"

Carlos had never thought of companions in terms of husband and wife, or bride and groom, but if the mortal terminology would please this young woman, he would comply. "Yes," he told her. "You would be my bride."

"Well, then, my groom, I am yours."

Jennifer leaned her head away from Carlos, offering her smooth, pale neck to him, and closed her eyes, awaiting the pain that would soon engulf her. Carlos looked at the lovely stretch of bare skin in front of him, a strange feeling coming into his groin, a feeling that he had not felt in a long time.

"This will only hurt for a short time. I promise."

His fangs pierced the lily-white skin, and a soft whine escaped Jennifer's lips. She immediately began to feel cold creep through her body as Carlos drank her blood. But before reaching the point of her death, he drew his head back, raised his wrist to his blood-soaked mouth, and bit into his own flesh. Offering his arm to Jennifer, he said simply, "Feed."

She gingerly reached out with her weakened and numbed hands and guided his arm with its self-inflicted wound to her own lips. She began to suckle, cautiously at first, but growing stronger as each drop of the fiery liquid entered her body. The more she drank, the more she craved. Carlos began to pull his arm away, but she only held tighter, her thirst for his blood increasing with each drop.

"Enough!" Carlos cried, pulling his arm forcefully away.

"I love you," said Jennifer unexpectedly. "And... thank you." She seemed to think that her mortal death and her transformation were already complete, and that the pain was over.

But then the pain began. The fire suddenly flowing through her veins burned to the depths of her soul, and she began to writhe in unbearable agony. Carlos held her closely and whispered, "It's all right, my love. Do not fight it. It will soon pass. You are becoming my bride."

Carlos continued to hold Jennifer as her body convulsed and thrashed about, eventually taking its last breath. Her transformation to the immortal world was nearly complete.

Jennifer lay still for a moment, the look of death on her face. Carlos watched her closely until her lids suddenly opened, revealing red-rimmed eyes beneath. Jennifer looked up at her "husband" and said, "I'm hungry."

* * *

The carriage wound its way back to the cemetery, and the crypt new husband and wife would now share. Carlos jumped down to help her out of the carriage, looking like any other couple arriving home after a night out.

"Uh…boss?" Nicolas interrupted hesitantly from his perch atop the carriage. He knew it was dangerous to speak unless Carlos addressed him first.

"What is it?" snapped Carlos. "Can't you see I'm busy showing my new bride her new home?"

"There's something in the doorway of your crypt."

Carlos walked to the rear of the carriage and looked around it to the entrance of the crypt. He saw that there was indeed something on the ground.

"Stay right here, on this side of the carriage," he instructed Jennifer, wanting to shield her from any potential danger.

Carlos strode purposefully around the back of the carriage to look more closely at the objects left on the ground. What he found were the heads of Grayson, Emile, and Davidson. He scooped them up by their tangled hair, still tied together, and held them up. This was a calling card he knew all too well.

"Oh, that bitch!" hissed Carlos. "I'm going to kill her myself!"

Just then, Jennifer appeared from the other side of the carriage, her curiosity having gotten the better of her. "What is it, my love?" She saw the three heads dangling from her husband's hand, and, shoving her fist into her mouth, stifled a scream. Carlos dropped the severed heads to the ground, threw his head back, casting his eyes to the sky, and screamed an unearthly scream of rage.

Vampires all over the city heard Carlos' scream. Birds and bats were disturbed and flew from their perches. Dogs howled. Rodents feeding in the trash-filled alleys stopped in their tracks and looked around for the source of the blood-curdling sound. Virginia, reclining on one of her favorite rooftops, knew that her "gift" had been received. She threw her head back and laughed. It was the one pleasant moment she had had all evening.

She had more in store for the fool that thought of himself as the "King of the Vampires". She was older than he, and well versed in this chess game that the ancients played amongst themselves. But, as with Nicolette, it was her responsibility to finish the game and rid the world of this troublesome vampire. No matter the cost in blood, be it mortal or immortal, Virginia was determined to declare "checkmate".

SIXTEEN

Mike lay on the futon in the basement listening to the movements of Jane and Meagan upstairs. His head was pounding, and felt like it would split in two at any moment, accompanying his stomach, the contents of which threatened to exit at the slightest provocation. The bright light of the sun shone through the small basement windows, blinding his tired, blood-shot eyes, and telling him it was morning. He didn't have much memory of the night before. He wasn't even sure it was just the night before. Had he been down here for more than a day? He had gotten so drunk in the past that he'd slept through whole days. He hoped it hadn't happened again. That would mean he could possibly have missed Sam's funeral. Would Jane have let that happen?

The only thing he was certain of at that moment was that his bottle of whiskey wasn't quite empty. He'd passed out before finishing the last of it. Thinking of the whiskey made his stomach lurch. He half stood and stumbled through the piles of cardboard boxes to the utility sink, where he grabbed the metallic lip with weakened hands, and heaved into the basin. He reached over to the faucet, turned on the cold water, and rested the side of his face against the cool surface of the sink.

* * *

Jane wasn't a stupid woman. She was certain she knew exactly where her husband was, and that he had been drinking again. That had been obvious from his slurred speech and the gruff way he acted toward her on the phone.

After the phone call, she'd decided to stay at Rachel's a while longer. It was late when she and Meagan finally returned home, and she had to carry the sleeping toddler upstairs to her room.

On her way through the house, she could hear Mike stumbling around in the basement. She hadn't noticed his car outside or in the garage, so she knew he didn't drive himself home. When she realized just how drunk he had gotten, she felt angry and betrayed at the same time. Angry that he had gone crawling back to the bottle he had promised to give up forever. Betrayed that just when they should be looking to each other for support, he'd chosen to go out and look for that support in a bottle.

She'd been through this before; she wasn't going to go through it again.

Her anger almost turned to pity for a brief instant. After all, the man had just lost his best friend. But then she realized that getting drunk was the last thing he needed to do to get over it. That wasn't the way to deal with the issue. It was a way to avoid it. And starting down that road once would easily lead to repeated trips.

It occurred to her that she wasn't sure that this was the first time he had gotten drunk since their wedding. There'd been many times he was out late, supposedly working. Had he been drinking behind her back all along? The anger and sense of betrayal returned at the thought that he could have been lying to her for years.

It didn't really matter if this had been his first fall from the wagon. It was going to have to be his last. If not, there would be only one result: he would drink himself to death. She was determined to not let that happen to him … or to her. Knowing there was nothing to be done while he was so obviously inebriated, she left him to his drunken misery and went to sleep alone in their cold bed.

* * *

In the morning, Jane stood by the locked door to the basement. She heard the sounds of movement below and knew Mike was awake. She was sure when she heard him retching. She got the spare key out of the kitchen drawer where they kept their odd and ends, and prepared herself to march down the wooden steps and drag her husband back up into the light.

But just when she felt ready for the confrontation, she heard a crash behind her. Meagan had been sitting quietly in her high chair eating breakfast, but leaned too far to the side, and tumbled over, taking the chair and her bowl of cereal with her.

Jane ran to the toddler to comfort her and make sure the baby wasn't hurt. Meagan seemed to be more scared than anything, so Jane knelt on the floor holding her daughter in her arms and rocking her until the tears quieted to sniffles, all the while singing what had become their song.

Once calm again, Meagan looked up at her mother and said, "I want Daddy."

At that moment a big part of Jane wanted Mike, too, but she wanted him sober and thinking, not drunk or hung over and swearing at the ceiling. Jane tried her best to be comforting, and said, "Sweetie, Daddy doesn't feel well right now. He's sick and needs to rest."

"Okay, Mommy," the little girl said between sniffles. "I hope Daddy feels better soon." Jane was amazed at the maturity shown by her four-year-old daughter. At times she acted like the little girl she truly was, but at other times her understanding of grown up concepts was astounding.

"It's almost time for pre-school. Why don't you run and get your backpack?"

Meagan ran off to get her Barbie backpack, one of the little treasures she kept hidden away in her room when she wasn't carrying it around. Jane walked back to the basement door and knocked hard, hoping for some response. She announced loudly, hoping he would hear her through the thick door, "Mike, I'm taking Meagan to school now. When I get back we need to have a talk!" She leaned on the door, pressing her ear to the wood, listening for footsteps coming up the stairs, or at least a groaning acknowledgment that she had spoken. But all she heard was silence.

Meagan came back into the kitchen carrying her backpack filled with some of her favorite toys. They were so precious to her that she couldn't bear to leave them home even for a day, so she packed them into her backpack and took them with her everywhere.

Jane took the little girl by the hand, led her out to the garage and put her in the car. She strapped the child into her safety seat, and climbed behind the wheel. She backed out of the garage and paused in the driveway before entering the street. She glanced at the house, her eyes drawn to the small ground level windows of the basement. In one of them, she saw Mike watching her. He looked like he had seen a ghost, and Jane realized that something was horribly wrong.

The drive to the pre-school was short, and Jane found an open parking space right in front. After walking Meagan into the building and kissing her goodbye, she started for home.

On the way, her head continued spinning with questions and all kinds of thoughts. Had Mike been drinking all this time on the sly? Drugs? Did it have something to do with the murder that he'd been called to on the day that Sam was killed? Did that murder remind him of his parents? What the hell could it be?

* * *

Mike had heard the crash in the kitchen. He could tell from the feet running across the floor and from the crying what had happened. He could also tell from his wife's lack of panic that everything was okay. He decided to stay where he was and let her handle it.

He heard Jane pound on the door and call to him, but he didn't think he could face her. Besides, he already knew what she would say.

The real problem was that she wouldn't understand. How could she understand? It wasn't just the loss of his friend. The macabre event had also brought back the painful memories of the other lives he had lost. He had long ago learned not to dwell on them, but now they were flooding his mind and wouldn't let go of his psyche.

Sam's death was just like the others: unsolved, an unnecessary murder of someone close to him. But this time there was something more. Something evil was lurking in the city after dark. Even his daughter seemed to sense it, and had given it a name. Mike doubted that anyone was safe from the Night People.

After he heard his family leave the kitchen, he stumbled through the boxes strewn about the basement and made his way to the small window that would allow him to look out onto their front lawn at ground level. From it, he had a clear view of their front driveway, and he watched as Jane backed the car out of the garage. He was surprised when she stopped and looked toward the house, catching his eyes in the window. Even from a distance, he could see pain, anger, and sadness mingled in her expression. He only hoped that he could make her understand. He also hoped he could protect his family from whatever it was that was out there.

* * *

Jane still wasn't sure how Mike had gotten home last night, but she was glad he hadn't driven after all the drinking he had apparently done. She got out of the car and nervously went inside the house, dreading the altercation she knew was coming. Once inside, she rummaged through their kitchen "junk" drawer, looking through the extension cables, light bulbs, birthday candles, and other stuff, until she found the spare key to the basement door. She unlocked it and slowly opened the door, listening to squeaking hinges in serious need of oil. She stepped cautiously onto the first step and called out to him, "Mike! I'm coming down!"

As she descended the creaking wooden staircase, Mike tried his best to hide the bottle, even though he knew he wouldn't be fooling her. It was obvious what he had been doing, even if their phone conversation — if it could be called a conversation — hadn't given him away. His tumbler was sitting on the makeshift table he had built out of boxes, the freezer door was still open from the last trip he made to it for ice, and the liquor on his breath couldn't be disguised. He tried to put the nearly empty jug behind him in a weak effort at subterfuge.

She looked at him with disdain clear in her eyes and said, "Don't try to hide it. It'll only make things worse."

There was nothing he could say, so he said nothing.

Jane broke the awkward silence. "I thought you'd kicked this habit. What the hell is going on?"

"Jane, you don't want to know and you wouldn't understand."

"Try me. I've been through too much with you to let you just slip back into this again."

"Jane, go away," he screamed, growing angrier. He didn't know why he was getting angry with his wife. She was only trying to help.

"If I walk out of this basement without us talking and you telling me what's going on, then I'll walk straight out of this house. And when Meagan gets out of school, I'll pick her up, take her, and leave. Mike, you won't see either one of us again, unless you let me try to help you. And I can't do that if you won't talk."

"Fine, bitch. You just do that. Take her and go," Mike sneered at his wife, the words and sudden fury shocking not only her, but him as well. He didn't think she would actually take his child away from him, but he also didn't know why he was acting this way. It was as if he had lost all control, and simply couldn't help himself.

Jane's shock was quickly replaced by the anger she had felt the night before. She couldn't tell if it was the drink making him say these things or if he really meant it. She ran back up the stairs crying and went to her bedroom where she began packing her bags, hoping Mike would appear in the doorway to stop her. When she finished packing and he still wasn't there, she went to Meagan's room and packed her things, as well, crying all the while. She just couldn't believe that the man that meant the world to her had told her to leave their home.

But she knew she couldn't back down now. If she did, he would be able to go on treating her the way he just had, and he would never stop drinking. If that were to happen, she didn't want to be around him, and she certainly couldn't expose Meagan to the monster that Mike could become when he was drunk.

She walked out of Meagan's bedroom, making sure she had packed the toddler's favorite teddy bear, picked up her own bags from the hallway, and began to walk down the stairs. She was still hoping that she would find him at the bottom of the stairs, ready to apologize for what he had just said to her. But still there was no sign of him.

It was indeed time to go. She yelled down the stairs, "Goodbye, Mike. The next time we talk it will be through a lawyer. You better get a good one, because I plan on taking full custody of Meagan, and you'll pay through the nose for child support!" Jane strained her ears, listening for some reaction to her threat. She didn't know if she meant what she'd said or if they were just empty words. But she hoped they would at least cause Mike to make some offering, some concession, some simple reaction that could be the start of fixing what was suddenly happening between them.

Instead, all she heard was the sound of snoring. She was used to hearing that sound coming from the body occupying the other side of her bed; it gave her comfort to know that her husband was there, and was at peace. But this time it wasn't a comfortable sound. It wasn't the sound of a man at peace, but, rather, one who had passed out again. And if she didn't stand her ground, it could be the man she would lose forever.

Jane carried the bags outside, put them into the trunk of the car, and backed out of the driveway, heading straight back to Meagan's pre-school. It had been barely an hour since she'd dropped her daughter off, but she didn't want to wait for the end of the day and give herself time to change her mind.

She told the teacher that there was family trouble and she needed to take Meagan out for the day.

"Where's Daddy?" demanded Meagan the moment they were in the car.

"How about you and me go on an adventure? We'll drive up to Grandma's house in Wisconsin."

"Yay! I love to see Grandma!"

Jane pulled away from the curb and headed for the Kennedy Expressway, northbound through the suburbs, and across the state border. Three hours after leaving their home, they arrived in Jefferson, Wisconsin, and the warmth of her mother's house.

SEVENTEEN

Chief David Duncan knew he had a long and hard day ahead of him. There had been three murders in two days, one of them an officer killed in the line of duty, and he had one raging hangover. And to top it all off, he had a nine o'clock meeting with the Mayor.

He hated going to the Daley Center to meet with the Mayor. It usually meant one thing: a serious ass chewing for something that he'd be caught unaware of, or had little to no control over. Additionally, he knew that he'd soon be asked to cut his budget more than he already had, and then he'd have to pull officers off the streets because there was no money for their salaries. But with what had happened over the past couple of nights, how could he pull officers? If anything, he needed more feet on the streets.

Of course, he certainly couldn't tell the Mayor his suspicions about what was happening. How could he tell the leader of one of the largest metropolitan areas in the country that the "unnatural" was running loose in its streets, and that he needed more foot patrol to keep the citizens from being attacked by vampires? It was hard enough to get extra officers during the summer to patrol the concerts and movies in the park, and all the festivals that went on. It would be next to impossible to put through a request to cover "guarding against immortals".

He bent down and reached under his desk to grab the bottle of aspirin he had dropped on the floor; on the way up he bumped his head on the underside of the desk drawer he had left open. He was leaning back in his chair with his hand against the knot already forming on the back of his head when his assistant walked in.

"Mornin' Chief," she said cheerfully. "Here's your coffee and yesterday's reports from all the districts." Irene's thick Jamaican accent cut through the room, and her dark skinned, athletic body practically floated across the floor to his desk. In their lighter moments, he teased her about her background, poorly imitating her more-than-a-little-put-on stereotypical speech. But today he was all business.

"Just put 'em on my desk. I'll get to them when I can."

She set down the coffee as he fought with the childproof lid of the aspirin bottle. Finally, he managed to pop the lid and shake out four of the chalky white tablets, washing them down with hot coffee.

Irene put the reports in the middle of his desk without another word, and turned to leave the room. The Chief sure was in a sour mood lately. She vowed to keep out of the line of fire, to do everything she could to avoid the terrible temperament he evidenced at times. He needs a vacation, she thought as she left his office and headed to her cubicle outside his office door. Lord knows I'd enjoy it if he took one!

Looking at the clock, David realized that he needed to leave immediately or he'd be late for his meeting. He sure didn't want to give the Mayor anything else to bitch about.

He ran out of his office and bumped into a sergeant headed toward his office. The sergeant began to talk, but David put his hand in the man's face and said "Not now, Richard. I've got a nine a.m. with the Mayor."

Outside, the bright morning sun stung his eyes. He searched his pockets for his sunglasses but, today of all days, when he needed them, they weren't there. It looked like everything in his day was going to follow the same miserable, uncooperative pattern.

Chief Duncan jogged across Clark Street, dodging his way through the line of cars stuck at the red light, and ran across the concrete courtyard that led to the entrance of the Daley Center. He hurried past the Picasso sculpture in front of the building, a piece of art that he thought looked like nothing more than a giant aluminum can sliced up the sides and twisted into a deformed mess. He stepped through the main doors, ignoring the imposing glass face of the building, and was quickly admitted through the metal detectors at the security checkpoints in the main floor atrium. He stepped around the dozens of people lingering in front of the banks of elevators as they tried to decipher which one would take them to the floor on which they were supposed to be.

The elevator that the Chief stepped into was unoccupied, and as he rose through the building his thoughts about the meeting to come were broken by the Muzak clawing its way through the tiny, underpowered speaker mounted in the ceiling of the car. Chief Duncan had involuntarily been humming along when he realized the song was "Muskrat Love," which he truly hated. His ex-wife had played that damn tune over and over again until he thought his ears would bleed.

Just when he was giving serious consideration to ripping the speaker out of the ceiling, the doors mercifully opened and he stepped out onto the Mayor's floor where he was greeted by yet another security guard.

"Morning, Chief!" the security said with a smile.

Does everyone have to act so damned cheery all the time, David wondered, knowing full well it was an act put on for his benefit.

He followed the plush carpeted walkway to the door at the end of the hall, wondering for the hundredth time how the mayor could squawk about expenditures by the Chicago Police Dept when the hallway leading to his own office was decorated so lavishly. More money had been spent on this walkway than had been spent on all of the CPD offices across the street combined. He pushed open the heavily lacquered door at the end and entered the outer office of the Mayor of Chicago.

"Good Morning, Chief," said Janet, the Mayor's assistant. Another cheery welcome for David, but one he had come to expect, and certainly didn't mind. He even saw a small twinkle in her eye, one that most people didn't get to see. It was reserved especially for David.

"He's expecting you. You can go right in." She nodded her head to the side, in the direction of the heavy oak doors behind her and to the right. David, and anyone else allowed to enter the hallowed grounds of the office of the Mayor would certainly know that "he" meant Larry Larson, the Mayor of Chicago, and which door led to him. But Janet always pointed the way unnecessarily, with a hand or with her head, out of habit.

David crossed the outer office in a few quick strides, and entered the inner sanctum of the most powerful man in Chicago. He had been there many times before, and was not taken in by the regal and majestic décor. The wall on the right was filled with framed photographs, a shrine displaying Larry shaking hands with hundreds of celebrities, his arm around the shoulders of hundreds of others, and numerous special events where the Mayor was a special guest or the guest of honor. The wall to the left was ceiling to floor with thick built-in mahogany bookshelves that, at first glance, looked to be filled with city codes books, law books, and other reference materials needed to run a large city. But a closer inspection revealed classic novels, recent NY Times best sellers, and many books being used as filler to keep the shelves from appearing empty and unused. The room was meant to intimidate and impress, and frequently did.

If David really looked around, he'd wonder if this was where the money cut from his department's budget was going. But he took little notice of his surroundings; he was too busy preparing himself for the epic ass chewing that he was sure was about to begin.

"Sit," barked Mayor Larry Larson, pointing to one of the small, wing-backed leather chairs that sat in front of his immense desk. He was standing next to his throne, a chair similar to those for guests but much larger, rifling through some papers.

Hmm, thought David, not even a 'good morning'. Must be something big.

Larry looked up. "Have you seen this?" he shouted, waving the morning paper in the air.

"Uh, no, sir, I haven't. It's been a busy morning, and I haven't had time to—"

"What do you know about this?" Larry interrupted, tossing the newspaper across the desk as he lowered his bulk unceremoniously into his chair.

The headline was not good. "Journalist found dead in dumpster. Police suspect drug deal gone bad."

"Mayor, I have no idea. I do know that we found a journalist's body in a dumpster on Rush Street between Chicago and Pearson. The body was burned from the waist down. We have a preliminary autopsy, but that's about all."

"What about the drug deal angle?" Larry had not lowered his voice.

"I don't know anything about that, either. Could be a rookie reporter trying to make a name for himself."

"Bullshit! Someone in your precious department is leaking information to the press. And not even correct information! You find out who it is and you hang them out to dry!"

"I'll see what I can find out, sir."

"Damn right you will! I want to know where this reporter got his information, and I want to know now. And I want you to trot your happy ass back across Clark and fax me over that 'preliminary autopsy' so I get it yesterday!"

"Yes, sir." There was nothing else he could say.

He got up and left the office, feeling berated like a dog. On his way out, Janet tried to engage him in the small talk that they normally shared, but David was in no mood for it today. He had a mission: do as he'd been told. That it would be his ass on the line if he didn't was the unspoken corollary.

* * *

David hurried back to his office and shuffled through the papers lying on his desk, looking for the autopsy report he'd been commanded to produce.

"Irene!"

She casually strode through the door and walked over to his desk.

"Where's that damned autopsy report?"

Irene reached out, slid two pieces of paper to the side, and picked up the autopsy report, handing it to the Chief without saying a word. Her smirk said it all.

He tried his best to ignore the look that said she knew his desk better than he did, and handed it back to her. "Get this faxed to Janet at the Mayor's Office ASAP. Mark it 'Urgent Fax, Mayor's Eyes Only.'"

Irene didn't hesitate, knowing that when the Chief asked her to do something like this it was probably because there was trouble brewing. And if it was one thing Irene tried to avoid, it was trouble.

She returned to her desk and quickly typed up the cover letter on her computer, hitting the "print" button before dashing down the hall to the room that held the myriad of printers, fax machines, and other computer equipment. Most of the paperwork generated by the PD was still done by hand, so this room was actually used by very few people for business purposes. When Irene stepped into the small closet-sized space, she wasn't surprised to find Sergeant Richard Tibbs and another office clerk leaning against one of the counters, their lips locked together and their hands groping and grappling at each other.

"S'cuse me please, but I have to get dis out," she said with as much authority as she could muster.

Caught in the act, the blushing pair hurriedly parted and rushed out of the room, straightening their clothes as they left.

Irene went to the printer, grabbed the cover sheet she had created, placed it on top of the autopsy report, and stuck the whole stack into the fax machine. On the first attempt to fax the information, the cover letter jammed and Irene cursed the paper, the report, and machines in general. She managed to get the cover letter free and did her best to smooth out the wrinkles before trying again. On the second attempt, the machine worked correctly and the report was on its way across the street. She stood there humming a song to herself as she waited for the fax confirmation to print out. When it did, she stapled it to the cover letter and stamped them with the rubber "Faxed" stamp, filled in the date and time, and went to put the papers back into the pile on David's desk.

"Will dat be all?" she asked.

"Yes," replied David. After a brief pause, "No. Wait. I've been here for a couple hours already and skipped breakfast. I guess I could use an early lunch. Why don't you go and order us some food from that Thai place that's over in the state building?"

"Sound good to me."

Once again, David wrenched his window opened and lit a cigarette. He sat on the windowsill, alone with his thoughts, and wondered what the Mayor would have to say once he read the information in the report from the coroner. Once the Mayor learned of the murders in Grant Park, there would be pure bedlam. And guess who'd be to blame?

David looked at his calendar with its list of reminders, and realized that tonight was "Movie in the Park" night. He cursed the event, as he would have to find a way to increase not only the foot patrols but the horse-mounteds, as well. If something unnatural was in the park, it was his job to make sure that the citizens of Chicago were safe.

EIGHTEEN

The machine was designed to operate quietly, specifically to be used in an office setting without interrupting workers, as opposed to its more industrial cousins that were generally placed in out of the way copy rooms where their train-loud sounds wouldn't matter. It hummed quietly to itself, starting up the motors and gears that would feed a few sheets of paper through its toner cartridge and slide the printed fax silently out onto its tray. It was so quiet throughout the process that Janet almost didn't notice a fax had even arrived in the machine sitting but a few feet from her desk.

It was a private fax line, only available to a few select individuals, and generally used only for extremely sensitive material. It was hardly ever used for sending faxes to others, out of fear that the number would appear on the transmission line and would become public knowledge. The information center received and filtered out the junk, the obvious "crank" letters, and the faxes sent to the Mayor by mistake or out of ignorance.

When Janet noticed the paper sitting in the output tray of the Mayor's private fax line, she went quickly to the machine, looked at the "urgent" designation on the cover sheet along with the Police Chief's office seal, and rushed it into his office without bothering to knock on the door. As usual, he was yelling into the phone at some poor soul who had the misfortune of incurring his wrath, so she stood in front of his desk patiently waiting for him to finish. She knew she hadn't put any calls through, so he must have made the call himself. Not a good sign for the hapless soul on the other end of the line. She watched as veins popped out on his forehead and his entire face turned the color of a fresh beet. She was surprised that his high blood pressure hadn't given him a heart attack by now.

He finally realized that she was standing there holding papers and motioned for her to hand them over without breaking his tirade or even pausing to take a breath. She reached across the massive desk, holding the small stack of papers out toward him, only to have them rudely snatched out of her hand. Larry motioned for her to leave the room, as if she were nothing more than a subservient child who had entered her father's private office without permission.

She walked back to her desk and decided she was hungry. She arranged for someone to cover her desk so that she could go out for an early lunch.

When she arrived at the food court, Janet decided Thai food was what she wanted. As she stepped into line at the counter, she noticed Irene, the

Chief's assistant standing a few positions ahead of her. Irene regularly picked up lunch for both of them, even though it wasn't really part of her job description.

The two women knew each other from meetings and phone calls between their respective bosses, so Janet called softly through the line of waiting customers, "Hey Irene."

Turning to see who was calling her name, Irene spotted the Mayor's assistant standing behind her in line, and smiled at the sight of a friendly face.

"Come up here," she waved the other woman to join her. Janet stepped past the couple of people between herself and Irene, and did her best to ignore the dirty looks she got for skipping line.

While they waited to reach the counter, they chatted about the new man in Irene's life, and the lack of men in Janet's. Irene knew that Janet harbored a crush on Chief Duncan, and she took every opportunity she got to tease her friend about it. They bantered back and forth until they reached the counter and placed their orders.

"Hmm…" Irene said with a mischievous glint in her eye.

"What nasty things are you thinking now, Irene?"

"I was just thinkin' dat maybe you should take the Chief's lunch to 'im. He hardly notice when I walk in, but he'd see. 'Specially if you wuz wearin' just the bag the food comes in."

The women laughed, knowing it could never happen. But it was certainly a pleasant thought for Janet, and she pictured the scene as she ate her lunch.

Irene crossed the street to her building, dodging traffic and trying not to spill the food she was carrying. Although many of the buildings were interconnected by the underground tunnels, the building that housed the Police Department Headquarters was not one of them.

She walked quietly into the Chief's office, careful not to disturb the phone call that he was on, and sat his lunch on his desk. She took her lunch back to her cubicle and ate while thinking of Graham, her new man. She tried to put him out of her mind during the day so she could concentrate on work, but she'd told Janet about him while waiting in line for lunch, and now he was all she could think about.

She'd met Graham at last week's "Movie In The Park" at Grant Park. The movie that night was Pillow Talk. She didn't think she would ever forget that night. For the first time since coming to Chicago three years ago, she'd met a man who seemed normal and didn't have excess baggage. He wasn't married, divorced, or homosexual, and he had no children.

He didn't seem obsessed with whatever work he did to make a living. She had noticed during her time in the States that a lot of people practically defined themselves by what they did for work. But during her first meeting with Graham, he never brought up the subject of work. He was actually quite elusive about it, changing the topic or sidestepping the question whenever she broached the subject. She hadn't really thought about it until Janet asked her what he did for a living. And now it began to bother her that he had avoided telling her something so basic about himself. It also dawned on her that in the week since that first meeting, he never contacted her during the day. Only at night. She started to wonder if he was a drug dealer or a pimp. Maybe he was a stripper in a club and was embarrassed to tell her.

Irene shrugged her shoulders and decided not to jump to conclusions. There had to be a good reason for his elusiveness and his nocturnal habits. And there was plenty of time to find out. She'd only known him for a week.

NINETEEN

When Janet stepped out of the elevator on the Mayor's floor after her lunch break, she found complete bedlam. Tiffany, the girl covering her desk, was almost in tears; assistants were rummaging through file cabinets looking for something, papers were beginning to be strewn about; and the phone had several lines ringing, some on hold, some not even having been answered. The Mayor was shouting at everyone.

"Where the fuck have you been?" the Mayor demanded when he saw Janet walk in the door. She was momentarily speechless at seeing the pandemonium going on around her.

"I ... I was at lunch. Didn't Tiffany tell you that?"

"When I need you here, I need you here. Not flitting around some lunch counter!"

The Mayor's shouting snapped her back to attention, and angered her at the same time. She had every right to take a break for lunch, no matter what he said. She wasn't a slave, and he had no right to talk to her as if she was. She was about the only person who could stand up to him and not get her head torn completely off. After having been his assistant for many years, they both knew he needed her more than he would ever admit. That knowledge gave her the power to bark right back at him, but she usually waited until they were alone in his office where no one else would hear her undermining his authority. But this time she couldn't seem to bite her tongue. "Well, I'm here now. What's so important that you have to scare half the staff into destroying the office? Your coffee get too cold?"

The office went instantly silent. No one moved. The other assistants had never heard someone talk back to the Mayor, let alone insult him the way Janet just had. She knew she'd probably gone a little too far and would pay for it later, but at the moment she didn't care.

The Mayor's face turned several shades of red as he tried to find some dignified way of responding. He couldn't keep screaming at her. She had just shown that she would scream right back and continue to embarrass him in front of the rest of the staff. After a moment he said, "Just get me the goddam coroner on the phone." He pointed directly at her and added, "And I want Mark Westwood, not one of those flunky assistants that call themselves coroners!" He turned and stormed back into his own private office, much to the relief of his staff, especially Janet. She didn't want a continuing confrontation in front of everyone.

Janet handed Tiffany a tissue. "Sorry about all of that. It wasn't your fault. Go to the water cooler and get yourself a drink. Then go and fix your face. And don't be afraid to take your time getting yourself back together."

As Tiffany left the room, still sobbing at the abuse she had just endured from the Mayor, Janet walked from the outer offices to her desk where she sat down and hit the speed dial button on the phone that automatically dialed the Cook County Coroner's Office. As expected, she got one of the "flunkies" on the phone.

"Yes, this is the Mayor's office. I need to speak to Coroner Mark Westwood right away," Janet said to the voice on the other end of the phone.

"He's not available," said the flunky. "But I'm one of his assistants and should be able to answer any of the Mayor's questions." His voice sounded young, but this young man had already taken on an air of arrogance and condescension. Janet could almost see the smirk on his face. He had a medical degree and had gotten a cushy job in the coroner's office, so he felt safe in talking down to a "lowly" assistant.

Janet gritted her teeth and tried to be pleasant. "The Mayor asked specifically to speak to Mr. Westwood."

"As I said," the voice came back, sounding like he was talking to a young child who didn't comprehend the words he had just spoken, "he's not available. But I'm one of his assistants and should be able to answer any of the Mayor's questions"

Janet was angered by his attitude toward her, but she was enraged by the way he repeated himself word for word as if she were deaf or dumb or both. She decided to take the kid down a peg or two, nearly hissing into the phone, "Listen up, buddy. I said the Mayor wants to talk to Mr. Westwood. Not you. So if you value your job, you'll get me Mr. Westwood on the phone right now. And if you question the Mayor's orders again, you may end up laying on that metal slab instead of operating over it."

She could hear the voice quaver a bit, as he stammered in surprise at the unveiled threat. "Uh … uh … okay. Okay. Um … hold on a moment and let me get him."

After a few moments, the talk radio she'd been forced to listen to while on hold was interrupted by a new voice. "Mark Westwood here, how can I help you?"

"Please hold for the Mayor, Mr. Westwood." Janet patched the call into the Mayor's office before going to check on Tiffany.

When the Mayor got Westwood on the phone, he immediately started grilling the man on the autopsy report he held in his hand about the journalist found in the dumpster. The two had spoken on several occasions; those meetings and conversations had been much more cordial and friendly. Westwood was surprised at the Mayor's gruffness and grouchy demeanor.

"What does this mean, 'Two neatly round puncture wounds on neck'?"

"Well, that means that the man had two holes on his neck. They were the apparent cause of death. Whatever was used to make them pierced the jugular, causing the victim to die of blood loss. With too little blood feeding oxygen to the vital organs, they simply stop functioning."

"Well, what made 'em?"

"The puncture wounds? That's hard to say. Items that could be used to make these wounds would have to be conical in shape, like a funnel. But to be driven in this deep, whatever was used would have to be hammered in, which would be very unlikely. Also, anything metallic would pull or catch on the skin surrounding the punctures. There was no pulling or tearing in this case. The punctures were incredibly clean."

"Okay, so you can't tell me much there," said Larry. "What about this 'blood at trace levels'?"

The coroner cleared his throat and said, "Well, Mr. Mayor, even when a person dies from extreme blood loss, the blood does eventually coagulate, stemming the flow and leaving quite a bit of viable blood in the system. It's usually found in the veins leading to the heart, which are less pressurized than the arteries leading from the heart. When we opened this body to drain out the blood for toxicology reports and in preparation for embalming, we found less than a pint of blood remaining. There was no blood in the heart, liver, or blood vessels surrounding the brain. It was as if someone had placed a high-powered vacuum over the puncture wounds on the neck and sucked out nearly every drop."

"How is that possible?"

"I couldn't even begin to explain it."

"What about the burns? Did they have something to do with the death?"

"No, the burns were post mortem. My best guess is that the burning was an attempt to destroy the evidence of the killing. This victim definitely died from blood loss, most likely through the puncture wounds on the neck."

"Oh, my God."

"And there's something else odd about this victim."

"What else can there possibly be?"

"It's not so much what there is, but what there isn't."

"What? What's that supposed to mean?"

"Well, sir, there are no apparent signs of struggle. Other than the burns on the legs, there are no lacerations, contusions, or abrasions anywhere on this victim. He didn't fight back."

"Are you saying he just laid there and let someone do this to him?"

"Either that or he was passed out. We'd normally check for drugs or alcohol in the system that would render the victim helpless or unconscious, but ...."

"But there's not enough blood to complete the tests," the Mayor completed the thought for him, a faraway look in his eye. "So, what's your best guess as to what happened to this guy? What are we looking for?"

"The only thing I can come up with is some sort of ritualistic cult killing. Nothing else makes any sense."

"So, some cult drugged the guy to make him pass out, stabbed his neck with some mysterious sharp tool that leaves no trace, and somehow sucked all the blood out of his body." The Mayor made it sound like the coroner was trying to convince him aliens had landed in the city.

"As incredible as that sounds, Mr. Mayor, it's the only explanation I can see."

Larry Larson had turned pale during the conversation. He knew exactly what had happened to the victim. He had been a Senior County Commissioner twenty-five years ago when David Duncan's mother was killed, and he remembered the details of the autopsy as if he had seen them yesterday, almost identical to these findings. He also remembered that David nearly lost his job on the police force because of his insistence that his mother had been killed by a vampire. The story had been buried, and shrinks had chased the foolish thoughts from Duncan's mind all those years ago, allowing him to rise to his current position as Chief.

What Duncan didn't know, what no one knew, was that he had been right about his mother. It had been a vampire. But they were all supposed to have gone, never to return. Had the nightmare come back? Was the past catching up to him?

"Mr. Mayor? Hello?" The voice on the phone snapped the Mayor out of the trance he had fallen into while thinking about what this could mean for what was now his city.

"Uh ... yes. Thank you for your time, Mr. Westwood," he managed to stammer, trying to regain his composure. "If I have any other questions, I'll have my office contact you." Then, almost as an afterthought, he added, "Oh, Mr. Westwood?"

"Sir?"

"The police may have to do some investigating into this case, so we don't want the findings made public. Please seal the autopsy report with the highest level of clearance required to gain access."

The Coroner hesitated momentarily. "I've never been asked to do that before, sir."

"Well, I'm telling you to do it now. Secure the file for only high level access."

He hung up the phone slowly, and stared at his wall of books, not really seeing any of them; for the first time in seventeen years he wished he hadn't quit smoking.

TWENTY

The Mayor stepped out of his office after folding up the fax containing the autopsy report and tucking it into his jacket pocket and walked past Janet's desk without saying a single word. His silent departure struck her as odd, since he never left without giving her some indication of where he was going or when he would likely return. She was sure he hadn't scheduled a meeting out of the office, but she looked down at his appointment book just to be sure. By the time she looked up to call after him, he was gone.

Larry got onto the elevator and descended non-stop to the main level, went quickly through the security maze, and down the escalator into the tunnel system. One level below the tunnels, he reached the parking garage where his aging Jaguar was parked. It always shocked him that he could park such an expensive vehicle in a publicly accessed parking lot that had little security and rarely have any trouble with thieves or vandals. His car had been run into by bad drivers who weren't paying attention to what they were doing, and a time or two his car was "keyed" by kids in some form of protest against the Mayor or some policy he had instituted, but those events were few and far between.

As he walked toward the car, he took the autopsy fax from his pocket and began tearing it into the smallest pieces he could. Next to the small dumpster placed in the garage, he bent down, placed the torn pieces on the floor, and held a struck match to them.

He stood and watched the paper burn. When he was convinced nothing remained but soot, he brushed the ashes away with the sole of his shoe.

He walked the remaining distance to his car, climbed into the Jag, and turned the key, listening to the muffled roar of the engine with a satisfied sigh. He began to wind his way through the ramps to the exit of the garage, and turned left onto Clark Street. He first thought about heading home, and then about stopping at his favorite bar. But home wasn't the best place. His twin sons would be arguing, and the confusion and mayhem happening there wouldn't allow him to think. Sitting at a bar wouldn't help, either. How could he think with a head slowed by liquor?

He turned the car east and headed toward Lake Shore Drive, past Grant Park, and, after fighting through the downtown traffic and reaching the lakefront, headed north. As he drove along Lake Michigan, he took out his cell phone and dialed a number he had not used in over twenty years. Somehow, it didn't surprise him that he still knew it.

"Yeah?" The voice that answered was rough and low.

"It's Larson."

"What is it?"

"It's happening again."

"You gotta be kiddin'."

"Nope."

"Which one was it?"

"Don't know. But the details are exactly the same as before."

"Name?"

"Paul Somethin'. Reporter found on Chicago and Rush a few nights ago."

"You didn't get a last name?"

"No, I destroyed my copy without looking at it."

"How many copies out there?"

"Three that I know of. I took care of the one I had. The Police Chief has one, and the Coroner's Office has one."

"Consider it done."

"Times have changed. There may be a computer record, too."

"I said, consider it done."

There was a click and the voice was gone. The Mayor turned on the radio and tuned in to the Oldies Rock station. He nearly laughed at the irony as he realized they were playing Blue Oyster Cult's Don't Fear The Reaper.

* * *

When he reached the northern end of Lake Shore Drive, the Mayor made a few quick turns, and headed south on Green Bay Avenue, passing a small "Mom & Pop" restaurant set into a strip of small storefront businesses. Looking around to make sure there was no traffic in his way, he made a quick U-turn and drove back to the restaurant, pulling into one of the open parking spaces on the street directly in front of the building.

Before getting out of his car, he used his cell phone to call home.

"Hi. It's me," he said.

"Working late tonight?" His wife had come to expect the long hours, and hardly needed to be told that he wouldn't be home for dinner.

"What's going on there?" He could hear their twin boys fighting over a video game. At that instant he was happy that he chose not to go home.

"Oh, just the usual bickering. I'll see you tonight."

Larry ended what was probably the most pleasant conversation he had had all day.

The restaurant was smaller than he had anticipated, but since it was nearly empty, that wasn't an issue. There was a long counter along the front wall with stools for customers who didn't want an entire table. A three-foot high dividing wall ran the length of the restaurant behind the stools, separating the counter area from the table area. There were small booths that could seat one and two person parties along the opposite side of the divider, and larger booths that could seat up to four along the back wall of the establishment. The Metra train could be heard rumbling by on the tracks overhead, but the building was sturdy enough that the train's passing wasn't felt.

Larry sat down in one of the small booths, and thought about the vampire threat had gone away nearly twenty years earlier. At the time he had thought it was gone for good.

"What can I getcha, darlin'?" The petite brunette had a thick southern accent, a friendly smile, and warm coffee brown eyes.

"Um ... I'll, uh ... I'll just have a burger, fries and a large Coke," he replied, knowing full well his wife would have a fit if she knew. But, he assuaged his guilty conscience, she wasn't here, and there was no reason for her to know of his dietary transgression.

He ate mechanically, barely tasting the food, lost in his reverie, not even noticing when the waitress returned with the bill.

"Sir, is there anything else I can get you?" she asked.

He looked up sheepishly and said "No, I'm done and ready for my check." She tapped the table in front of him where his check laid. Embarrassed, he paid the bill and then left her a twenty dollar tip.

The Mayor walked out of the diner into the darkening evening. He began to feel real fear in his heart, noticing that the sun was down and the time for these demons of the night to come out and play had arrived. He knew there was a free movie playing in Grant Park tonight, and his boys often went to the show. He quickly grabbed his cell phone and called his house.

"Hello?" To Larry's relief, it was Tommy, the older of the twins. He could hear Jimmy in the background back-talking their mother.

"It's Dad. Tell your mother I'll be right home." The relief he felt knowing that his sons would not be out, and in possible danger, was evident in his voice.

"Okay, Dad. Is there anything else you want me to tell her?"

"No, but tell your brother that if he doesn't quit talking to his mother like that, I'm going to kick his ass when I get home."

TWENTY-ONE

Irene filed away the last of the day's paperwork, locked the office, and hurried home. It had been a long day, and she wanted to change before heading for Grant Park. She'd gotten a call from Graham asking her to meet him again for the Movie in the Park. She was excited about seeing him again, and wanted to look her best.

She entered her one-bedroom apartment, threw her bag on her bed, and quickly undressed. After showering, she put on her prettiest summery dress, a dark pink gauzy affair with thin spaghetti straps, perfect for the humid summer weather. She really didn't have time, but took a moment to sit down and put on a bit of makeup; she wanted to look as perfect as possible.

On her way out, she opened her linen closet, and grabbed a large plaid blanket that she could lay out on the grass, a way to claim a little territory for herself and Graham on the lawn where they could lie and watch the movie, and she could try to find out more about this mysterious man. She also thought it would be nice to have a bite to eat, so she grabbed a small picnic basket. At a convenience store just down the street from her apartment building, she filled the basket with hummus, pita bread, peaches, grapes, and a bottle of merlot.

She met Graham in the grove of trees at the corner of Monroe and Columbus. It was an area that was often used as a meeting place, because it was a small enough location and made it easy to find someone, as well as being right off one of the main entrances into the park. He was standing in the deep shade beneath a cluster of trees when she arrived. The sun was reaching for the horizon created by the tall buildings to the west, casting enormous shadows through the park. The movie would begin just as soon as the last rays of the sun withered away for the day and the shadows were exchanged for the darkness of night.

He complimented her on her dress and the wonderful way it hugged her body. "You look good enough to eat," he said, eyeing her lithe body.

She looked into his dark black eyes with gratitude. She loved being complimented, especially by a strikingly handsome man such as this. He stood about five-foot-nine, rather thin and lean, without an ounce of fat anywhere on his body. He was muscular, as if he worked out at the gym, but only to the point of being firm. His long blonde hair fell straight to his shoulders, but didn't give him that "hippie" look that some men with long hair seemed to have. He kept it neat and trimmed, and looked very professional, while remaining stylish. He was dressed in a pair of black jeans and a tight black shirt that seemed to outline every muscle on his chest. Through the shirt, Irene could see the solid muscles that reminded her of a saying that her mother used to repeat whenever she saw a muscular man. Something about having a "washboard chest that you could do a week's scrubbing on."

Graham took Irene's hand and gently placed it through his right arm. He escorted her through the shadows like she was a duchess on her way to a formal ball. They found a spot near the back of the growing crowd and he helped her to spread out the blanket. Both of them kicked off their shoes and sat, Graham stretching out and reclining on his elbows, Irene curling her knees underneath her and sitting upright. She felt absolutely giddy as they became lost in a world all their own, completely unaware of the hundreds of others people present in the park.

Graham asked about her day, and she could tell that he was truly listening to every word she said, not just making small talk. He was charming, attentive, and entertaining all at once. Irene reached over to the basket and began to remove the contents of the small feast she had so thoughtfully chosen and brought along. When Graham saw the bottle of merlot, he hesitated.

"Oh, I am dreadfully sorry. I should have told you before. I do not drink alcohol."

Irene was slightly embarrassed, but quickly regained her composure. How could she have known? He hadn't told her much about himself. Perhaps he had been an alcoholic at one time.

He noticed that "the tent" had been opened. It was a semi-permanent structure with a canvas covering located at one end of the park. Inside was a small vending area, where movie-goers could purchase soda, water, coffee, and various snacks, including the traditional movie popcorn.

He excused himself and said, "Please remain here, enjoy the wine, and the opening credits. I will fetch myself a bottle of water, and return before the movie begins." Irene noticed that Graham seemed to have an old world way of speaking. Rarely using contractions, preferring to pronounce each word, and using phrases like 'dreadfully sorry'. She almost expected him to have a British accent, but his voice sounded purely American to her ears.

She watched him walk away, admiring the way he moved beneath the skin-tight clothing, and noticed several other women watching him, as well. She swelled with pride that a man that could attract that kind of attention was at the movie with her.

She began to set out the picnic food she had brought, and cursed herself again for being so bold as to bring alcohol without finding out first about the man's past. Oh, well. Live and learn, she decided.

Well before the movie began, Graham returned with three bottles of cool sparkling water. He kicked off his shoes once again and reclined on the plaid blanket. He took notice of the food that Irene had brought and he complimented her on each selection she had made. They were all of his favorites, he told her. Irene had stardust in her eyes and didn't seem to notice that he barely nibbled.

She did notice, however, that as the movie played on, Graham inched closer and closer to her until she could almost feel his breath upon her neck.

He whispered into her ear, "Irene, I have never met anyone like you before, and I doubt I will again."

Chills went up and down her spine, as though a sudden breeze had blown in from the lake, trying to cool the sexual attraction she felt toward this man. But even a hurricane wouldn't have mustered enough cold wind to chill the desire she felt building inside her. She was barely in control of her own actions when she reached toward him with both arms, took his face into her hands, and kissed him full on the mouth with all the passion that had been pent up inside of her for years. This was not the time or the place to let it out, especially with a man she knew so little about, but Irene could simply not stop herself.

Graham returned her kisses, pressing his lips against hers, and sliding his arms around her back, pulling her closer to him. When he probed her mouth with his tongue, she willfully parted her lips to allow him in, meeting him with a hungry tongue of her own. She felt as if an ice cube had entered her mouth, causing her to jump a little, but they did not part from one another. His hands began to roam and explore the body beneath the light material of the summery pink dress.

"Hey, you two, get a room!" Irene vaguely heard a voice calling out to them. She noticed that Graham's hands were chilled like ice; she could feel their coldness through the thin fabric of her dress. Probably from the cold bottles of water he had been holding; at that point, she didn't care. She only knew that she wanted this man. And she wanted him now. She began to reciprocate his fondling by running her hands across his muscular body and moaning, her face buried in his neck.

"Let's get out of here and go back to my place," she suggested. It was far bolder than she expected from herself, but she didn't fight it. It felt good to be bad for once.

Graham pulled back from her, looked her in the eye, smiled, and said, "Good idea."

TWENTY-TWO

The silence within the crypt where Virginia slept away the days was broken by the creaking of her coffin lid as she opened her coffin and sat up, ready to roam the night streets of Chicago once again. She took the locket that now hung around her neck and kissed it before climbing out of her comfortable satin bed.

She stretched and thought about spending the evening looking up an "old friend." She knew Elizabeth was in town; she had seen her picture only a few days ago.

It had been a night when Nicolette was off being her foolish, childish self, before Virginia had finally made the decision to end the young vampire's life. Virginia was strolling along a dark street, looking into the windows of the closed shops, when she passed an art studio with a small photography exhibit on display. She stopped to look at a picture of the new Millennium Park structures that were under construction, and thought she recognized a figure in the background of the photo. Virginia turned herself into mist and slipped through the cracks under the locked doorway to enter the Modern Art Gallery so she could look at the photography exhibit more closely. In one of the crowd scenes, she saw the figure again. She was certain it was Elizabeth. She'd recognize that face anywhere, Somewhere in this large city was another vampire, one that she couldn't call her minion, her companion, or her lover, but one she could definitely call her friend. Virginia knew that Elizabeth had lived in Chicago many years ago, but she seemed to have disappeared after the last bit of trouble in the city, when Carlos nearly gave the vampire secrets away to the mortals. Many assumed Elizabeth had been destroyed, caught either by mortals or by Carlos himself. Her appearance in these photographs told Virginia otherwise. She was still here. And she was caught on film.

Virginia stepped out onto the rooftop of the church that served as her home and thought back to the first time she had met Elizabeth.

* * *

It was the night of Catherine the Great's wedding, the same night Carlos killed Dominick. Virginia was an invited guest at the wedding, but was getting tired of watching the mortals gorge themselves at the food tables. She had gone outside to look for a more suitable meal when she spotted Carlos and Dominick leave the main parlor. She knew that those two in the same place could mean only trouble, but she didn't feel the need to interfere. Instead, she continued to hunt her chosen prey, a young man who had left the celebration for a breath of cool night air, taking a stroll in the garden nearby.

After following the young man to a lonely, solitary spot in the garden, Virginia approached, walked with him for a bit, and eventually sank her teeth into his flesh. She drank until she was satiated, and left his body in the shrubbery within a grove of trees far off the normal footpaths.

As she returned to the main manor, she saw Carlos again leaving from the front entryway, this time with Elizabeth in tow. Virginia hadn't met the young woman, but she had seen her earlier with Dominick and had assumed this was his latest companion. But why, then, would she be walking with Carlos?

Out of curiosity, Virginia followed, staying unobserved in the shadows. She didn't want Carlos to sense her presence. That would only result in a confrontation in front of all the mortals inside.

She watched them enter the stables, saw Elizabeth suddenly stop, gasp, and falter. Carlos laughed at the sight of whatever was in the stables and returned to the wedding feast, leaving Elizabeth sobbing on the ground.

Virginia hurried and arrived just in time to see the body of Dominick, pinned to the wall with his entrails removed and piled at his feet. The dissolution had just begun, and she watched in horror as he melted away into a puddle. She knelt down next to Elizabeth, and took the younger woman into her arms.

Elizabeth didn't know who this woman was, but she could tell it was yet another ancient vampire. She sensed the same presence she had felt emanating from both Dominick and the evil vampire who had just destroyed her mentor. What she was unsure of was whether this new arrival was there to help her or to hurt her. She gave in to her immense sadness, and allowed the strange woman to hold her.

They cried together, but for different reasons. Virginia cried for the loss of another fellow ancient. Elizabeth cried because she was unsure of what she would do now that her companion was gone.

In time, they composed themselves and returned to the celebration. They managed to avoid Carlos for the remainder of the evening, Virginia disappearing whenever he came near. He didn't speak to Elizabeth, but he would occasionally throw a smug, leering glance her way. He thought it strange that the sensation of a nearby immortal had not gone away with the dissolution of Dominick, but put it down to the fact that the other had been a powerful ancient, and perhaps his presence would take time to disappear completely.

As the evening came to a close, Virginia offered to take the young vampire under her wing and teach her the things that Dominick had not had the time to share. But Elizabeth realized that, for the first time in her life, she was free to do as she pleased, on her own. When she had been mortal, her father was always there, taking control of her life. And even when she had flown away from Dominick, she still felt his presence guiding her. Now she felt completely and totally independent, and the thought exhilarated her.

"Thank you very much, Virginia, but I'd rather not. It has nothing to do with you, or the Code. I just need time to myself."

"I understand," said Virginia as she patted away the last of Elizabeth's tears. She knew there was more to it than simply needing time to grieve. And she had a feeling they would meet again.

* * *

Their paths crossed over forty years later, in Vienna. The year was 1787. The two women had adjacent box seats for the premiere of Mozart's new opera, Don Giovanni. With all of the attention diverted to the stage, each would have spent the night entirely unnoticed by the other, except for the sense of presence.

Virginia leaned over the railing and peered into the box occupied by Elizabeth and her evening meal.

"Boo!" she said playfully.

Elizabeth laughed when she recognized her friend; her escort was taken aback by the unheard of act of someone leaning into another's box in such a fashion.

During the intermission, the two women rushed into the carpeted mezzanine to hug. Elizabeth couldn't help notice the jealousy forming in the eyes of the young woman who stood at Virginia's side.

"Elizabeth, this is Nicolette," Virginia introduced the two women. Elizabeth knew that the introduction meant the woman with her was not a mortal who would later become an evening meal. It was a fellow vampire, a companion like she used to be to Dominick. Elizabeth didn't bother to introduce her escort.

Instead, she stood on tiptoe, embraced Virginia again, and whispered into Virginia's ear, "I think your young protégé is becoming jealous. I guess we had better stop."

"Better than that," whispered Virginia, "watch this!"

Virginia grabbed Elizabeth and forcefully dipped her, planting a kiss full on the mouth. The on-lookers gasped, Elizabeth's escort fainted, and Nicolette went running back into their box in a fit of jealous fury. Virginia and Elizabeth doubled over with laughter as the other opera patrons simply stared at the odd scene.

* * *

They shared a strange, though distant, bond through the centuries. Virginia respected Elizabeth's decision to not ally herself with other ancients, even though she had been given the opportunity many times in the past. It was her independent quality that Virginia admired about Elizabeth

But tonight, she felt the need to speak with her. She was becoming sloppy, and was endangering the vampire community. Two bodies had been found, obvious victims of vampire attacks, and her face had appeared in a photograph in an art gallery. It just wouldn't do.

How Virginia knew the bodies were victims of Elizabeth, she couldn't quite say. But somehow she knew that it wasn't just a coincidence that the bodies had appeared at the same time as the photograph.

Virginia floated back down through the darkened tower to the catacombs below and looked with longing at Nicolette's coffin. She couldn't decide whether to find another companion or try to convince Elizabeth to move in with her. If Elizabeth did move in, she would still need to remove Nicolette's coffin, a task she hadn't been able to bring herself to face.

The when/where/how decisions of coffin removal would have to wait. Right now, she had to find Elizabeth and somehow convince her friend that she needed the protection of an ancient, someone to guide her before she became any sloppier with her victims. Her independence and stubbornness were things that Virginia loved about her friend, but this time could be at the cost of the entire vampire community.

* * *

Virginia left the catacombs and flew to the base of the church. She didn't want to attract undue attention, so she walked around to the front entrance and climbed to the top of the stairs, giving the sharp whistle that would call her followers to her side.

"I know it's early and I know you're hungry, but I need you to comb the city and look for someone. Many of you know Elizabeth. Many of you don't. Those that do, we need to find her. The rest of you, keep your senses alert for a vampire unknown to you. If you find her, bring her to me on top of the Sears Tower. Our friend is alone, in possible danger, and, whether she knows it or not, she needs us."

They nodded their understanding, then, with the sound of a thousand birds suddenly taking flight, they left, spreading out in search of the elusive Elizabeth.

TWENTY-THREE

Carlos woke as dusk settled on the city, with his new bride still asleep at his side. He took her hand and kissed it lightly. Her eyes fluttered open and she smiled through the darkness.

Jennifer had not been told of the significance of the upcoming event, the event that Carlos was eagerly looking forward to. Soon, the Earth's shadow would eclipse the moon, the dust particles in the air refracting the light rays and making that orb appear dipped in blood. This phenomenon, the "Blood on the Moon," occurred twice every year. But only once every decade during the lunar eclipse did the ancients feel an uncontrollable need to mate.

Carlos knew that the Code forbade the mating of an ancient with a made vampire, and he knew the risks of such a union. He would end up with yet another ghoul, another deformed or mentally unstable child, another Graham.

Most ghouls were easily spotted, with obvious physical deformities, much like the ghouls of modern folklore, the hideous creatures who guard cemeteries and feast on the recently dead.

But Graham had the looks of his ancient vampire father, and could not be easily distinguished from other vampires. His ghoulish deformity was hidden deep within, in the way he feasted on his victims, by not just sucking the blood out of their veins, but by eating their flesh and bone entirely. He was the vampire world's answer to Jeffrey Dahmer, Eddie Gein, and Albert Fish all rolled into one.

It was a revolting habit, but he was Carlos' son, so the others simply turned a blind eye. At least his fellow hunters never needed to worry about disposing of their victims. Once Graham was finished, there was nothing left to hide. He was, at times, thought of as the family mongrel. Give him the leftovers, and he'd devour the smallest of scraps.

Carlos was certain Graham was still awake, prowling the streets. He had left his son to sleep in the old cavern, the one where half of his followers now rested. Unlike those in the cemetery, close by Carlos, the vampires in the cavern would not awake before the last stages of the Blood on the Moon. Being a ghoul, not a vampire, Graham would stay awake and keep watch over Carlos' sleeping army. The hidden entrance could only be opened by Carlos, but he was certain Graham had found the other way out, and was roaming the streets.

Carlos was so overcome with lust during the mating period he didn't care that his children were ghouls. He was driven by the upcoming eclipse, and felt a need to have another child.

And the energy he gained by mating under the Blood on the Moon was power he desperately desired, power he would need to achieve his goal.

Jennifer, new to the vampire world, had no knowledge of the Code that all vampires lived by. And Carlos intended to keep it that way. There was no reason for her to know that he had made her only to serve a purpose, to be the mother of his next child. He also didn't want her to know that in almost every case, after an ancient and a minion mated, the mother died during childbirth. She might resist, and that would diminish his pleasure.

* * *

The birth of full bloods, created by the mating of ancient to ancient, and referred to as "ancients" themselves because of their lineage, was generally celebrated throughout the vampire world.

Carlos did not feel the same about the birth of a new ancient. While the rest of the vampire community saw a new member of the family, he looked at the newborns as threats, potential drains on his vast hordes of potential followers, and another obstacle to cross in his ongoing quest to rule the vampire world with absolute power. He did everything he could to destroy newborn ancients, preferably before they were old enough to defend themselves. Most were hidden, sometimes unsuccessfully, until they were grown.

Carlos knew that the Code only allowed for one pair of ancient vampires to mate and create an offspring. He'd had passing thoughts of simply abiding by the rules for a change, waiting to see if he was inexplicably drawn to one of the female ancients that were in North America, within his reach. But the Blood on the Moon was drawing near and he had felt no such sensation, so he decided to ignore the Code, its prophesies, and his past, near-disastrous experiences, and give in to the lust he always felt during this time.

He justified his decision with the rationalization that had he been drawn to one of the nearby ancient females, he was unsure if he would be able to mate with them without fear for his own safety. He had been involved in past squabbles with each of them, and they each still felt vengeful toward him.

No, Carlos would mate with Jennifer, his new companion. He might miss her company after she died giving birth to their child, but his desire and his seed were ready for planting.

TWENTY-FOUR

With the incredible speed of an immortal, Virginia went south toward the downtown area of Chicago known as "The Loop", a district made up mostly of high-rise office buildings and businesses that were closed down at the end of the day. Virginia looked around to make sure she was not being watched, but at this late hour, there were few people about, other than the vagrants and the homeless that roamed the lonely streets throughout the late night hours. Certain she was not going to be seen, she approached the tallest building in the country, the Sears Tower.

She jumped straight into the air, reaching the top of the tower in a single bound, the feat having taken almost no effort.

Virginia loved being high above the city. The view was unmatched anywhere, and the breezes coming in off the lake were fresh and unbroken, having nothing else this high to interrupt their path. In the distance, the surface of the lake shimmered in the moon and starlight, its waves carrying to the shore the secrets of the ships and sailors that lay entombed in its icy waters deep below the surface. And far below, the entire city lay like a glimmering gemstone, sparkling at just the right moments, in just the right places.

Virginia enjoyed being alone with her thoughts. It gave her the opportunity to reflect on all the things she had learned during her extended existence. She knew the Code as well as anyone, as did all of the ancients that remained to dwell the earth. She tried her best to teach the Code to her minions. Some caught on, and lived peacefully, almost in harmony with the mortals who ruled the day. True, they still needed to feed on the blood of the mortals, but by following the Code, they could do so unobtrusively, without causing panic in the lesser beings.

And then there were vampires like Nicolette, who did not accept the Code as what it was meant to be, a way to keep peace between the mortal and immortal world, instead viewing it as a set of parental rules meant to be broken. These wayward ones were not long-lived. Virginia still grieved over what she had been forced to do.

Virginia's thoughts were interrupted by the arrival of one of her favorites, proudly announcing that she had found Elizabeth.

* * *

They embraced, old friends who been apart too long.

"How have you been?" asked Elizabeth.

"Doing well. Better than you lately, it seems," answered Virginia.

"What do you mean?" Elizabeth was confused.

"You're becoming sloppy, my dear. I've seen your image twice in photographs, and the newspapers are filled with the stories of the journalist and the woman in the park. And, in the midst of all this, did you kill the cop, too?"

Elizabeth hung her head, ashamed at her recent behavior, and quietly answered, "Yes, I did kill him. But I can't figure out why. Something made me snap."

Virginia held her friend while Elizabeth began to cry. "There there, lovey. We'll find a way to make it all better."

"Do any of the other ancients know?" Elizabeth's sadness was suddenly replaced by fear.

"What's wrong? What are you afraid of?"

"I broke the Code. They'll be after me! And Carlos! He's here in Chicago."

Virginia looked at her friend, blue eyes meeting violet, and tried to offer reassurance. "Elizabeth, you need protection right now. And I'm your only hope. I'm the oldest remaining ancient, and I can protect you. If Carlos finds you, I can't imagine what that bastard would do. Let me put you into hiding until I can decide what to do next."

"If you think that's best. But what of Nicolette? Won't she get jealous?"

Virginia became obviously somber. "Nicolette is of no more concern. She has moved on from this world."

Elizabeth grew suspicious, wondering what had happened to the young vampire, afraid that she was being coerced into becoming a replacement for the departed Nicolette. "I won't use Nicolette's coffin," she said, perhaps a bit too defensively. "I'll want my own."

"No, we won't have you using her coffin. It's already being taken care of. You're still staying in the old Water Tower? Even after all these years? I have people heading there now, preparing to move your things. Carlos doesn't know where I live, so you will be safe there as long as you hunt with me and stay by my side."

Elizabeth agreed on the condition that she would stay by Virginia's side for protection only. She was not interested in becoming anyone's minion, companion, or lover. She only wanted to be protected from Carlos. And with the coming of the Blood on the Moon, she felt the same sense of impending trouble she'd felt for the past few days. She wasn't sure what it meant, but she knew she would need the protection of her friend. As long as they remained friends, she would reside with Virginia. But if things changed, if Virginia tried to make Elizabeth into more than she wanted to become, she would take her chances in the outside world.

TWENTY-FIVE

After feeding on a local boy in the Logan Square neighborhood, Carlos and Nicholas disposed of the body in a back alley.

When they returned to the carriage, Jennifer had rolled up the side curtains and put them back in place, like a new homeowner tidying the house before her husband came home from a hard day of work. She gave the two men a smile, but Nicolas sensed that something was wrong. He could sense that she hadn't had her fill, and would need to feed again soon. He was certain Carlos could sense it as well, and they would drive through the streets hunting until she was satisfied. Nicolas wouldn't get to feed for himself until much later.

In the meantime, though, Carlos had a very important matter he wanted to discuss with Jennifer. He took her in his arms and announced, "I want you to have my child."

Jennifer was taken aback. It was sudden, unexpected, and she didn't know what to say. She didn't even realize that vampires could reproduce. She knew no details of this new life into which she'd been inducted.

"The Blood on the Moon is almost here, and it is only during this time that I can impregnate another vampire." He repeated to her, "I want you to have my child."

It was the most romantic thing Jennifer had ever heard. Never in her mortal life had anyone felt this way toward her, or made any offers to do more than help her walk down the stairs. And here was a man wanting to have a child with her. She grabbed him by the back of the head and kissed him deeply.

"Yes! Oh, yes!" she exclaimed, continuing to rain kisses on him.

Her reaction was more than Carlos had hoped for. It heightened his every feeling, stirring his desire to mate during the upcoming eclipse. It had been almost two decades, but it would not be long now.

* * *

The carriage came to a stop and Nicolas threw open the side door, reaching in without a word to either Carlos or Jennifer, and effortlessly grabbing the body of their latest victim from the floor. Carlos and Jennifer leaned out the open door, watching curiously as he placed it in a pile of overgrown weeds. Looking around, they saw that they were stopped near the freeway, next to an obviously neglected patch of land, grass growing wildly, and trash lying strewn about. No one would find the body for a long, long time.

Nicolas brushed his hands off on the back of his pants and turned back to the carriage. After a short walk through the overgrowth, he climbed back up to the driver's seat, and started back into the city.

He tried his best to ignore the giggles coming from the carriage below, but he couldn't ignore the conversation. The carriage was far from soundproof. Even though Nicolas had been what mortals would have called "mentally impaired" during his mortal life, he was not a fool. And the more he heard, the more the conversation began to bother him.

Carlos could make a companion any time he felt the need. Other minions had companions as well. Why was Nicolas never allowed to make a companion? Was there something wrong with him wanting someone to share his eternity with? He could try to talk to Carlos about this, but he feared the wrath such a conversation would undoubtedly bring down upon him. He also knew the significance of the upcoming lunar eclipse.

In the back of Nicolas' brain, a thought was forming. He couldn't focus on it, or understand it. He felt as if he were being called upon by a Higher Power to serve the vampire community. But when the time came, would he be ready? He thought he would; he had spent most of his life trying his best to please those around him, and a Higher Power such as he felt would surely lend him strength.

TWENTY-SIX

In search of prey, Nicholas soon came across a young girl sitting alone on a park bench, her head held in her hands, sobbing.

Nicolas sat down next to her and offered her his handkerchief. She took it and, without a word, placed her head on his shoulder. He put his arm gently around her shoulder and held her tenderly.

Nicolas couldn't help but notice the perfume she wore. It was a Jasmine scent that reminded him of the jasmine bushes back in Louisiana, the home of his long past mortal life.

Her short hair was stylishly cut, and even though most of her eye makeup had run down her face from all of the crying making her look like a raccoon, Nicolas felt something he couldn't explain. Maybe this was the person that was sent to him to be his companion. Maybe this was what the Higher Power was offering to him, in return for whatever it was that would be expected of him in the near future.

He knew how to turn a mortal into his companion. It was something that all vampires learned through the Code, and, although he had never done it, he was certain he was meant to now.

He stood up, and, still having spoken not a single word, took the girl by the hand, leading her into a solitary spot. He thought about telling her what his plans were, what he meant to do to her. But he was afraid that if he offered her immortality, she would run from him, or try to attract the police. Then he would be forced to simply kill her, something he didn't want to do. This woman was more than a meal. He felt it deep inside. She was much more.

She didn't bother giving him her name, because after his silent comfort, and unspoken way of leading her to the rose garden, she assumed he was deaf or mute. If that were the case, she wouldn't know how to communicate with him. So she remained as silent as he, comforted by the simple attention he had given her. He didn't even know why she was crying. He just held her, allowed her to cry, and walked with her in companionship.

Cindy, for that was her name, had no idea what Nicolas really was or what was about to happen to her. She was a bit surprised when he pulled her close to him, something he had learned from watching Carlos hundreds of times. She wrapped her arms around Nicolas and laid her head on his shoulder, content in the arms of this total stranger, feeling utterly relaxed and at peace.

Nicolas could see her jugular vein pulsating with every beat of her heart, and fought the urge to drink to his heart's content, wanting to prolong the culmination of this unprecedented experience . When his anticipation reached its peak, Nicolas dipped his head and sank his fangs into her throat. At first, all he could taste was her perfume. But then he felt the warm blood reach his tongue, and he found the taste he sought.

When she was close to death, he released her and laid her gently back onto the bench. Barely alive, her body going cold from lack of oxygen, she was sure she was dying. Her physical pain was far outweighed by her emotional pain; death would be a welcome relief.

Nicolas bit his own arm, drawing blood from his own veins. He held his wrist to her lips.

"Drink and live."

After a time, Cindy's body stopped convulsing and she relaxed once again. She ran her tongue across her teeth and was surprised to find that she had fangs.

She glanced at Nicolas and, with the smile of a Cheshire cat, said, "I'm hungry."

Nicolas laughed.

* * *

After Cindy fed on the blood of her ex-fiancé, Edward, who had made the fatal mistake of breaking off their engagement earlier that day, explaining that he had fallen in love with another woman, Nicholas led her back to the carriage.

"Who's this pretty young thing?" asked Carlos, assuming she was the meal Nicolas had chosen for the evening and that he was simply leading her on, toying with her before he finished her off.

"This is Cindy. She is my companion," came the curt reply. Carlos was surprised by the abrupt response, and decided that such a display of disrespect would require addressing. At a later time, however. He had other, more important matters on his mind, and was ready to return home.

Nicolas sensed his master's hesitation. But now that he had taken the brave step of making a companion for himself, he felt a bit of vampire arrogance flowing through him; one step toward greater self-confidence and a lesser fear of Carlos.

At that moment, they heard a woman scream in the distance. Cindy began to laugh. Carlos and Jennifer looked at the young woman, wondering if they had missed a joke. Cindy looked up at Nicolas and said, "Well, I guess Shannon found Edward!"

Carlos immediately realized that a recent vampire kill had just been discovered, and he hissed, "Quickly, get us out of here!" as he climbed into the lower cab, pulling Jennifer through the door behind him. Nicolas untied the horses before helping Cindy climb atop the carriage, and then followed her up into the driver's seat.

Carlos called to his driver, "Home, James!" It was his joke, one he had used for all the years that Nicolas had served him. It had nagged at Nicolas in the past, being treated like an inferior and having Carlos joke about it in such a blatant manner. But with his new, growing independence, he was sure he would draw up the courage to put an end to it in the near future.

TWENTY-SEVEN

Before Carlos stepped through the entrance to the crypt he now shared with Jennifer, he paused to look up at the moon. He could already see the reddish tint beginning to appear across its surface, the "Blood on the Moon" beginning, and he felt the need to mate growing stronger within him.

"Just one more night," he reminded himself, finally stepping into the crypt behind his bride.

* * *

Elizabeth and Virginia spent the evening hunting on the southwest side of downtown, not far from the Sears Tower that Virginia loved. They strolled past an Italian restaurant, the aroma of the fine food wafting to the walkway, enticing passersby to enter and enjoy the succulent dishes prepared within. Virginia stopped and inhaled deeply, grabbing Elizabeth by the arm.

"What is it?" Elizabeth asked.

"Do you smell it?"

Elizabeth inhaled, and began to suffer a spasmodic fit of choking as the strong scent of garlic passed her nostrils and filled her lungs. "Stop, Virginia! Do you have a death wish?"

The older Vampire smiled. "No, no. It won't kill me. But it does remind me of the years I spent in Rome." Virginia's eyes took on a faraway look, as if she had suddenly been transported back in time.

"It really was a lovely city. And that same smell was everywhere. The people there loved garlic. It was why I had to leave. I felt ill every time I would feed on one of them. There was just too much of it in their system."

"I'm surprised you were able to feed at all, if that were the case. How did it not kill you?"

Virginia snapped back to the present, and began walking away from the restaurant, Elizabeth staying with her, stride for stride, a young student eager to hear of the adventures of a favorite professor.

"Didn't Dominick teach you about garlic, the 'bane of our existence'?"

Elizabeth shook her head sadly, looking down at the concrete that passed by their swiftly moving feet. "No, he never had time. He was gone before getting to many of the smaller details of the Code. I only learned the basic lesson that garlic was deadly to immortals."

Virginia stifled a small laugh. "Deadly, no. But certainly something to be wary of."

"How so?"

"Well," Virginia took on her role of teacher with ease, "the scent of garlic can do nothing to you, as you just learned back there by the restaurant. Neither can the touch. But all vampires are, in our own way, allergic to it. If you ingest a small amount, you may become ill. If you ingest a large amount, it would cause you extreme discomfort."

"How extreme? Death?"

"Probably not. But it's possible. Your throat might swell shut, your little black heart might stop temporarily, you might feel intense pain throughout your body. You would need to sleep for many days until the effects go away. And of course, then you would be weak from not feeding. But death from garlic is rare."

The night continued, Virginia filling in blanks in the Code that Dominick had not had the opportunity to teach. Virginia was impressed with the amount of knowledge Elizabeth had learned in her short time with her maker. It was the reason she had so successfully lived on her own for so long.

But she was still young, and she did still occasionally make mistakes. Allowing the journalist to be found, as well as the girl in the park, were major ones. Being photographed was another.

And later in the evening, she made another silly mistake by selecting a victim who had had far too much to drink; when she drained his blood, she became rather drunk as well.

The women enjoyed the evening immensely, Elizabeth stumbling and walking a fine line of consciousness from the effects of the alcohol, with Virginia constantly laughing at her friend, knowing full well she might have to carry the drunken vampire home.

In the back of Virginia's mind, she thought that, given the state Elizabeth was in, she could most likely have her way with her friend without too much of a struggle. But she had promised that she would be good, and she didn't want to lose a centuries-old friendship for one night of lust.

Virginia turned to see Elizabeth slumped against the wall, drunk from her meal. Effortlessly, Virginia picked her up, cradling Elizabeth in her arms, and flew them both home. She carried Elizabeth into their crypt, and laid Elizabeth in her own coffin. "Sweet dreams," she whispered.

TWENTY-EIGHT

With Elizabeth secured, Virginia climbed the tower to the rooftop to enjoy what remained of the moon's rays. She glanced up at the nearly full orb, and noticed the red dust reflecting off its surface, the beginnings of a lunar eclipse. She knew that the moon would be full the next night, and that the Earth, moon, and sun would be in perfect alignment, creating the Blood on the Moon.

She was certain that Carlos had by now taken a new companion. And she was certain she knew why. He meant to mate during the eclipse and reproduce again.

It wasn't often that a vampire, cold and dead on the inside, could feel an icy chill. But the thought of Carlos creating yet another monstrosity like the ones he had created in the past, sent shivers up her spine.

She knew she would have to prevent Carlos from bringing another ghoul into the world, but she also knew it would be foolhardy to try to stop him on her own. That was why she had summoned the other ancients. She had reached nearly all of them, and they would begin arriving before daybreak.

The plan to destroy Carlos could mean the death of many vampires, and possibly mortals as well, but she saw no other option. She had to warn her followers of what was going to happen the next evening. And time was running out. It was almost dawn.

Virginia opened her mouth, and with a mighty breath let out a sound that was heard throughout the entire city. Those who had served her well recognized it immediately and went to her. Within moments, she was surrounded by the familiar sounds of wings and breeze. She flew down to a small garden in the center of the church pavilion and waited. The garden, with a fountain and a narrow walkway, was set back from the street by a tall brick archway. It wasn't the most private place, and she was wary of convening there, visible to the public eye. But it was the only nearby place large enough for them to gather.

When Virginia spoke, her presence held such command over those around her that not another sound was heard.

"My darlings, you know that tomorrow night is the lunar eclipse. It is the 'Blood on the Moon'. You are also aware of all that I have taught you of the Code, that once a decade, during such an eclipse, a vampire may reproduce. In this decade, we are faced with a terrible danger. Somewhere, here in our beloved city, Carlos has taken a companion. He plans to mate with this 'made' vampire, something we all know is a strict violation of the Code, something that can only result in a horrible tragedy.

"Those of you who have witnessed Graham and his methods know of what I speak. We must destroy him, along with Carlos, and put an end to his horrible reign. There will be massive bloodshed, both mortal and immortal, but it is for the greater good of the vampire world.

"I have summoned the other ancients, and those who are closest will be arriving soon. I do not know if they can reach Chicago in time to stop the reproduction of another abomination, but they will try. It will take longer for the others to reach us from overseas.

"Any of you who have not yet fed tonight, be wary of anyone loyal to Carlos. If you cross paths with such a one, do not hesitate to tear their hearts out, or bring them to me alive.

"If you run across Carlos himself, keep your mind clear. He can read your thoughts. Do not let on that you know what he is up to. And do not reveal my plans.

"The last of the ancient wars is about to be waged, the final battle to destroy Carlos and his kind. He will be forced to answer to those of us left, and pay for the many crimes he has committed against mortal and immortal alike.

"I love each and every one of you. I will be saddened to see any of you fall, but I want you to keep your knowledge of the Code in the forefront of your mind at all times. You will be rewarded here, or in the place of the Prophets."

Glances and murmurs passed through the group. They all knew the power of Carlos. They also knew that if they banded together in groups, they could destroy three or four of what was now considered to be "the enemy" at one time.

They were outnumbered eight to one, thanks to Carlos' uncontrolled creating, but they would fight for each other, for Virginia, and for the entire vampire kingdom. They would not simply lie down at the feet of someone like Carlos. Their benefactor was kind and wise, and they adored her.

They also respected the other ancients and they would fight to the death to protect them, as well.

She turned to the young vampire who had found Elizabeth earlier. "I want you to be ready to be the handmaid to Elaine when she arrives. She will need a very strong chain. Break into a hardware store to gather two or three large spools of chain. The chain must be strong, so the spools will be heavy. Take someone with you if you need assistance in carrying them."

Virginia turned to another. "I will need you to assist Erik when he arrives from New York City. Anything he wants, you get and get quickly." He nodded, and dashed off to feed for the night.

"The rest of you, make yourselves available as the others get here.

Gideon has already arrived by airplane and is waiting to be set free. I need a volunteer to go to O'Hare Airport, enter the customs area where you will find his crate, and break the seal. Anyone?"

"I'll do it," said a voice behind Virginia. She turned around to see Elizabeth standing up against the wall of the church.

"But, my love, you are not in any condition for this mission."

"Oh, cut it out, Virginia. You just don't want me to meet Gideon and steal your thunder," came the smart response from the younger vampire.

Virginia could tell from the smile on Elizabeth's face that there was no disrespect intended in the comment. She was relieved that her friend had so quickly recovered from the effects of the alcoholic blood she had consumed earlier and was ready to help in the fight against Carlos. She smiled, shook her head and said, "Go," sending Elizabeth off to free Gideon of his bonds.

As the other vampires scattered throughout the city with the knowledge that the next night would bring them to a battle the likes of which they had never seen, Virginia sat on the bench in the garden, placed her head in her hands, and cried.

She cried for the loss of her favorite lover. Not Nicolette. She had loved Nicolette, but Nicolette was just a plaything. She cried for Dominick, whom she had loved long ago. And she cried for the child they had conceived under the Blood on the Moon so many decades ago, the child Carlos had killed.

She also cried for the other baby ancients Carlos had killed over the centuries. She cried because at that moment, for the first time in her existence, she felt powerless over the events around her, events created by someone she knew that, given the chance, she would not hesitate to rip out his heart and show it to him.

Virginia was afraid that with so many of the ancients converging in one place, any minor event that went wrong could place Carlos in a position of unfathomable power. If that were to happen, the entire Code and all it stood for would be destroyed. Forbidden abominations would take over the entire world, and the ancients would be able to do nothing but watch silently as chaos ensued.

* * *

The lock on the filing cabinet opened as easily as the one on the office door had moments earlier. The strong hands, encased in thin plastic surgical gloves, quickly flipped through the file folders, finding the tab marked "To Be Entered". He was in luck. Neither report had been entered into the permanent computer system, something that would have slowed him drastically, as he would not only have to wipe out the record, but also hack into the server to remove any evidence that he had been tinkering with the files.

He laughed at the ease with which he had entered two government offices and located two sets of reports. He was a master at gaining access to locked offices and bypassing security systems.

Had the main offices of the Chicago Police Department been located in one of the precinct houses, it would have been much more difficult. The round-the-clock activity would have made entry into the office files next to impossible. But a downtown office that closed its doors to everyone but the custodial staff made his job so much easier.

It also helped that over the thirty years that he had been doing these jobs, the systems with which the files were organized never seemed to change. Office managers, assistants, and clerical workers would come and go, but the system stayed the same. It made it quick and easy for him to find what he was looking for.

In the office of the Police Chief's assistant, he had found the copies of the autopsy reports right where they belonged, in a neat stack of sent faxes, properly stamped, dated, and stapled together. Here in the Coroner's Office, they were awaiting entry by one of the data processing clerks from the office one floor below. Now both sets would cease to exist. It had been twenty years since he had been asked to destroy autopsy reports of this nature, and he couldn't believe he had been asked to do it again. But the phone call from Larson made it clear this was no joke.

He knew that the last time he'd been asked to perform such a service, Larson was a city congressman. Soon after, Larson was elected Mayor, and had held the office ever since. He also knew it was some kind of cover-up, but he never understood the reason for it. The autopsy reports seemed to indicate vampire attacks. But since he didn't believe in vampires, he knew it had to be something else, like a ceremonial or sacrificial cult killing. But why would a small group of city officials want to cover up a cult? Were they secret members?

Luckily for him, the only member of the cover-up who knew his real identity had died five years ago, so now he was a totally anonymous sideman, nothing more than a hired gun and barely a shadow. The rest of the committee knew him simply as their "magician," because he could make unwanted reports disappear.

And now, thanks to his anonymity, no matter what went down, he couldn't get fingered and dragged into the mess. He could simply make himself disappear.

That was always a good position to be in.

TWENTY-NINE

Detective Mike Green woke in the basement of his house, wondering where he was. Blinking at the harsh light from the single bare bulb hanging down from the ceiling, vague memories of the previous evening and the earlier morning came rushing back to him.

"Jane!" he called, the volume of his own voice causing starbursts of pain to erupt in his skull.

There was no answer, and no movement from upstairs. He looked at his watch, the digital readout proclaiming it 7:30 p.m. Normally at this time his home would be filled with the sounds of the two women he loved working in the kitchen and chatting with each other as Jane made dinner and Meagan worked on her latest masterpiece of crayon art. The smells of dinner cooking should have been wafting throughout the house, filling the rooms with the aroma of the latest delicious meal that Jane had discovered in one of the many magazines that filled their mailbox on an almost daily basis.

Slowly he sat up, the pain in his head pounding as if his entire brain was about to burst out through his eyeballs, his stomach doing its own version of calisthenics. He sat for a minute and wondered if the nausea would make him throw up on his shoes or if he could stand on his unsteady legs long enough to make it upstairs to find out where Jane and Meagan where

He briefly considered some "hair of the dog" to get him off the futon, but the moment the thought crossed his brain, his stomach did another series of flips and vetoed the idea with a swift stamp of disapproval. He carefully grabbed the end of the futon and slowly pushed himself up onto his feet. The world swirled for a moment, the ceiling spinning, the floor swaying like a roller coaster, the solid furniture around him warping in ways only possible in science fiction movies.

When the moment passed, he slowly made his way to the stairwell, clutching any solid piece of furniture along the way to try and keep himself steady.

"Jane?" he yelled up the empty stairs again.

Still no answer from the darkened rooms above.

As slowly as he could, each step resulting in another miniscule explosion inside his head, he made it out of the basement and into the kitchen. The lights were off and the stove was cold. There were no signs of life. He looked around the table for a note, a message, anything from Jane to let him know where she was, but, again, nothing.

He began a deliberate room-to-room search for Jane and Meagan. He didn't dare turn on the lights for fear that the sudden flash of brilliance would blind him and set off his head like a nuclear reaction reaching critical mass.

But amidst all the pain, the fog cleared ever so slowly, revealing bits and pieces of the conversations he had before passing out earlier in the day. He remembered Jane trying to get him out of the basement. He remembered getting angry with her for no reason. And he remembered calling Jane a bitch, when all she was trying to do was help. When the memory of his verbal attack on his innocent wife surfaced, he pushed aside the agonizing pain in his head and went bounding up the stairs to the upper floor as fast as he could.

When he reached the bedroom they shared, he pulled open the drawers of her dresser and saw only a vast emptiness. All of her clothes were gone, magically transported to another dimension. He turned to their walk-in closet, its doors made of full length mirrors where Jane had spent so many hours making herself look absolutely perfect before leaving the house to attend a policemen's ball or other event where she wanted to exude a look of elegance. Mike slid the doors to the side along their squeaky rails, rails he had failed to oil even after repeated requests from his wife, and found that the only clothes remaining were his own. The sections of the closet reserved for his wife were bare. It was obvious that he had been out for quite some time. The completeness of the packing would have had to take time. This was no fast pack-and-dash.

He left their room and ran unsteadily down the short hallway to the baby's room, where he found a similar scene. The dresser was bare, except for a few pieces of outgrown clothing. The blankets favored by the youngster had been removed from the shelf in the closet, along with the few pieces of hanging clothes that had been there before. Gone also was the child's teddy bear, the bear that stayed on the bed during the better part of the day, and which the little girl would absolutely not sleep without.

Mike sat on the edge of his daughter's bed and dropped his head in defeat. He began to recall the full conversation he'd had with Jane, and he knew that she was gone because of it. He was certain she would have gone to her mother's house in Jefferson, but he also knew that he couldn't call her there.

By now his mother-in-law knew why Jane left him, that he had started drinking again. It was something Jane's mother had always been wary of, and now it had come to pass. There was no chance she'd allow Mike to talk to his wife that night.

He also knew that if his mother-in-law had her way about it, he would never see Jane or Meagan again. She was against all forms of alcohol, had been ever since her husband, Jane's father, had died from his drinking. Jane had always threatened to leave if he started drinking again, but he never thought she would seriously go through with it. Unfortunately, he was now finding out just how serious about it she was.

He wondered what to do next. He couldn't go back to work for the next four days, his wife and daughter were gone, and his best friend had been viciously murdered. He pulled his knees up to his chest, hugged his legs, and cried.

He had to find a way to get his wife and daughter back. He knew he could go to AA every day to show that he didn't want to start drinking heavily again, that this was a one-time thing. But he couldn't take back the hateful way he had spoken to Jane or the horrible things he had said to her. He knew that she was hurting inside just as he was, and he needed her now more than ever.

* * *

Elizabeth arrived at O'Hare Airport with plenty of time to rescue Gideon from his crate. It was easy for her to slip through the airport, even with the heightened security. Security guards and baggage handlers were far too busy to notice a mist floating near the ceiling, or even a levitating vampire, if Elizabeth decided not to take the less visible form.

Inside the terminal, past the metal detectors and long lines of passengers waiting to have their carry-on baggage screened, Elizabeth wandered past the gates, the shops, and the overpriced airport restaurants crowded with people waiting for flights to arrive or simply passing time during a layover. Engrossed in their own activities, they paid no attention to the woman walking amongst them.

When Elizabeth was sure the customs inspectors would be at their busiest, she made her way to the international terminal, choosing to ride with the mortals on the electric rail that connects the terminals. She stood just inside the sliding doors, hanging on to one of the looped leather straps dangling from the ceiling.

At this time of the early, pre-dawn morning, there were few people on the train, and they were either traveling at the odd hour in order to get reduced fares on their airline tickets, or were businessmen who had uncomfortably early meetings in the city. Elizabeth, with her lack of luggage, and very un-businesslike attire, didn't fit into either category, but still managed to remain unremarked by her fellow passengers.

At the last stop, the international terminal, Elizabeth disembarked and walked a short distance past the customs gate. Few people were paying attention to those on her side of the gate, being mainly concerned with people coming from the terminal. The customs officials were vigorously checking for contraband, and everyone else was watching for their particular disembarking loved one.

Elizabeth stood as far back in a corner as she could, and looked around to be sure she was unnoticed, paying special attention to any security cameras that could possibly capture her image. When she was sure she was unobserved, she flew up to the ceiling, turned herself into a mist, and floated past the "exit only" sign into the receiving area of customs.

She moved silently through the aisles of cartons, packages, and crates that had been shipped through international freight but which had not yet been cleared for delivery through the gates and into the country. She nearly laughed out loud when she found what she was looking for: a large wooden crate, sealed tightly on all sides, and addressed to "The Devil Himself." Amused by the obvious joke, she knew that Gideon must be inside.

Quickly breaking the seal and lifting the lid, Elizabeth revealed the lid of an ornate casket made of solid oak. She reached down into the crate and lifted it open.

Inside, she found the pale skinned corpse of a man who looked to have passed away in his mid-twenties, arms crossed on his chest, hands meeting and clasped above the sternum. The best mortician in the world couldn't have created a more stereotypical pose for a wake. His hair was slicked back, revealing a high, unlined forehead above closed eyelids that looked unstrained, and were without crease. If this man had worked a day in his life, it didn't show in his face. The slightly flattened nose reached down to a pair of deep red lips that had a slightly upturned smile upon them.

Elizabeth leaned down into the crate, coming to within inches of the face, and, with a broad grin, whispered, "Gideon."

Gideon opened his eyes and the smile broadened, spreading across his face. "Why, Elizabeth, my darling, I knew you wouldn't be able to resist my charms!"

He sat up and the two vampires embraced. They looked around to make sure they still could not be seen, and quickly closed the coffin, replaced the packing material, and reassembled the shipping crate. They left the customs holding pen the same way Elizabeth had entered, and were soon on their way to the church where Virginia anxiously awaited their arrival.

THIRTY

The Hummer H2 sped down the dark streets, fighting the centrifugal force that tried in vain to tip the sturdy vehicle each time it careened around a corner. The quiet of the dawn was broken by the screech of tires against pavement, the acrid smell of burnt rubber following closely behind.

The driver seemed unconcerned with the dangers of his driving. His long blonde hair fell past his shoulders, flowing out from under the Stetson hat tipped low enough in front to completely hide his light blue eyes.

The vehicle came to a sudden stop at the curbside, and the driver unfolded his six foot three inch muscular frame from the seat behind the steering wheel. Dressed in tight jeans, steel-tipped cowboy boots, and a tight white T-shirt underneath his long denim duster, he stretched his arms above his head before almost getting knocked over when Virginia rushed out the door and barreled into him.

"Grant, darling! You made a seventeen hour drive in one night?"

"Naw," came the reply. "I stopped in St. Louis when the sun started to show and slept the day next to a dead hooker." He added with a twinkle in his eye and a sly grin on his lips, "After I had her for dinner."

Grant was one of the few ancients who seemed to have the uncanny ability to commit blatant acts that should attract the attention of mortals but still remain unseen. He loved driving his Humvee at breakneck speeds, never concerned about what would happen if he crashed. Police never stopped him. He could be loud and boisterous, and no one noticed.

Virginia threw her arms around Grant, and led him around the side of the church, through the courtyard, and to the base of the tower that led down to her catacombs.

"Did you bring your own coffin, or do we need to find one for you?"

"Aw, mine's in the back of the Hummer. The back seats fold down, ya know." He said this with the wide-eyed enthusiasm of a young child showing off his newest toy with all its special features.

Virginia couldn't help but laugh at her dear friend and his odd ways before snapping her fingers to summon two of her followers.

"Please unload the coffin in the back of his vehicle and take it down to the tunnels."

* * *

Susan had never met Elaine, but knew it was an honor for her to be asked by Virginia to be her handmaiden. Rumor had it that Elaine had given birth to a new ancient, but Susan was skeptical; she knew that Carlos had killed any new baby ancients born in the past two centuries. Then again, she ruminated, maybe it's the story of Carlos' actions that's the real rumor.

She suddenly heard the sound of wings above her hear. Before long, a striking figure stood in front of her, dressed in a blood-red cape that covered a dress which was more reminiscent of the Renaissance than modern day. Jet black hair pulled sharply back exposed the most incredible widow's peak that Susan had ever seen

She found herself unable to speak.

The figure seemed to float toward her effortlessly. She was even more beautiful than Susan had first realized.

"You must be the handmaiden that Virginia arranged for me," came the sultry alto voice. "I am Elaine."

Susan nodded, still unable to make a sound. Elaine wondered for a minute if she was mute.

"You don't have to be worried about me. I won't bite you." This brought a laugh from Susan, who began to relax for the first time since Elaine had appeared before her.

The two women began to walk through the park, Susan leading the way. Dawn was quickly approaching, and they would have to take flight soon to reach the church before the sun rose.

* * *

As Erik walked the city block that held the church where the ancients were slowly gathering, he admired the architecture surrounding the church: the gothic appeal of the church itself, reaching high above the rest of the neighborhood; the intermingling of the old fashioned streetlights on one side of the street and the more modern style on the other; the precise planting of trees along the boulevard, forming a perfectly straight row along the pavement; even the slight angle of the criss-crossing streets in need of repair, but continually ignored by the city decision makers

Mostly, he was drawn to the Victorian homes, their occupants safely tucked inside, sleeping, never dreaming that, right outside their doors, the most dangerous creatures they could ever imagine were gathering.

A dog began to howl as Erik approached. He snapped his fingers at the dog, instantly reducing the beast's ruckus to a soft, shy whimper. He secretly loved the ability and power he had over lesser animals.

And he held hatred in his black heart for the man who was the reason for the gathering of the ancients, the man who would soon be held accountable. Erik had fathered two beautiful baby girls, baby ancients who could grow and continue the ways of the vampire world and to foster a new generation of co-existence with the mortals. But they had been ripped from his life by Carlos, the uncontrollable monster.

He decided was going to savor seeing Carlos brought to justice.

Each one of the ancients had their own justification for wanting to be rid of Carlos, but Erik knew that despite the growing and ongoing hatred, destroying Carlos would also be difficult on Virginia, as he suspected she must be experiencing terribly conflicted feelings. She was, after all, his mother. Still, she had seen how Carlos had killed Dominick, his father, centuries ago, and had detested him for doing it. And, of course, Virginia, being one of the oldest of the ancients, always did what was best for the overall vampire community.

Erik stood in front of the church and looked up at the majestic building, which, to his trained eye, he knew must have been constructed shortly after the "Great Chicago Fire." Lost in his thoughts, he let his guard down, never feeling the icy hands creep across his face until he heard a familiar voice whisper in his ear.

"Fiona!" he exclaimed, turning and swinging the lithe vampire off her feet.

They complemented each other well, and they knew that, according to the prophesies, they were the next ancients in line to mate and create another purebred vampire–in only ten short years.

Pieces of plaster suddenly began to rain down on them. They looked up to see Grant's grinning face peering over the edge of the rooftop at them.

"Hey, you two, get your carcasses up here! We have some planning to do if we're going to be two short."

They began to climb the marble steps that led from the paved sidewalk to the oak door that held the numerous secrets of the building. Just as Erik reached for the door handle to open the heavy door, the sound of scores of wings filled the air. The two vampires on the church steps looked up, almost expecting to see Carlos' minions arriving to force a confrontation. All they could see was darkness. Instinctively, Fiona stepped closer to Erik.

Two figures draped in black robes, heads covered by dark hoods, alighted from the skies squarely in front of Erik and Fiona, who prepared themselves to meet face to face with the enemy. The new arrivals slowly drew back their hoods, revealing the faces beneath.

Erik and Fiona embraced them. "Leslie! Peter! How? Why?" These two had not been expected.

Leslie answered, saying, "Well, the 'Blood on the Moon' happens here in Chicago, too. So why can't we mate here and still be available to help?"

Peter's thick Scottish accent joined in. "We knew that Katherine couldn't be here, and we knew that you would need every pure blood available to abolish this monstrosity."

"Humph," came a voice from behind Leslie and Peter, "I could crush his head with my bare hands."

The voice came from a man who stood six foot five, with a close-cropped beard, flowing locks of reddish brown hair, and a style of dress that mimicked that of a Spanish Conquistador.

"Antonio!" Both Leslie and Fiona threw themselves into his outstretched arms.

More plaster chips came raining down from above as Grant, the prankster, called to the small crowd gathering on the steps. "Okay, stay down there and let the sun fry your stupid brains out. Then Virginia and I will not only have to mate tomorrow night, but we'll have to kill Carlos and all his lackeys on our own!"

Laughing, the five new arrivals entered the church and began to climb the stairs to the belfry where Virginia, Elaine, and Grant waited.

The eight of them wondered where and when William would make his entrance. Known for his dramatics, they took turns guessing where he was. They knew Gideon would be there soon. They had not heard from Maria, but Greece was a long way off, and they didn't expect her to arrive until early that evening. And no one ever knew when or how the ever-elusive Morgana would arrive. At that point, their gathering would be complete. Twelve of the fifteen living ancients, banded together against Carlos.

Susan moved among them, keeping their wine glasses filled with fresh blood that she had gathered earlier, suspecting that the ancients would probably enjoy a little refreshment after their long journeys.

Above them, the winds began to pick up, and the sound of laughter filled the air. But it was not the laughter of the eight who waited. The laughter came from above.

They all looked up and saw two pair of eyes glowing at them from the tallest steeple, fear at whose eyes they could be beginning to enter their cold hearts. Surely Carlos wouldn't start an attack now, with dawn so close at hand. The battle would be short-lived, with the only casualties the stragglers caught in the first rays of the sun. But who else could the glowing eyes belong to?

Their question was answered when the owners of those glowing eyes flew down into their midst. William and Maria had managed to approach their family without being detected until the last moment.

Almost complete, the group chatted amongst themselves, relaxed in each others' company, enjoying the reunion. But always in the back of their minds was the reason they were gathered in this one place. The job ahead of them would not be an easy one.

They lacked only the last of their number, Morgana, who loved to travel the world and re-explore the ruins of ancient civilizations where she had spent her younger years. Grant said that his last knowledge of her whereabouts put her in Mexico, at the pyramids of the Aztecs. William commented he would not be surprised if she were already in Chicago and near Carlos, watching his every move.

Virginia couldn't repress the pangs of jealousy she felt while watching Leslie play with tendrils of Peter's hair. It had been a long time since she had mated with an ancient and, according to the prophecy, it would be a much longer time before she would again. Out of the corner of her eye, she caught sight of Erik placing a hand on Fiona's thigh in a manner that was much more than just a friendly gesture. And, once again, she felt alone.

THIRTY-ONE

In the cemetery on the north side of town, Carlos and Jennifer neared the end of their stroll, expecting to return to their crypt well ahead of the first rays of the sun. Jennifer had complained throughout their walk, wishing she could go out in the day time and shop Michigan Avenue with its trendy stores. She had only been an immortal for a short time, and she still missed some mortal pleasures.

Carlos, for the most part, ignored her. She was young, and the memories of walking in the sunlight would fade over time. But even more, he was preoccupied with a sickness he was feeling in his stomach.

He felt like someone was watching them, someone as pure of vampire blood as he.

Ridiculous, he thought. The ancients are scattered around the globe. The only other in Chicago is Virginia, and she has no idea of what I have planned for her or any of the others.

Following the death of the last vampire child, Carlos had managed to sneak back into Chicago, and prepared himself for a long sleep. He knew that as long as he slept, he could not be sensed by the other vampires. And as long as his minions were asleep, they would not kill a great number of the city's mortals, upholding the deal he had made with a small band of corrupt city officials. Now that he was so close to his goal, he could break his deal with the mortals, destroy the other ancients, and become the ultimate ruler of the entire world.

Carlos did not know, could not know, that the other ancients had, in fact, already caught up with him. He only knew that Virginia had found him. But how long had she known where he was? He was sure he had plenty of time to gather his followers, mate with Jennifer, create another new ghoul child, and move to a new home far away where they could begin their conquest of power. By the time the other ancients found him, it would be too late.

Moving would be no novel event. Every few years Carlos' band would drain the life from a local population and then move on to a new killing ground. It was the way Carlos felt the entire vampire world should be. Move in, feed on the lowly mortals, and move on. They should not be forced to hide in the shadows. They should be the rulers of the world.

* * *

He never realized that hidden high in a willow tree, up against the bark, was indeed another ancient. Morgana was watching every move he made. Her presence was the cause of the sick feelings he was experiencing. She was far enough removed that he couldn't sense her, but his body responded on a much more subliminal level.

At one time she had loved Carlos and would have gladly mated with him every decade, whether it was according to the prophesy or not. She had been so in love with Carlos that she was almost willing to break every rule of the Code.

But all that changed with the killing of baby Dharma twenty years ago, with the killing of Simon, the child born ten years earlier to Katherine and Antonio. Carlos had become a monster, and Morgana had realized how wrong she had been about him. He had seemed so innocent when each new ancient born was mysteriously destroyed. Some of the ancients believed it to be a punishment for their kind, the destruction of any new life they created, the end of their race. Others postulated they had been discovered by mortals who found it impossible to kill the full-grown ancients, but managed to destroy the newborns. None had suspected it had been Carlos killing a new ancient child every decade for nearly two centuries.

As she gazed down at Carlos and his "bride" she wondered what it was about the girl that would make Carlos break the Code and risk having another child like Graham.

Her heart pained her to know that she had to take part in what was to come. She wished that she could flee the city, but couldn't turn her back on her family, her duty to them, to the Code, and to the entire vampire world.

Above all else, she was a vampire.

THIRTY-TWO

Chief David Duncan arrived at his office promptly at seven a.m., as was his habit. He got coffee and walked to his office, morning paper in hand. He sat down behind his desk, spread the paper out in front of him and began his daily ritual of searching for obscure missing persons reports. Although rare, there were times when an overzealous reporter managed to get a story about a missing person, or some other crime, into the paper before a police report had even been filed. Duncan went after those reporters with a vengeance. It was one thing to show blatant disregard for the family of the victim by splashing their horror all over the paper, but it was even worse to put all the details in print, making a successful investigation almost impossible.

Today, he read even more closely, because he had a feeling that soon the stories would multiply exponentially, and he'd be thrust into something larger than anything he'd ever experienced.

He had already finished off his fourth cup of coffee, still engrossed in the paper, when his intercom buzzed. It was one of the clerks from the outer offices asking where the daily reports from the other precincts were. Irene normally distributed them by nine a.m., but when the Chief looked at the clock he was thunderstruck to see that it was already ten thirty. He had been so involved in the paper that it hadn't occurred to him that he hadn't seen his assistant that morning.

He left his office and went to her desk, where he found everything in its usual place. Irene's organizational skills were what had landed her the position as his assistant, and they'd joked frequently that he wasn't allowed to touch anything on her desk, since he lacked the same skill. Additionally, she'd always been punctual.

He walked across the carpeted office, and poked his head out the door into the outer office, where he asked if anyone had seen Irene. When the answer was no, he became even more puzzled.

He returned to his office, and called down to personnel to see if perhaps Irene had called in sick. It was possible that she'd called him and he missed the call, or she just hadn't been able to reach him. No, they hadn't heard from her, either.

Something began to tug at his subconscious. There could be plenty of good reasons why Irene would be away from work without calling in. Some kind of emergency, a family tragedy, a simple case of oversleeping. But some indefinable sense told him there was something else wrong, and that he needed to check into it.

He did something he had never done before in his life. He walked out of the office, took the elevator all the way down to the underground parking lot, got into his unmarked cruiser and drove to her apartment. There had never been a personal relationship of any kind between David Duncan and his assistant; always strictly business. But he had given her a ride home on occasion when they'd both been working late, so he knew where she lived. He pulled to the curb outside her building, and walked to the front door. He didn't know which apartment was hers, but the apartment buzzers outside the main entrance were labeled.

He pushed the buzzer for Irene's apartment, and waited impatiently for a response. He tried the buzzer three more times, just to be certain. Somehow, he wasn't surprised that she didn't answer.

An older woman left the building carrying a small dog, and he grabbed the door before it could close, gaining access to the building. So much for building security.

Remembering the apartment number listed next to Irene's name, he climbed the two flights of stairs and checked each door until he found hers. He banged on the door as hard as he could, hoping none of the neighbors would be nosy enough to ask him what he was doing, or worse yet, to call the cops.

Finding the door incompletely latched, David entered the apartment. Inside he found an over-turned picnic basket, a crumpled blanket, and Irene's apartment keys on the floor. He immediately drew his weapon and began searching from room to room, calling her name.

As he neared the bedroom door, a foul but familiar odor hit his nose. He gingerly opened the door with his foot, careful not to disturb anything. The sick feeling in his stomach told him that he was about to discover a crime scene.

His fears were confirmed when he discovered a pool of blood, one arm, some fingers and what could have been part of a leg. His stomach wrenched and he had to turn away before he vomited. He ran back to Irene's living room and sat down in an overstuffed chair, lowering his head between his knees. There was no way of knowing who the body parts in the bedroom belonged to, but he was fairly certain he had just found what was left of his missing assistant.

Gathering his wits, he took a handkerchief from his pocket, and used it to pick up Irene's phone and dial 911, careful to not leave his fingerprints anywhere, or smudge any that might be present from the person who had done whatever had been done to the body in the bedroom. He gave his gruesome information to the dispatcher and told her to send a coroner, as well as a forensics team. He then called his office and told the officer in charge to find Detective Mike Green.

The feeling in his gut that had told him Irene's absence was something more than just an absent employee also told him that the strange murders of the past few days were somehow connected. And since Mike Green was the only officer who'd gotten a good look at the first victim, the journalist in the dumpster, he was going to be needed on this investigation.

The Chief was reminded that he had sent Detective Green on vacation after his friend Sam was found murdered. "I don't care where I sent him," he growled into the phone. "Find him and get him back. Send him straight to this location."

He couldn't bring himself to go back into the bedroom where the bloody remains of his assistant lay strewn about the room, so he sat and waited.

He continued to sit in the chair, refusing to move, even when the teams arrived. All he asked was if they had found Mike Green. One of the forensics officers had said he was on his way.

Mike Green walked through the door looking haggard and exhausted. David motioned him over. "Take a walk with me out onto the back porch," he said.

Once outside, David turned to Mike and said, "You don't look so good. What's up?"

"I sort of," Mike looked at his unpolished shoes, "fell off the wagon."

"Pretty hard?"

"Yeah. A whole day. I'm still feeling it."

"Your wife okay?"

Mike looked up at the Chief, amazed that the man could sense the real trouble so easily. "She's gone. Took our daughter and left. Said she couldn't be around me if I couldn't stop drinking."

"You'll work it out."

"What I really need to do is get my mind on something else ... like a case."

"Well, that's exactly what you're about to do." Then the Chief asked him a very odd question. "Do you believe in the unnatural?"

"I'm not sure I know what you mean, Chief."

"Mike, in that bedroom you're going to see something worse than the night in the park with Sam. I want you to be prepared. What I think we're dealing with is the supernatural, not a typical murderer, serial killer, or psychopath. I want you to go in with an open mind, and then, when you're done, come back out here and tell me what you think."

Detective Mike Green couldn't believe his ears. This wasn't something he'd have ever expected from the Chief. But if it was true, then maybe what he saw in the alleyway the other night was more than a drunken hallucination.

Mike braced himself and walked back into the apartment. He made his way through the maze of forensics personnel and detectives and approached the bedroom with caution. Even with the Chief's warnings, he could never have prepared himself for what was in that room; he had to steel himself in order to not vomit. His mind registered the bloody sheets covering the bed, and the pieces of hair and grey tissue, undoubtedly brain matter, lying near the head of the bed. Little flesh remained on the scattered bones, and it was obvious that what was missing had not been removed with any kind of surgical tool, but, rather, had been ripped away; it almost looked as if they'd been chewed on by a rabid dog.

Just before turning from the room, he noticed something that struck him as odd: a pair of women's black panties turned inside on the floor next to the bed. Whatever killed her had most likely removed those panties before the act; and the fact that they were intact, not torn, suggested to him they'd been removed with the consent of the woman wearing them. This was not the act of an attacker. That they were inside out suggested they were probably removed quickly, perhaps in a moment of passion.

Looking across the room at the bedside table, Mike noticed a small square package perched next to the lamp. Walking closer, he saw it was an unopened condom. Had the victim been planning ahead, leaving this available for the man she was bringing home with her?

She hadn't been attacked by a stranger; she'd had him here consensually.

The chewed remains were confusing. The Chief had made it sound as if this one were tied in with the other recent murders. But this was far different.

If the Chief was hinting that this was a vampire attack, it was a very abnormal way for a vampire to kill. But the woman ripping the heads off those three people in the alleyway and sucking their blood out wasn't normal, either, from what little he understood of their ways.

Mike walked back out onto the back porch where David was puffing away on a cigarette and looking blankly into space.

"Whose house is this?"

"It's my assistant, Irene. And what's on that bed is what's left of her."

The thought that the remains were of someone he knew put Mike over the edge. He leaned over the railing and vomited. David stood in silence, knowing what the detective was going through.

"Did you notice anything that might help," the Chief asked once Mike had regained his composure.

"Yeah, black panties turned inside out next to the bed, but completely intact. No tears or rips. They were taken off without a struggle. And there's a condom on the bedside table, ready and waiting. It's as if she had a lover with her."

David looked at Mike and said, "Irene and Janet, the Mayor's assistant, were friends. I want you to go down to the Mayor's office and interrogate Janet. Find out everything she knew about Irene, particularly any relationships she was in. Tell her that Irene is dead if you have to, but do not tell her how or what we found."

THIRTY-THREE

Mike arrived at the Mayor's office to find Janet sitting at her desk, typing away on a computer keyboard.

"Are you Janet Martin?"

Janet looked up from her typing and said, "Yes, I am. Where do I sign?" The man was dressed in a rumpled suit coat with the tie loosened and pulled partway down his chest. His eyes were red, and his face looked tired.

Janet suddenly realized he wasn't wearing a deliveryman's garb; the perplexed look on his face told her that he didn't know what she was talking about.

"I'm sorry. Do you have a delivery for me or something?"

Whipping out his badge, Mike said, "I'm Detective Mike Green with the Homicide Division. I have a few questions to ask you about Irene Ibenez."

Janet paled, and the flying of her fingers stopped.

"Let's see if we can use the Mayor's office for this," suggested Mike. "We may want a little privacy."

Janet nodded. She knew that Chief Duncan had called the Mayor earlier, but she had no idea what for. Now she realized the Chief had been forewarning the Mayor and asking for permission for his detective to speak to Janet in the privacy of the inner office. "I'll go get you two some coffee," the Mayor suggested as he left the two of them alone in his spacious office.

"Janet, I know this isn't going to be easy for you, but I need to speak to you about Irene."

"What's wrong? Did something happen to her?"

Mike knew there was no gentle way to break the news. "Irene is dead. She was murdered in her apartment last night."

Janet began to cry, her shoulders shaking with the effort to stop the tears. "Is there anything that you can tell me, anything about Irene that no one but you would know?"

Janet's fight became a small victory as her sobs turned to much smaller sniffles. She told Mike about Graham, the man Irene had just met that past week at the Movies in the Park. She didn't know Graham's last name, but she knew Irene was smitten with him, and that Irene had called her the night before to tell her she had another date with Graham. She had asked Janet for her advice on what to take as a romantic picnic dinner.

The Mayor returned with two cups of coffee and set them down between Mike and Janet before quietly sneaking back out of the office.

Janet began to cry again. It was hard to find a close friend in this city, especially one that had a job as equally demanding as hers and understood the day in/day out. She and Irene had formed an instant bond the first time they met. Janet cried for the loss of her friend, and, before he knew what he was doing, Mike rested her head on his shoulder and let her cry.

When Janet's hard crying again turned to sniffles, Mike handed her one of the cups of coffee.

"Is there anything else you can tell me about this Graham person?"

"No, I really didn't know that much about him. Irene only had two dates with him." The tears began to well again in Janet's eyes.

The Mayor walked back into his own office and sat in the chair next to Janet. He handed her a Kleenex, and patted her hand. It was the first time he had shown any sort of compassion toward her in all the time she had worked for him.

"Take all the time you need, Janet. I'm sure that Tiffany or a temp can handle things until you're ready to come back to work. Do you want me to arrange for someone to take you home?"

Janet didn't reply, as if she hadn't heard a word.

"I'll drive her home," said Detective Green.

"Thank you, Detective. I really appreciate this. Janet has been with me for a long time now, and I know this is very hard. It must be quite a shock to her."

Janet stood up, walked out of the Mayor's office and back to her desk. Her movements were jerky as she gathered her purse and sweater. Her best friend had been killed last night, but she didn't know how or why. She knew that if a homicide detective was asking questions, especially about a boyfriend, they had to have some sort of a clue as to what happened. She also knew from her experience in working in city government that if she asked Detective Green any questions, he wouldn't answer. She had a own key to Irene's apartment—they'd swapped for emergency purposes—so she decided she'd just wait a day or two and then go see what she could see.

* * *

Mike watched Janet enter her building before putting his cruiser in gear and heading back to headquarters. He reached his office just as the phone began to ring. He grabbed it and said, "Detective Mike Green here."

"Mike, is that you?"

His heart leapt for joy. "Jane, I'm so glad to hear your voice!"

"Well, at least you're out of the basement." The anger mixed with sarcasm quickly dashed his hopes. "Mike, I'm not calling you to try to patch things up. You said some horrible things that I can't forget or forgive. And you promised me you'd never drink again."

"But, Jane—"

"I only called because I can't reach Rachel, and I wanted to find out if you know when Sam's wake is. I want to pay my respects."

Mike's heart sank. "No, Jane, I haven't heard anything about the wake or the funeral. But as soon as I do, I'll let you know." After an awkward pause, he tried again. "Is there any way we can get together and talk this out?" The next sound he heard was the click of the connection being broken. He swiped at his tears with the back of his hand and did what he had to do: put his personal life on hold while he worked on his case.

THIRTY-FOUR

The Chief was driving back toward his office from the crime scene when his cell phone rang. "Chief David Duncan here."

"David, it's Larry. We need to meet for lunch. I have something I want to talk to you about."

"Where at?"

"The Signature Room. One o'clock."

"I'll be there."

David was a fair distance away, so, in order to keep his word, he flipped on his lights and sirens.

The Maitre de recognized him and led him to the private section reserved for the city's dignitaries. The Mayor sat staring at a martini; David wondered what the dead soldier count was. David placed his drink order and looked at the colorless face across the table.

"David, you and I go way back, so I'm not going to pull any of the normal 'Me Mayor, You Chief' crap."

David's face relaxed. At least he wasn't in trouble this time.

Larry continued, "I know what's been happening in our city. It might sound strange to you, but hear me out before you decide to commit me to a mental institution." He paused and took a hit of courage from his glass. "I think we have vampires in our city."

David didn't laugh. Instead, he took his whiskey sour and downed the drink in one swallow. He motioned the waitress over and ordered another, his eyes still fixed on the Mayor, who, with the heightened perception of a political shark, realized that his guest knew something, and that he was about to find out what it was.

After the waitress deposited his second drink, David said, "What I'm about to tell you can be looked up on my police records and can be validated. When I was a rookie, just out of the academy, I was assigned to foot patrol. One night I heard something in an alleyway and went to check it out. I saw a man with his arms wrapped around a struggling woman. When I shouted at them, the man flew straight up into the sky. I walked over to the victim, and realized it was my own mother. There were puncture marks on her neck.

"Before the forensics team or anyone else could get there, her body began to decompose, like she'd been dead for a long, long time. But I'd seen her murder only moments before.

"When I reported all this to my superiors, I got the therapist and shrink course. I spent years trying to deal with it. I even lied and said I must have been mistaken, that the therapy had helped me to see the truth. But, in all honesty, I never forgot what I saw, and I never changed my opinion of what had happened."

David leaned back and downed the second drink, allowing what he'd said to sink in. Larry had known all about that experience, having been part of the cover up. That knowledge was why he was confiding in David now; he knew the other man would believe him.

David could sense that the Mayor wasn't telling him everything. If only he could get Larry to tell him what he knew, maybe he could find a way to stop what was happening. He could only hope he got the whole story before it was too late.

They both knew what lived in their city. Larry and his cover up committee had believed the vampires were gone for good and so had disbanded long ago. But now he knew that he had just formed a fraternity of two, a new committee, linked by the knowledge that vampires were roaming the streets of Chicago.

Larry and David ate in silence, lost in their thoughts. They both jumped when David's cell phone rang.

It was Mike. "Chief, we have a problem here at the crime scene, and I think you should come as fast as you can. You need to see this right away, before it leaks to the press or goes to the Coroner's Office."

"What did you find?"

"In the blood on the bed, every Polaroid we take has a facial imprint in the blood. It looks more like an animal than human."

"I'm on my way."

Larry leaned in. "What is it? Another victim?"

"No, but how'd you like to go to the crime scene at Irene's apartment with me? I think you know more than you're telling me—call it cop's intuition—and maybe you can help."

The two men left the restaurant; the signed bill would be sent directly to the city's Accounting Department, and hurried to the police cruiser.

* * *

Reporters had been gathering in the lobby of Irene's building, trying to get a scoop. It had to be something big, because the police weren't giving the slightest of details. Their curiosity was further heightened by the arrival of not only the Chief of Police himself, but the Mayor of Chicago.

The two men muscled their way past the reporters, cameramen, and photographers, leaving in their wake a string of terse 'No Comment's and ignored questions. When they entered the apartment, they found the forensics photographer sitting on the couch looking at stacks of Polaroid pictures.

"Show me what you got." The Chief had no time to waste.

The photographer reached down, grabbed three of the photos and handed them to David. When the Chief looked at the first picture, he saw a face-like image in the blood on Irene's bed. It wasn't clear, but he thought it resembled the nose of a dog. He handed the picture to the Mayor and he looked at the second one.

The image was from an angle, a full-on view of the bed. The impression in the blood on the bed turned his stomach. Eyes slanted drastically backwards, nostrils flared, and long teeth that looked canine.

Larry took the second picture from David, along with a third, and saw the exact same thing. Whatever it was, it was not the product of anyone's over active imagination.

The three men stood in the living room, caught in the final act of some horrible play, waiting for the curtain to come down. Larry suddenly dropped the pictures, raced for the back door, leaned over the railing, and vomited his expensive Signature Room lunch over the side.

There was a dirty plastic chair to his left. He had the fleeting thought that the filth it had accumulated would surely ruin his Armani suit, but he didn't care. He had to sit down.

He reached for his phone and pressed the speed dial button that automatically called his home number. Debora answered the phone.

"Where are the boys," he asked her.

"Timmy's mowing the back yard and Tommy is helping me by doing the dishes. Why?"

"Good news, honey. I can take next week off. Why don't you and the boys pack your things right now and head to the cabin and I'll meet you there. I should be about five hours behind you." He hated lying to her, but he felt an immediate need to get his family out of Chicago.

Debora agreed enthusiastically. She called to her sons told them to pack for the cabin and to be ready within the hour. Soon, the trio was headed north into central Wisconsin.

Larry looked up at David standing in the doorway, staring at him. "So ya lied to get the family out of town, huh?"

Larry nodded.

David said to him, "I just went back into the bedroom and looked at the blood on the bed again. Nothing but bloodstains. That face only shows in the pictures."

After a brief silence, David said, "Do you know anyone who could explain it?" It wasn't a subtle hint, but the Mayor's response wasn't what he'd expected.

Larry thought, trying desperately to pull a name from his memory, trying to remember who from the old committee was still around, and if they could help. The face in the photographs was something new, but it had to be connected somehow. Just as Mike stepped out on the back porch, Larry said, "Yes, I think that there is someone that can help. Tonya Stewart."

"From the Field Museum?"

"Yeah. She's a curator there. And her personal specialty is religious artifacts."

Tonya Stewart hadn't been involved in the prior cover up, but she was the only person he could think of who might be able to give them a clue.

"Religious artifacts," repeated Mike.

Larry looked at the young detective and said, "Yes, take her the pictures, show them to her, but do not under any circumstances tell her where they came from." Then he decided it was best to handle it personally. "On second thought, David, drive me over there with those pictures."

When he had gathered all the photos in one envelope, he passed it to the Chief. Mike heard Larry calling ahead to make sure that Tonya hadn't disappeared into the depths of the museum, as she often did, and would be available.

Mike was annoyed. This was his case and he wanted to know every little detail of what was going on. And he wanted to know what the cops were dealing with that could cause not only such carnage, but also result in the direct involvement of the Chief and the Mayor. When the reporters asked him for information, he was truthful when he said, "I can't comment on that right now."

THIRTY-FIVE

David and Larry walked through the grand front entrance of the Chicago Field Museum. The security guard, a 'Rent-A-Cop', called for Tonya.

After a brief telephone conversation, the security guard said "Chief, Mr. Mayor, if you'll follow me, I'll take you to Ms. Stewart's office."

* * *

The room they were shown into was less an office than a laboratory, with large porcelain tabletops, bright fluorescent lights, and various glass and metal containers and tools. Everywhere the two men looked, they found artworks, relics, and innumerable figures from different time periods, all in some way considered religious in nature. There was everything from pagan deities to translated and preserved scrolls, to small gargoyles resting on shelves near the desk at the back of the lab.

As the pair of men made their way through the large room, the woman at the desk turned and walked toward them.

"David! Larry! It is so good to see you again." Tonya Stewart's smile showed her well-cared-for teeth, their gleaming white set off against the dark complexion of her sun-baked skin, the result of many hours outdoors on archeological digs, searching for the smallest of religious artifacts to add to her already impressive collection. But it wasn't the collection itself that drove her. It was the quest for greater knowledge that came from each and every piece she acquired. She was truly a scholar, and a woman of science. Her goal in life was to find a scientific explanation for every religious belief in existence.

"What have you got for me?" she said with a twinkle in her eye.

David held out the envelope he still clutched in his hand, and offered it to Tonya. "Inside are some Polaroids taken at a crime scene. It's pretty gory stuff, but we figured that if anyone could identify the imprints in the blood, you could."

"Oh, David, you old flatterer." She looked authentically embarrassed by the praise. "Why, I haven't worked a crime scene with you since before Larry was elected. Back then, you were just a pissant detective!"

The men followed her as she turned and walked back toward an open work area at the back of the room. She cleared off a space on her desk for the envelope, which she opened with the same care she'd use in removing the smallest and most fragile piece of art from the dirt of a fresh dig site.

"You said the image doesn't show up looking at it with the naked eye?"

"That's right. We even had one of the guys look close, with a magnifying glass. Nothin'."

"Okay, give me a few minutes alone with these. You want coffee, help yourself."

She pulled out the pictures, and tried to look at them with the unbiased and trained eye of a professional. But she couldn't repress her shock and disgust. Once the initial reaction passed, she started to look at the photos one by one, studying them closely, pulling out a small magnifying glass from a desk drawer to get a closer look at the fine details.

David and Larry passed the time by looking at the artifacts that shared the space. Larry stopped dead in his tracks, staring at one.

"David, come look at this," he whispered loudly.

David walked over and found himself face to face with a six foot tall statue bearing facial features that matched those in the photographs.

"Tonya!" they both yelled at the same time.

Tonya ran across the room. She squeezed between the two men and looked first at the statue and then at the photo still clutched in her hand. An almost identical match.

"I knew I recognized it!" she said with quiet excitement.

"What is that?"

"Well," she said, "as soon as I saw the image in the pictures, I knew I'd seen it before. I was just trying to figure out where. Then you two manage to stumble across this. I should have recognized it sooner. It's been sitting here for years!"

"That still doesn't tell us what it is." David was getting a bit impatient.

"That, my dear, is a statue that was unearthed in Israel. It has been carbon dated to the year 600, and we believe it is a statue representing the deity of a ghoul."

"A ghoul?"

Tonya jumped at the sudden outburst from the men on either side of her.

"What the hell is a ghoul?"

Tonya sighed, "The textbook definition of a ghoul is an Islamic folklore that eats freshly buried bodies, often abducts children, and attacks unwary travelers. Of course, we haven't been able to prove it, and have never found an actual ghoul. There are a lot of bits of folklore from around the world that can't be explained or proven, though."

David grabbed Tonya by the shoulders, and said, "The photo and that statue, would you say that they are one and the same?"

"I would say they definitely are one and the same," she stammered, wincing as his fingers dug into her shoulders. "Now, please let go. You're hurting me."

David let go and apologized.

"So," Larry asked hesitantly, "how did the image get into the photo?"

"My guess is it's a sort of spiritual signature." She was walking back to her work table, David and Larry following close behind, hanging on ever word. "Sort of like an other-worldly fingerprint."

"I don't follow." David looked a little lost.

"Think about a crime scene. There are fingerprints everywhere, but to the naked eye, they can't be seen. Or if they can, they appear to be just smudges. So, what do you do? You dust. The dust makes the fingerprints show up more clearly. But they're still just dusty smudges until someone examines them with a high-powered microscope, or feeds them into a computer. Only then, under the right conditions, can the fine details be seen to separate one fingerprint from another."

"Okay, that I get. How does that fit in with this 'ghoul' image?"

"It's along the same lines. It's there in the blood, but you can't see it with the naked eye. The camera flash and the properties of the film act like the fingerprint dust and the magnifying glass. When seen through the right conditions, it appears."

"Okay, that sort of makes sense," Larry said slowly. "But how did it get there?"

"I'd say," Tonya took a long moment before making a bold assessment, "that the image is there because it's the face of your perp."

"You think this... thing is what killed the victim?"

"Based on what I've seen, yes, I do."

No one spoke for what seemed an eternity. Tonya was the first to break the silence. "So, guys, what do we do now? Do you want me to continue working on these pictures, or do you need them to put back into evidence?"

David looked like he'd seen a ghost. He cleared his throat and said, "I guess we'll take those back into custody and turn them in to the evidence techs."

"One more thing," Larry said.

"What is it?"

"Could this ... thing, this ghoul, could it have any connection to vampires?" He expected her to give him a flippant answer but, instead, he received a thoughtful look.

"How did vampires get involved?"

"I'm not saying they are, but could there be a connection?" He knew he was going far out on a limb, broaching the subject of vampires with someone who hadn't been part of the little inner circle, but he didn't see a choice.

"Well, for years, people assumed vampires were demons or works of the Devil himself. Ghouls were thought of as keepers of the dead and the underworld. I guess that could be a connection, even though there's no evidence to support either of those myths."

"But the two are similar? If one exists, the other could very well also exist?"

"With the things I've seen in this room, Larry, I'd be hard pressed to say that anything does not exist. But to answer your question, they do seem to be similar, so they could be connected somehow. I just haven't seen anything to prove it one way or the other." Tonya returned the photos to the envelope. "Do you need me to get you an escort back out or do you remember the way?"

"Oh, I think we can find our way back out," David lied. He figured some time wandering aimlessly though the corridors might give them a chance to sort out what to do next.

The two men spoke barely a word as they found their way back to the elevator that would take them to the main level of the museum.

Larry looked at David and said, "I think I need to get really drunk."

* * *

The forensics and crime scene techs had finally finished and left, and Mike was alone in the apartment. A lot of time and effort hadn't yielded any useful results. There were no fingerprints other than the victim's, and no other clues.

Mike stood in the doorway and took a final look around. Glancing down, he noticed a small, odd shaped twig on the floor. He bent down to pick it up, wondering if it had already been examined and discarded as useless. It was the tip of a stalk, with a few small hairy, grey-green round leaves on one side, a bud of purple petals on the other. Mike, on his haunches, looked around the room, not looking at what was there, but instead noticing what wasn't. There were no plants in Irene's apartment.

"So, my little friend," Mike said to the bud as he twirled it in his fingers, "where did you come from?"

His intuition told him it was important, so he took the tiny stalk with him, hoping that by keeping it close by, its presence would help trigger the elusive something he sensed in his memory.

* * *

Larry and David walked out of the museum and went to drop off the envelope at the lab, where David covered for having made off with the evidence by acting grouchy and screaming at random techs that were unlucky enough to be nearby, blaming them for not properly marking the envelope to keep it from being 'misplaced'. Everyone was glad to see him leave.

David drove the pair to their next destination. In a small neighborhood pub, far enough away that he felt they'd be anonymous, the two men grabbed a table in back and ordered two beers.

The waitress returned with two bottles of Miller and set them down in front of the guys. "You runnin' a tab or will this be it?"

"We'll run a tab."

"I need a credit card for that."

David pulled out his wallet without hesitation to get his credit card. He knew that if Larry gave her his, she'd recognize the name and soon everyone in the bar would know that the Mayor of Chicago was about to get hammered.

The two men sat and drank quietly, beer after beer, keeping entirely to themselves. But even after seven beers apiece, neither man felt drunk. It was as if they had been drinking water the entire time.

They had both witnessed some gory things in the past days, and if what Tonya told them was true, they had to figure out how to fight a ghoul, as well as vampires. And they had to find a way to do it without the general public finding out. All they had to go on was folklore.

They talked very little, but when they did, they avoided talking about the case. Each knew what the other was thinking.

And neither noticed when the sun began to set.

THIRTY-SIX

The sun sank slowly into the western sky. The brilliant purples and red painted a canvas of splendor on the darkening cityscape. The immortals began to wake, eager to return to their playground, the city at night.

All over the cemetery, Carlos' army was beginning to rise, not suspecting what lay ahead for them that night.

Everyone in the cemetery knew not to bother Carlos. Tonight was the night of the lunar eclipse, the "Blood on the Moon", and he had chosen a bride with whom to mate. It would be their duty this night to find food not only for themselves, but also for the couple.

Inside Carlos' crypt, he swung open the coffin that he shared with Jennifer and sat up unsteadily. He couldn't explain the continued uneasy feeling, but he knew that something was not quite as it should be.

The queasiness could be because this mating would be different than the rest. He knew that each time an ancient vampire mated, he gained strength. It was as if the act of mating provided a permanent energy influx.

Carlos felt the urge to mate at every opportunity, and did so in an effort to make himself the most powerful of the ancients. And with tonight's mating, he would be powerful enough to track down and destroy each of his fellow ancients. Not one of them would be able to stop him, or prevent him from becoming what he saw as his destiny: the Ruler of the World.

He shook his head to clear his thoughts, and looked down at Jennifer with longing. He wished he loved her more, like he had loved Miranda, or Zora, or even Tatiana.

As if on cue, Jennifer's eyes opened and she looked up at Carlos, completely in love. He knew that she loved him. But to him, she was there to serve a purpose, to quench the urge that he could not resist, the longing and desire to mate under the Blood on the Moon, and give him the last piece of the puzzle to an all-powerful existence.

"So, do we eat first, or what?" It was meant to be an innocent question, asked by one who was new to the vampire world, and unschooled in the Code. But the way she asked, the tone of her voice, reminded Carlos of an unruly child, petulant and unafraid of those in authority.

"Do not worry about food, my love." He tried to ignore her tone and focus on what was to come. "The others will provide for us. We can begin now, or we can wait until after you feed. But it will be much better if we mate now, while the evening is young. The Blood on the Moon has already begun."

In fact, there was no need to rush their mating. The Blood on the Moon would last all night. But he saw no reason to wait.

As flesh pressed against flesh, Jennifer realized how cold Carlos' skin was. It was one of the many things for which she was ill prepared. The feeling of lying in a freezer covered in ice nearly overwhelmed her. As a mortal, she had very little experience with sex. But from that little experience, she had a distinct memory of the feeling of heated passion, of the warmth of bodies, of the combining of hot sweat. Those sensations were all peculiarly absent.

Jennifer ran her fingers down his now bare chest, slicing his skin ever so slightly with her sharpened nails. When her hand grasped his manhood it was like wrapping her fingers around an icicle in the dead of winter.

It was at that moment she fully understood what they were: undead, and without warmth.

* * *

Jennifer felt cool tears of blood fall from her eyes as Carlos thrust himself into her again and again. The excitement, the cool passion she had felt were gone, along with the thrill of being the bride of a powerful vampire. Now, she felt like the victim she was.

* * *

Sitting in a booth at the downtown branch of the Chicago Public Library, Mike twirled the tiny stalk in his hand. He had a small mountain of botany books laid out across the desk in the small cubicle, and was wondering if he would ever find the origin of the small, purple flower. He had looked up purple flowers, hoping to get lucky with the color of the bud. He noticed the little plant gave off a strong minty scent, so he had looked up mints in a book on herbs and spices. He even tried to look up plants that had small, round, hairy leaves. But he was having no luck.

He sat for a moment and stared at the severed stalk, concentrating as if trying to hear its voice speaking to him. Oddly enough, that seemed to work. A vague memory began to take shape in his mind.

It had been a few months earlier, when Jane and Rachel had been going through what they now referred to as their "crazy plant phase." They were trying to make all sorts of unusual plants grow in their homes, most of the attempts resulting in dead brown plants dumped out in the trash. The plants they were trying to grow were not meant to grow in the climates of their houses.

But during that time, the women had dragged Mike and Sam along on numerous expeditions to the Lincoln Park Conservatory, where many of these exotic plants did well. They were window shopping, they explained, looking to see what they wanted to try next.

Mike remembered seeing this particular plant on one of those excursions.

"Penny-something," he said aloud, racking his brain for the name of the plant, or for more information. "Or Nickle-something. I know it had to do with money. I remember Sam joking about all the money it'd cost and waste."

He decided to give up on the library and go back to where he'd seen the plant. They'd certainly be able to tell him more about it.

* * *

Suddenly the lid to their coffin flew open and hands reached down, roughly pulling Carlos up and out, away from his unnatural act. Carlos' shock combined with fury that anyone would interrupt him at such a delicate time. They would pay for their intrusion.

Jennifer screamed and tried to cover herself with her discarded clothes. Part of her was relieved to have Carlos' frozen member out of her, but she was surprised at the sudden invasion of their private moment.

Carlos looked past the hands holding him to see the faces beyond. His fury subsided—and turned to pure hatred—when he recognized the faces of Grant, Antonio, Erik and William staring back at him. Peter and Gideon were standing further back acting as sentries at the doorway to the crypt.

With a force unknown to the mortal world, the four men threw Carlos into the corner, nearly knocking down the brick structure. With loosened mortar raining down on his head, Carlos looked up to see that his attackers had drawn their favorite weapons: scythes, katanas, broadswords, and, of course, the ever-popular stake, sharpened to a deadly point.

Elaine entered the crypt. The men held Carlos down, while she enclosed him in steel cabling, effectively preventing him from moving.

"You cowards," Carlos shouted, suddenly regaining his cockiness and self-assuredness. "I'll have my minions kill you all!"

"Oh, drop it, lover boy," Grant said, not bothering to hide the disdain in his voice. "We know about your mating rituals, you scum. You send all of your lackeys off to find food for you and the unlucky thing that you mate with. That way you can be alone and none of them can hear her screams."

From a dark corner, in the recesses where no light seemed to reach, came Morgana. In her hands she held a potion for Jennifer to drink.

"Here, darling, drink this. It will help with what you just went through."

Jennifer looked at the beautiful woman, wanting to trust her, but unsure.

"Carlos is an ancient. You are not," the woman explained to the frightened young vampire. "If he impregnated you, you will certainly die a horrible and painful death during childbirth."

Jennifer glanced at Carlos, and could tell by his pained expression that it was true. She realized that all of his talk of love was nothing but a façade, words to get what he wanted.

"This potion," the woman said bringing Jennifer's attention back, "will ensure that you do not become pregnant."

Jennifer suddenly felt compelled to drink, even as Carlos filled the air with his protests. She believed the woman. She drank every last drop and immediately felt a warm sensation deep inside. It was the first warmth she had felt since Carlos had made her, and it was the last thing she felt before black goo started to ooze down the side of the coffin where she had been leaning.

"I guess it's a little late to mention the severe side effect," Morgana said, referring to Jennifer's instant death.

The smell of burnt coffee filled the crypt along with the howling "No!" that escaped from Carlos' lips.

Grant backhanded him, snapping Carlos' head to the side. He hated Carlos terribly and took great pleasure in the act, telling him "Shut up, or you'll be the next to go."

Carlos tasted a drop of blood on his lip and said with a sneer, "Well, cowboy, I see you haven't lost your strength."

"Why should I? I'm not the one who spends my energy making ghouls"

"Let me go, Grant, and we'll see who has more strength," Carlos said, once again self assured and ready to take on the world.

"Oh, we have other plans for you," Grant said, squatting down in front of him, mere inches away. Carlos could feel the cold breath of his adversary with each word he spoke.

"And what a shame, too," Morgana chimed in as she strode over to the corner where Carlos had been secured. She looked at his naked and bound body. "I had personal plans for you."

Gideon poked his head into the crypt and said, "Well, boys and girls, here comes our carriage!"

They heard the hooves of horses on the gravel road that ran through the cemetery and a woman's voice say "Whoa there!" It was Virginia at the reins. She had led the others to Carlos' front doorstep, and then gone off to find transportation.

Maria, Fiona, Elaine, Morgana, Grant, William, and Erik grabbed the bound naked Carlos and threw him unceremoniously into the carriage, climbing in and onto the conveyance themselves before Virginia snapped the whip to drive the four pure white horses on.

THIRTY-SEVEN

Arriving at the Lincoln Park Conservatory, Mike made one loop around the nearby streets, hoping desperately for a parking spot close by. When he had no luck on the street, Mike pulled his unmarked cruiser into the employee lot near the rear entrance.

Before Mike was even out of his car, a tall thin man with grey wisps of hair stretched across his balding head was leaning out of the back door of the Conservatory's offices.

"Can't park there. Private lot!" he yelled. "Employees only!"

Mike held out his badge and shouted back as he closed the car's door and strode toward the old man. "Police business. I need some information."

With the approach of a police officer, the old man became just a bit nervous. He had never, in all his 73 years, been interviewed by the police. He was relieved when Mike reached into the pocket of his rumpled jacket, one that looked like it had been slept in, and produced a small twig. He held it out to the caretaker saying, "I need to know what this is, and where it may have come from."

The old man invited Mike to the back door, where they could get a better look at the little plant. He seemed eager to help, as if he were afraid that by not helping, he would be in serious trouble with the authorities.

"Now," he said, "let's take a look at your little plant."

Mike handed him the twig he had found in Irene's apartment. With almost no hesitation, the man said, "This appears to be a Pennyroyal."

"Pennyroyal!" Mike nearly shouted, slapping himself on the forehead. "That's what it was. I knew it had money in the name."

The caretaker looked at Mike as if he were one of the strangest men he had ever seen, but continued, "This appears to be only the tip of one stalk, because the branches are usually much larger. But I'd say it's definitely Pennyroyal."

"How can you be so positive?"

"We have some on display here in the Conservatory. I see it every day."

"So what else can you tell me about it?"

"Here, let me look it up," he said, moving toward a large filing cabinet that held basic information on every plant currently displayed. He pulled out a lower drawer, and quickly flipped through the file folders, removing the one he was looking for. "Ah, here we are."

"Pennyroyal, or Mentha puleguim," he continued, as if lecturing a student, "is an herb that has weak, prostrate stems, bluntly quadrangular, three inches to a foot long, which readily take root at the lower joints or nodes." This was all information that Mike didn't really need, but although he was impatient to get to what he did need, he was hesitant to interrupt the old man, who seemed to be enjoying his informational role. "The leaves are shortly stalked, more or less hairy on both sides, roundish oval, grayish green, about one to one and a half inches long and half an inch broad. The flowers are in whorled clusters of ten or a dozen, rising in tiers one above the other at the nodes, their color reddish purple to lilac blue, and in bloom during July and August. The seed is light brown, oval and very small."

"So it should bloom any day now," Mike said. He really wasn't interested in the blooming of the flower, but he wanted to seem interested for the sake of keeping the old man going.

"This species of mint, a native of most parts of Europe and parts of Asia—"

"Europe and Asia?" Mike interrupted.

"That's right."

"So it's not native to North America?"

"No, it doesn't really grow around here. Although I have heard of it growing deeper in the southern part of the country."

"So where would someone find a stalk like the one I brought you?"

"Well," the man thought for a moment. "I guess someone could buy it. But they'd most likely purchase it as an herb, with the leaves already plucked and dried."

"Could someone grow it themselves?"

"Not likely in this climate. It needs a very specific habitat."

"Like here in the Conservatory?"

"Exactly. It's what we do here. Grow plants that otherwise would never be seen in this area. In fact, I'm not sure where you found that little piece of the plant, but I'd venture a guess that it came from here."

"Can you show me where this plant is displayed?" Mike knew that if the only place to find the plant was here in the conservatory, then there was a good chance that whoever, or whatever, had killed Irene had been here as well.

The old man led Mike through rooms filled with all sorts of vegetation, rooms Mike remembered from his trips with Jane.

On the eastern side of the Conservatory, the man stopped on the path and looked across a small expanse of various plants and flowers. A look of dismay crossed his face as he shook his head sadly. "Well, there's your Pennyroyal."

"What's wrong," Mike asked, seeing the old man's grim expression.

"Look there," he said pointing into the jungle of leaves. Someone trampled right through the plants. If I find that it was an employee, heads will roll."

Mike saw what the old man was looking at. There was a definite path made where there shouldn't have been one. Some of the branches of the larger plants had been pushed aside, and a few of the smaller plants had been stepped on. It wasn't obvious without looking directly at it, so there was no telling how long the destruction had gone unnoticed. "Could someone have walked through there to tend to the plants toward the back?"

"No need. There's a service tunnel under the Conservatory that allows access to the back of these larger display areas. If you look right through there," he bent and pointed between two of the larger plants, "you can see the access door."

"So someone could walk from this path, through the plants, and out the access door?"

"Yes, or vice versa."

"I'd like to see this service tunnel, if you don't mind."

"No, no, no. Not at all. It's almost time to lock up, so there's hardly anyone here anyway. It's this way." He headed off in the direction from where they had come.

THIRTY-EIGHT

In the dark corner of the tiny bar, the Mayor of Chicago and the Chief of Police gave up their quest to get drunk. No amount of alcohol was going to make them forget the things they had seen and heard. David reached for his cell phone and hit the power button, turning it back on.

"Whatcha doin'?"

"Figured I'd see if anyone tried to reach me. Never know when somethin' might break."

He looked at the illuminated display: one voice mail message waiting. He pressed the buttons to retrieve and listen to the message, and put the phone to his ear, waiting patiently for the recorded voice to go through its litany of redundant options. Finally he got to the message. When it ended, he broke the connection, and immediately began dialing.

"Who was it," Larry asked impatiently.

"Tonya. Said she found somethin'. Could be important."

She answered on the first ring. "Tonya Stewart."

"Tonya, it's David."

"Glad you called. I found something in an old book on vampire legends."

"What is it?"

"Well, it's kind of sketchy, but it could be important. About a couple of things."

"Like what?"

"Like for one, there's a reference to the 'Children of the Undead' and then it goes on to talk about ghouls. Now, depending on how you want to interpret that, the 'Undead' could be your vampires, and the ghouls could be the 'Children'. That would be the ghoul-vampire connection you were looking for earlier."

"Makes sense, but it doesn't really help us."

"No, but this might. It says that a vampire's greatest power comes during the Blood on the Moon."

"What's the Blood on the Moon?"

Larry gave him a quizzical look, hearing only David's half of the conversation.

"It's a special lunar eclipse. Dust particles make the moon look like it's bleeding."

"So that's when these things are at their most powerful?"

"According to what I read, yes. And according to my handy dandy almanac, that's tonight."

"What?" David nearly leapt out of his chair. "Tonight?"

"Tonight."

"What's tonight," Larry asked. David held up a hand to silence the Mayor, so that he could listen.

"I can't believe I found this book. This is so exciting!" Tonya was clearly thrilled with her new discovery.

"Where do we find them? How do we stop them?" David was practically screaming into the phone, much less enthusiastic about Tonya's newest addition to her book collection. He was also beginning to draw attention to himself and the Mayor, so Larry led the Chief out of the bar and back to their car.

"Where to find them should be fairly easy. It would most likely be a large park, near water, lots of statues around."

"Well, gee, Tonya, that narrows it down to about a hundred locations in Chicago." His trepidation quickly took the form of sarcasm.

"Think lots of shaded area surrounding a large clearing, probably a central statue as a focal point. It's likely near all the elements. Earth and Air don't narrow it down, but Fire and Water do. Probably near the lake."

"Okay, so if we find them, how do we stop them?"

"That's not so clear. It doesn't really say. This book is more about rituals and customs than it is about how to kill. But I'm sure you can use the old tried and true stake-through-the-heart method. That is, if you can get close enough."

"I better get going. We have some hunting to do."

"Oh, one last thing."

"What else could there be?"

"This book. It's not some ancient text or lost scroll."

"Whaddya mean?"

"I mean it was written about ten years ago. And it was written by a guy from Chicago."

"And?"

"And he seems to know some pretty detailed stuff. He'd have to have direct contact to get this kind of info. And he makes reference to some pretty powerful people knowing about the vampire existence for years. Almost like it's some sort of government conspiracy or something."

David looked at Larry. He'd had a persistent feeling there was something the Mayor wasn't telling him. Now that same gut feeling was telling him that this was it. The Mayor knew about these vampires all along. He'd known before the killings began a week earlier. He'd known before he became Mayor of Chicago. He'd known when David's mother was killed by one of them. And he'd helped to cover it up the entire time.

"Thanks, Tonya." He pushed the end button as he and the Mayor reached the car.

Larry buckled himself into the passenger seat, and turned to David.

"Where are we going?"

"You tell me." The look on David's face was serious. "Where do they gather on the night when their power is the greatest?"

Larry was stunned for a moment, but gradually the accusing look on David's face meant that he'd learned more than he should have. "You know? You know I knew all along?"

"I do now." David turned forward and drove away from the bar.

* * *

The display room in the northeastern portion of the Conservatory was for short-term displays. Currently it held a display of roses. The room was filled to capacity with roses from around the world. The spectacular array of colors was astounding, as was the overwhelming aroma. Mike followed the old man along the gravel path that had been created specifically for this display.

Among the exotic varieties, Mike found what he considered to be a basic, home-grown bush of red roses. It looked just like the ones that Jane was always trying to grow around their house. The plant brought back painful memories of the things he'd said to his wife, and the fact that she had left, along with their child.

"Mommy likes roses, don't you Mommy?" he remembered his daughter saying. Her voice was so clear and vibrant in his head. "I like roses, too. I think they're pretty."

"Please don't do that," the old man said, interrupting Mike's reverie. He saw the old man looking at his hands and realized he had absent-mindedly plucked two of the roses from their bush.

His face reddened slightly with embarrassment at having defiled this man's work right in front of his eyes, and he sheepishly shoved the roses into the pocket of his pants. He knew it would squash the flowers, destroying their beauty, but it was the best he could think to do.

Shaking his head in sadness at seeing his plants abused, the old man led Mike to a white door along the back wall. Similar to the ones he had seen in other rooms, the doors the old man had called "access doors" blended into the wall surrounding them, making the doors nearly invisible.

Opening the door, the man led the way down a flight of metallic stairs, the sound of their shoes clanking against the metal and echoing through the tunnel below. At the bottom, the old man waved his hand down the tunnel.

"This is it. It's storage space, plus a service tunnel. It runs under the whole place, with stairwells like this one," as he pointed at the stairs they had just descended, "leading up to the different access doors. The employees are supposed to use it to tend to the plants near the rear of the displays." The scorn in his voice was evident, remembering the trampled plants of the Pennyroyal.

"Which way to the door where we saw the trampled plants?"

"Follow that way," he said, gesturing, "and turn right at the end. It's about halfway down."

"I'd like to take my time looking around down here. I don't want to miss something that could be important. Mind if I stay down here alone?"

The old man hesitated, not really wanting a complete stranger to be left alone in what he considered to be his facility. "Well, I guess I do have to get back upstairs." He looked at his watch. "I need to lock up. I guess it'll be okay. When you're done, you'll have to leave through the office. The front doors'll be locked."

"No problem. And thanks for your help."

They shook hands, and the caretaker made his way up the stairs. When the door above closed, Mike turned to look down the service tunnel. The concrete walls were painted solid white, with florescent lights glowing every ten feet from the curved archway that formed the ceiling, making Mike feel as if he was walking through a giant tube. His footsteps echoed to the far reaches of the tunnel.

At regular intervals, Mike crossed a metal grate set into the floor. He took the flashlight from its pouch on his belt and shone it through the grates, revealing a drainage ditch that followed the service tunnel, presumably to catch runoff from the watering of the plants throughout the facility. As he neared the stairwell that led to the access door behind the Pennyroyal, Mike suddenly stopped. Something was different about the last grate he had crossed.

He stepped backward over the grate, and shined his flashlight through the crisscross pattern. Unlike the others, where he could see the wet, grayish sludge that flowed through the drainage ditch a mere six inches below the floor of the tunnel, this one exposed only blackness. The drainage ditch seemed to be gone.

Getting down on his knees, he looked more closely, shining his light straight down. What he saw was a straight drop of what he guessed was about twenty feet.

Setting the flashlight aside, he put his fingers through the grate and pulled. It came away easily, as if it had been removed and replaced often. He set it on the floor, and, picking up his flashlight again, looked into the yawning hole.

It looked to be a shaft carved from rock, with hand and footholds carved down one side. It certainly wasn't the same smooth architecture prevalent in the rest of the Conservatory, or even in the service tunnel. It appeared to have been hand carved, or blasted away, like the raw edged tunnels of a mine.

Mike considered climbing down the shaft, but remembered what it was he might be dealing with. If there were vampires down there, and he suspected there were, he was going to need more than the bullets in his standard issue police weapon.

He stood up and checked the door to the nearest storage room. Luckily, the staff wasn't afraid of anyone stealing plant supplies, so they didn't bother to lock the doors. Inside, he found potting soil, various sizes of planters, and rolls of plastic sheeting. Nothing he could use against the undead. He checked the next room and found what he was looking for. Metal spikes used for holding up long stemmed plants that weren't strong enough to stand on their own.

Mike had another use for the stakes in mind now. He took one in each hand and returned to the open shaft.

Each spike had a small hook on the top end, meant to hold a display sign, giving visitors all the information possible about the plant that they were looking at. Mike used them to hook the spikes through the belt loops of his pants, freeing his hands to grab the hand/footholds hewn into the rock. Putting his flashlight back into its holster, he sat on the edge of the shaft, and put his feet into the first holds. Taking a deep breath, he shifted his weight off the security of the tunnel floor and onto his feet, surprised that it held. He began to make the difficult climb down the shaft.

THIRTY-NINE

The carriage carrying the pure blood vampires arrived in Lincoln Park and rolled easily over the curb, stopping between a row of elm trees and a statue in an open grassy area. The ancients in the carriage were surprised to see Leslie and Peter waiting for them, but Virginia could tell by Leslie's demeanor that their enjoyable and enviable duties had already been fulfilled.

"Hey, you two. Wanna help us get this scum into place?" she yelled at the two young lovers.

They ran hand in hand toward the carriage, reaching it just as the side door was flung open from inside.

Carlos was pulled roughly out from the carriage and taken to the base of the statue, where his bindings were adjusted, adding chain to the cord that constricted his movements, securing him to the statue. Antonio ripped the blindfold off so Carlos could see the group forming a circle around him.

"The least you could do is to cover me!" he bellowed, bemoaning the fact that he was still completely naked.

Maria spat at him and said, "You should feel lucky we are giving you the chance to be questioned. We could have just waltzed into Chicago and tore you apart bit by bit like you did to Dominick."

"I don't know what you mean," Carlos had the audacity to lie to their faces. "I didn't do a damned thing to Dominick. Have you questioned the little toy he played with for all those years?"

Virginia stepped forward and slapped Carlos so hard that he tasted blood. Out of the darkness of the trees stepped Elizabeth, the "little toy" Carlos had tried to blame for the death of Dominick.

She looked at Carlos, crossed her arms across her chest and said, "Oh, so now I'm nothing more than a toy? What about all your little toys? Is our world nothing but a game to you? You make vampires any time you like, you mate whenever the desire strikes, and the creatures that you have created have almost destroyed this world."

"Someone shut her up," Carlos said with undisguised venom in his voice. "She's not one of us, and I don't have to listen to her accusations!"

"No, but she might as well be pure blood," Erik chimed in. "She's followed the Code much more than you have."

"You have created abominations, violated the Code," said Gideon. "She hasn't even mated because Dominick taught her that it would be wrong for her to do so."

"You haven't done nearly as well living by the Code," Grant added. "Look how we found you tonight: about to plant your seed and create who knows what!"

Erik stepped close to Carlos and waved a katana in his face. "I ought to slice you up right now," he hissed through clenched teeth. "But I think that the others have something to say before you are ripped apart."

William joined the litany of accusations. "You killed our pure blood babies as soon as you found them. You even endangered the mothers while the seed was developing. You are a danger to both the mortal and immortal world and you need to be destroyed."

Morgana stepped between Erik and Carlos and with the palm of her hand pushed the katana out of Carlos' face. "I would have loved you for eternity. We could have mated every ten years under the Blood on the Moon and had a pure blood baby every decade, prophesy or no. But you rejected me.

"Then, when the prophesy said it was our time, you rejected me.

"Know this: one by one, the spawn of your seed will be hunted and killed. Each and every one was a violation of the Code that we all hold to, and each and every one must be destroyed. Before I leave Chicago, I will kill Graham myself. If I find him before this night ends for you, I will bring him to this place and kill him in front of you so that you can watch the blood of your child spilled to the ground, your offspring turned into dust."

With that, Morgana turned away from Carlos and flew off in search of Graham.

Michael stepped forward, raising the broadsword he had carried for centuries since taking it from a knight in a tournament in France in the 1700s. The man he faced had slipped and fallen directly onto the tip of Michael's sword, earning Michael his opponent's weaponry, as were the rules.

Without a word, Michael used the razor-sharp edge of the blade to slash Carlos' side. Maria rushed forward and held a chalice to catch the black blood that poured forth.

Carlos howled in pain, a howl that could be heard throughout the city, a howl that was recognized by the minions who had spent years, decades, and even centuries serving him. When they heard their master's scream, they knew that something was terribly wrong. It should have been his bride who howled in pain. They ceased their feeding and began traveling in the direction of the scream.

Virginia was prepared for their arrival. She had already assembled and instructed her own followers, who were now stationed around the perimeter of the park.

At her quick whistle, they stepped out of the shadows, each with a weapon in hand. Their eyes glowed with the excitement of what lay ahead. They were many, nearly fifteen hundred, and each was anxious for the privilege of destroying at least one of those heading toward the park to defend their evil master. No one knew how many Carlos had created, but they would all have to be destroyed. No trace of his evil could be allowed to survive.

* * *

He was sweating by the time he reached the bottom of the shaft, and took a moment to catch his breath before continuing on. He shone his flashlight through the dim corridor. The light penetrated the darkness far enough that Mike could see where the short tunnel opened up into a larger cavern. He followed the tunnel to the opening and was shocked at what lay beyond.

Slowly panning the room with the light, he saw an immense cavern. Across the floor were hundreds, maybe thousands, of stone pedestals. On each pedestal lay a body, some with their arms at their sides, some with hands crossed over their chests. A few were inside caskets, but most were lying directly on the stone in silent, tranquil poses of sleep—or death. Mike was fairly certain it was both.

Walking slowly along a row of sleeping corpses and noting their thin, pale skin, Mike realized that a few of them were faces he recognized. He hadn't seen them in several years, but they were faces from old missing persons files, nearly unchanged since the time of their disappearance.

Stepping up to one of the bodies, he pulled one of the stakes from his belt loop and raised it over his head, holding it in both hands. He hesitated. He wasn't sure he could bring the stake down into the chest of the creature lying on the stone pedestal. What if he was wrong and it wasn't a vampire after all? What if he was about to kill an innocent human being?

Then he remembered the scene in Irene's apartment. His memory flashed from there to the alleyway, to the woman who had sucked the life from three headless bodies. He saw Sam lying in the bushes, head twisted at a grotesque angle. And he knew he had to rid the world of these creatures while he had the chance.

He scanned the cavern again, looking at the sheer number of bodies. These could not be innocent humans. This number of people would surely have been discovered. No, these bodies had to be something else, something inhuman.

He raised the stake above his head, again holding it with both hands. He tightened his fingers around the metal stake, closed his eyes, and brought it down with as much force as he could muster. He felt a jarring sensation, and heard the clank of the metal strike the stone pedestal as the tip of the stake penetrated the flesh of the creature. Black blood spurted, spraying cold and wet against Mike's face and arms. Mike looked down at the face of the creature and saw its eyes flash open, red irises staring up at him, bewildered, wide with shock. The mouth opened as well, displaying a sharp set of fangs and letting loose a terrible shriek of pain. The sound echoed off the stone walls of the cavern, and quickly died away. Mike looked around, expecting to see the other bodies rise at the noise, but they remained still and silent.

When he looked back down at the stone pedestal, he saw the creature melt away, becoming a black, tarry substance with a stench like burning coffee. He had to pull the collar of his shirt up over his nose to ward off the smell. He still held the stake in his hand, a bit of the black substance dripping from its pointed end.

He carried the stake with him as he stepped to the next pedestal, where another creature awaited him. He took another look around the cavern at the number of bodies that seemed to stretch to infinity. This is gonna be one long night. With a confidence born of so easily killing his first vampire, he raised the stake and drove it into the heart of the next.

FORTY

The sounds of flapping wings and whispering winds signaled the coming of Carlos' legions. Nicolas and Cindy arrived and surveyed the situation. They hesitated, sensing that something evil was about to occur. Nicolas had been one of the few to see the severed heads that had been left as a warning, and knew that Carlos' enemies were close at hand. When he looked in their direction, he could see the ancients gathered around the statue, Carlos bound to it, and he knew that this a trap set to destroy not only Carlos, but his faithful followers, as well.

Nicolas turned to Cindy, grabbed her by the shoulders, and said, "This is trouble for Carlos and those of us that follow him. It could result in the end of us all." Cindy looked afraid. "I never liked him, even though he was my maker," Nicolas continued. "He was an unkind master who only thought of himself."

"Are you saying we should abandon him," Cindy asked, a glimmer of hope in her eyes.

"We have three choices. We can leave Chicago, and hope to never again see those that we abandoned. We can join the fray with Carlos and his followers. Or we can convert to Virginia's side, which will be terribly outnumbered. But with our help, Virginia could learn the weaknesses of Carlos' army. You have not been part of the vampire community for long, so I leave it to you to decide what we should do."

Cindy thought for a moment, the weight of the decision heavy on her recently blackened heart. "What happens if we help Virginia? Would we later be allowed to leave this city and start over someplace else?"

Nicolas grabbed Cindy in a tight embrace and said softly, "Only if we win the battle, my dear. If Carlos is triumphant, he will destroy us for having turned on him."

* * *

In a cluster of trees on the south end of the park, Nicolas found a group of vampires being instructed on the strategy to be employed against the arriving horde. He approached warily, whispering his words as the group broke up and prepared for the coming onslaught.

"We have decided to defect to Virginia's side. We do not wish to fight for Carlos. I can give you information about his weaknesses."

The vampire looked at them skeptically. Surely this was a ruse to get her to lower her guard.

"All we ask is that once this terrible battle is over, Cindy and I be allowed to leave Chicago and start anew someplace far from here."

Seeing nothing but sincerity in his eyes, as well as in those of his young companion, she nodded. "Welcome, brother and sister. We are happy to have your assistance. Any information on the weaknesses of the others can be given to us. But we must hurry. Time is growing short."

They stood in the cluster of trees while Nicolas relayed all he knew of Carlos and his strategies. He spoke in the ancient language, a language used long ago by the vampire world, one that could be used to convey his meaning much more rapidly than any of the languages used by mortals.

He told them that there were two groups. One slept in the cemetery where Carlos' own crypt was located. Those vampires were awake and feeding, probably on their way to the park after hearing their master's anguished cries.

The other group would still be asleep. They wouldn't awake until the last stages of the Blood on the Moon, later that evening. They were even greater in number than those who were awake, and would be difficult to fend off. If they woke before Carlos was destroyed, they could overpower the park defenders, and possibly even the ancients themselves. That would be what Carlos would be counting on.

Unfortunately, Nicolas had no idea where that group would be sleeping. He knew there was a cavern somewhere in the city, hidden far below ground, but he didn't know its location. And only Carlos could open the secret entrance.

He also let them know that the greatest weakness was simple: They hated roses. They hated the smell, the color, the beauty, but most of all, the thorns. Rose thorns caused immeasurable pain to Carlos, and therefore inflicted the same to those that Carlos had made.

Word of the rose defense spread through the trees to each member of the guard. And just as quickly, rose stems began to disappear from the rose bushes around the park.

The sound of beating wings came ever closer.

* * *

Speeding south along Lake Shore Drive, Chief David Duncan tried repeatedly to raise the only other police officer in the city who would believe his story. But Mike Green wasn't answering his home phone or his office phone. When the Chief tried calling the detective's cell, all he got was voice mail. He called the police dispatcher, and requested that Detective Green be hailed on his cruiser's CB, but, like the telephones, those attempts went unanswered.

"Where the hell could he be?" David said in frustration as he slapped the lid of his phone shut. He had to be careful to keep the car pointed straight down the four-lane road. A couple too many beers with the Mayor had slightly slowed his reaction time.

He had coaxed the location of Carlos' old gathering place out of Mayor Larry Larson and was on his way there. Twenty years earlier, before Larry had been elected Mayor, the same park had been used on numerous occasions to hold secret meetings between the members of the cover up committee and Carlos. At the time, Larry hadn't known, as none of the committee members had, that the park held special significance.

As they sped past the rear of the Conservatory, David noticed what looked to be an unmarked police cruiser in the employee parking lot. He thought it odd, but assumed it was a member of the night security force and gave it no further consideration.

Across the street from the Conservatory, David skidded to a stop at the curb that bordered the open grassy area. Behind them along Stockton Avenue, and further ahead, the edges of the park were bordered with rows of trees; the rest of the park had been filled in with rose bushes. In the direct center was a statue of William Shakespeare reclining in a chair of solid granite. They could see a small gathering already forming around the statue, their shapes lit by the reddish glow of the unusual lunar eclipse and the streetlights that lined the boulevard between Stockton and Lincoln Park West Avenues.

Several figures were standing in a semi-circle surrounding another figure that seemed to be bound to the base of the statue. David unbuckled his seat belt and was about to get out of the car when Larry put his hand on the Chief's arm.

"What is it?" David said, turning in his seat to look at the Mayor.

Larry stared vacantly ahead, as if entranced. He slowly raised his arm and pointed toward the sky above the group gathered at the statue. "There. Look there."

David turned his head just in time to see several large shadows move across the sky. Looking closer, he saw what appeared to be large birds circling the park, blocking out the light of the moon, and creating odd shaped shadows on the ground. As they descended, David realized they were not birds at all, but the figures of men and women, dressed in dark robes and long black coats, slowly floating down from the sky. Many of them landed at the edges of the park, using the safety of the trees as temporary cover, before they started to move stealthily toward the statue.

David looked back to the Mayor, who was staring without blinking at the gathering in the center of the park and at the statue where he and his committee had met and made a deal with an immortal being, a vampire.

When David looked back across the park, he saw more and more of the figures land from above, as well as others that seemed to materialize out of the shadows and the trees to confront those from the sky. It reminded him of a gang rumble, the members of opposing factions facing each other in a fight over territory, the victors claiming the area as their turf. Seeing the numbers arriving from both areas, he had a feeling this was not just a "rumble", but an all-out war between opposing gangs of vampires. He had a feeling it wouldn't be pretty.

* * *

Morgana flew high enough that no mortal could see her. With the vision of a hawk, she could see the tiniest detail far below. Having met Graham, she knew what he looked like. She also knew what kind of an uncontrollable and unpredictable animal she was going against. But she had a secret weapon in her arsenal: a vial of ground nightshade that would render the creature immobile without killing him so that she could transport him back to the park where Carlos was standing trial and deposit him at the feet of his father.

She caught a glimpse of Graham below, standing on a platform of an "El" train. He either had not heard Carlos' howl, or else did not realize its significance. He seemed to be in no hurry to rush to his father's aid. Perhaps it was the fact that he was a ghoul, and not a vampire, that the cry had not registered. It didn't matter to Morgana. She had found him.

She descended from the sky and swooped past him, so fast that the other passengers waiting for the train thought her passing nothing more than a sudden shift in the wind. The train came, accompanied by its usual rush of air as it pulled into the station. But masked by the train's arrival was another passing of the mysterious breeze, which this time knocked Graham nearly off his feet, and prevented him from entering the train. The other passengers assumed he was drunk. The train conductor had little patience, and he closed the doors and began moving away from the platform toward his next stop. As the train accelerated, it created another rush of air. And with it, another gust hit Graham, who collapsed, unconscious.

Each time Morgana flew, unseen, past Graham, she left more of the nightshade floating in the wind in front of his face, where he unknowingly inhaled it and quickly succumbed to its effects. She had completed the first step of her vendetta against Carlos.

Landing easily on the nearly empty platform, she reached down and picked up the unconscious ghoul, cradling him as a mother would a newborn baby. As she took off again in flight, his head lolled against her shoulder. She wasn't sure if she were more disgusted or saddened by this creature born into such an existence.

She felt his weight shift. He was beginning to come out of his drugged state, so she quickly propped his head against her shoulder, pried open the vial with her teeth and passed it under his nose again until she felt her burden return to the heavy dead-weight of the completely unconscious. Then she resumed her journey to where his father was being held.

FORTY-ONE

Slowly, one by one, the followers of Carlos began to arrive at Lincoln Park. Victor was the first, landing where a pair of Virginia's guards stood waiting.

Victor strode toward them, sneering, "What are you two going to do? Am I supposed to fear you? You know I could easily kill both of you with one swipe of my hand."

One of the guards laughed, raising Victor's ire another level. He was certain the older vampire's statement was nothing more than bluster hiding fear.

The other took a step forward and said, "You have every reason to fear us."

Victor was taken aback momentarily, but recovered quickly. "I have nothing to fear from you. I am centuries older than you. I was perfecting my craft while you were still a mortal, crapping in your diapers."

They both laughed. Victor paused, uncertain. The vampires attacked, plunging the rose branches they'd kept hidden behind their backs deep into Victor's heart.

* * *

Once Nicolas and Cindy had passed their lethal information to those defending the park, they were led near the center circle where the ancients were holding Carlos' trial. Virginia left the circle for a few moments to speak with her new friends.

Nicholas asked Virginia not only for her protection, but her permission to leave the city as fast as they could. As much as he had grown to hate Carlos, he didn't want to take part in the fight. He had already contributed what he could.

Virginia laid a hand on each of their heads and said, "Thank you for your assistance. As long as you exist, you have my protection. Please leave this city now, before your former brethren catch you. I will ask Elizabeth to watch over you until you are a safe distance away."

She summoned Elizabeth. "Be certain that those of our family know not to harm these two. They are now with us. And if any of their own try to attack, call for help if you need it."

They both hugged her before taking flight.

* * *

An army of undead was converging on the park, ready to defend their master. They knew they had superior numbers, with others en route. They were confident of victory. But their confidence also made them careless.

They could not have known that their enemies had already discovered their common weakness and had stripped every rose bush in the park of its strongest branches and sharpened them to fine points.

The petals were spread in a giant circle around Carlos and his accusers, the scent enhanced by an essence of rose oil potion, effectively forming a protective ring that none of Carlos' followers would dare to penetrate.

As Carlos' troops arrived in the park, they saw their master bound to the statue. They approached, prepared and eager to fight, their progress slowed only when they detected the rose scent that permeated the air.

With whoops of joyful anticipation, Carlos' minions attacked as one, certain that they could easily destroy those that stood in their way. But the overconfident vampires were quickly cut down as the rose branch stakes were driven into their hearts.

Those who managed evade the stakes fought back with every weapon in their arsenal, but could not pass the circle created by the rose petals and the potion. The ancients within the protected center knew they would eventually have to join the fray, but they had a job to do first: pass judgment on Carlos and hand down his sentence.

* * *

Watching from the safety of his cruiser, Chief David Duncan could only stare in awe at the ferocity of the attacking vampires. He had long since lost track of which were the defenders of the park, trying to protect the inner circle, and which were the attackers, trying to penetrate it.

Beside him sat the Mayor, still in a trance-like state.

When one of the figures in the center set fire to the ring that had been formed around them, David grew concerned for the safety of the neighborhood. The fire would spread quickly, the nearby buildings and their sleeping occupants would be in grave danger.

That was enough to make him spring into action. He screamed, "Larry, let's go." Larry looked around, shaking off the dizzy bad dream feeling that had held him.

Their progress was slow, stepping through the sticky black goo that covered the ground where bodies had fallen.

Suddenly, one of the figures dropped straight down from the sky, and landed, standing on her feet, directly in front of them. Her intense violet eyes burned into them, reaching down to their souls.

"You must leave, for your own safety and for the good of your kind.

This place is not for you." Elizabeth had returned in time to see them leave the car, and knew they would surely be killed. She had no desire to see innocent lives lost.

"We need to stop that fire," David yelled. "It'll burn down the whole neighborhood!"

"The fire is no danger," she said calmly, just before a figure in a dark robe flew at her from the side. She easily side-stepped the attack, and produced a sharpened rose stem from inside her long black duster which she thrust into the chest of her assailant. David and Larry watched the figure fall to the ground where it writhed in agony before melting away and adding to the growing lake of black tar.

"That is the only danger to you. You cannot fight them. You do not know their secrets. You are in danger."

"I'm the Chief of Police of this city," David said, trying desperately to sound indignant and self-assured. "I have to stop this."

"There is no way to stop it, Sir Chief. There is only to let be what must be. Otherwise your world will fall under the realm of Carlos, the evil one."

David had no idea what the woman was talking about, but he couldn't stand out in the open with the Mayor any longer. The flying creatures were getting closer.

"So how do we help defeat the 'evil one'?"

"You cannot. You can only return to the protection of your vehicle and await the conclusion of the trial."

"This is a trial?" David said incredulously. "What happens if the guy's found guilty?"

Elizabeth ignored the sarcasm and said, "Go now."

David turned back just in time to see two vampires, locked in battle, fly through the front windshield of his car before bolting straight up, tearing the roof apart, and destroying the vehicle. The car no longer offered any protection.

"You cannot fight them," Elizabeth repeated. "You must wait until it is done."

She grabbed each of them and lifted them easily into the air. Setting them down in a small grove at the edge of the park, she commanded, "Wait here. I will return for you when it is over."

FORTY-TWO

One of the conventions of the Code was that in case of trial, each accusing ancient had to approach the accused and state not only what portion of the Code had been broken, but also were allowed to air any grievances against the accused before the passing down of final judgment. Inside the protected ring, the ancients stepped forward one by one and set forth the litany of heinous acts committed by Carlos against mortal, immortal, and ancient.

* * *

When the battle was winding down, Morgana returned and unceremoniously dropped her heavy load at Carlos' feet.

Carlos showed fear for the first time. "You've killed my son!"

"Not yet. He is only feeling the effects of essence of nightshade. I saved the best part so you could watch," Morgana told him, "This 'thing'," she said with contempt, "lying at your feet is the result of you taking matters into your own hands and mating with a vampire who was not pure-blood. You created this atrocity.

"It runs around the cities and villages that you drag it to and feeds off the young women and children. Being a vampire is an honorable thing. It is what we are, an immortal race, a part of the natural order. But you continue to mate with lesser beings, creating ghouls, abominations, unnatural things. These "children" of yours are an affront to both the mortal and immortal world. And now I take from you the love you have denied me."

With that, Morgana took a lit torch and touched it to the ghoul's feet. As she ran the flame across the body, the air was suddenly filled with screams of agony and the smell of burning flesh.

Carlos' face was red with bloody tears. "Why? Why are you doing this to me? What have I done to any of you? I stayed out of your way. I stayed out of the towns you inhabited. Virginia is the one that should be here chained to this statue, not me! I didn't follow her here; she followed me." His final attempt to save himself was ignored. The ancients knew the truth; no matter how he pled his innocence, his fate was assured.

As Carlos hung his head and cried, Graham's body turned to dust and was blown away by the wind.

When Carlos lifted his head, his eyes burned with hatred. "You will pay for this. All of you!"

"Look around," Gideon said. "Your army has been defeated."

"As have you," Maria added.

"You have no idea," Carlos snarled. "The battle has only begun. My other followers will rise, and your lives will come to a painful and tortured end."

The ancients looked at each other in confusion. Only Virginia seemed to understand. She had been told by Nicolas that there was another army nearby, and that they would soon arise. She had allowed herself to hope that it wasn't true.

* * *

His arms were tired. The floor was covered in the sticky black oil that came from these sleeping creatures when they died. Mike had spent hours thrusting the steel spike from the Conservatory's storage room into the chests of hundreds of the creatures that slept on the stone pedestals. At first he had counted, in awe of the sheer numbers, but he soon stopped keeping track. There were just too many. Shining his flashlight ahead, he could see that, while he was well over halfway through, he still had a long way to go.

He sat down on the next pedestal, nearly immune to the fear he had felt when he realized he was in the presence of deadly vampires. He was sweating, and needed a break.

The vampire lying on the next pedestal made no sound when it woke. It sat up quickly and effortlessly and turned its head, baring its fangs, eager to take its first meal after twenty years of sleep.

Feeling a bit refreshed, Mike stood, ready to continue his mission. He rose from the stone just as the creature lunged for his neck, missing by inches. Mike spun, hearing the creature's hands slap down on the stone as it sought to break its fall. The face, serene in sleep, had transformed into the ugly, snarling face of a hideous beast.

And Jane thinks she looks scary when she wakes up, Mike thought in a flash of humor.

Quickly moving his light, Mike saw that the rest of the vampires were also starting to rise. And he knew that he was in trouble.

He started backing away slowly toward the shaft where he had entered the cavern, and slipped in the black puddle that had formed on the floor. The vampires, able to see easily in the dark, began to approach.

Frantically trying to recall everything he'd ever read about vampires, Mike tried to think of some way to keep them back. The stake worked, but he could only kill one at a time, and he was pretty sure they'd attack as a group. He hadn't brought any garlic or holy water, two other supposedly sure-fire protections.

Maybe a cross would work. Mike wasn't religious, but he did have a small metal cross on his keychain, a small trinket his wife had bought him long ago because she had been attracted to the design of the tiny jewels and the etchings in the metal. Mike thought it just might save his life.

He reached into his pocket with one hand, the other trying to get leverage on the ground to push him back up to a standing position. He managed to back himself through the black tar to one of the pedestals he had visited earlier and pull himself up. On his feet, he faced the oncoming vampires, the cross held out in front of him.

The nearest beast took the cross from his hand and looked at it as if it were an interesting piece of art. Mike didn't understand why nothing seemed to happen. Weren't vampires supposed to fry or something when they touched a cross? The creature dropped Mike's keys into the black puddle and took another step toward Mike. Apparently, the protection of the cross only a myth.

Mike lifted his small flashlight, and shined it in the face of the monster. That helped, if only a little. Having been asleep for twenty years, the vampire's eyes were accustomed to the dark, and although the light didn't hurt the creatures, it momentarily blinded them, giving Mike a little more time to back toward the entrance to the cavern.

Inch by inch, he edged closer to escape, flashing his light in the faces of any creatures that got too close, and jabbing at them with metal spike he still held in his other hand.

By the time he had backed all the way to the shaft where he had entered, he realized he was completely surrounded. The walls behind and to the sides of him were solid rock. In front of him was a band of nearly a hundred snarling, hungry vampires.

"Hey, guys, I'm flattered," he said. "But you all looking at me like that makes me feel like a piece of meat." His attempt at humor was lost on the creatures, who stepped closer.

* * *

The dust had settled, and the ancients had awaited the arrival of Carlos' "other minions" long enough to know that they were not coming.

"Looks like you're on your own, Carlos," Antonio said mockingly.

"Maybe they all realized what an evil bastard you really are," said Virginia, who had remained quiet throughout the trial.

Carlos could not explain why he had been abandoned. His time had run out, and his quest for the ultimate power was not to be. His fate was sealed.

The ancients exchanged glances; it was time to pronounce sentence.

Grant tipped his Stetson back and approached Carlos, stating very formally, "We have listed for you every aspect of the Code that you have broken. We have given our reasons for judgment. You have killed pure blood babies, bred abominations, violated the prophesized mating rituals, and then blamed others for the crimes that you have committed. You killed one of our own kind, one of our ancient brethren. You murdered Dominick. We pulled you out of your very own coffin, in the process of mating with one of your creatures. You are despicable."

Grant spat in Carlos' face before stepping back.

The ancients joined hands and looked to the sky as they began to chant in a language few had heard. It was the language of "those who came before"; the chanting called for the swift punishment of Carlos.

Carlos began to writhe in pain, screaming. Smoke began to rise from his feet. As the chanting became louder and louder, his agony grew.

* * *

Mike heard the noise from above, like a thousand windows exploding in unison.

The Vampires ceased their attack, clutching their heads and ears to block out the terrible sound. Mike's mortal ears heard only the staccato tinkling of glass shards falling to the pavement above. Whatever it was that was causing the beasts such pain, he was thankful for the opportunity to escape. He turned to the wall and reached for the first handhold.

His arms felt like jelly and his legs were weak with fatigue and fear. Despair washed over him as he realized that he didn't have the strength left to climb the vertical wall of the shaft.

He didn't know how long they'd be incapacitated, but he didn't think it would be long. He remembered the saying, 'the best defense is a good offense,' and decided to attack while he had the chance.

Thrusting the stake through their hearts was not as easy when the heart was a moving target, but he did his best. He could tell when the tip of the stake found its mark, because the creature would stop cringing from the ear piercing noise, and start howling in pain. When he missed, there was no reaction.

He managed to destroy several before they began to recover.

One by one, they regained their wits and began to advance once again. And once again, Mike feared he'd reached his end.

* * *

From their vantage point near the edge of the park, Larry and David could see nearly everything that was happening. David was concentrating on the activities at the Shakespeare statue, the circle obscured from view by the ring of fire. His concentration was broken when another snarling figure began to fly straight at them, their hiding place among the trees temporarily discovered. Larry ducked beneath a shrub, and David dropped to the ground, covering his head with his arms.

Suddenly, all glass around them shattered. Windows, storefronts, even the roof of the Conservatory. Shards flew everywhere, littering the ground. Looking up at the tree next to where he lay, Larry saw a huge sliver of glass embedded in the bark where his head had been moments before.

When they looked up, the attacking vampire had stopped in his tracks, and held his head in pain. Larry and David observed all of the warriors in the same state.

Larry spotted the beautiful vampire who had saved them earlier, rolling on the ground. He ran to her before David could stop him, and slid to his knees next to her.

"What's happening to you, to them," he asked.

David followed and arrived in time to hear her trying to speak. "Get … back … to … the trees. Carlos … is almost … gone. Won't … last … long."

David pulled Larry by the shoulder, motioning for him to return to cover. A few lights were starting to come on in the condominiums where the windows had shattered, and it wouldn't take long for calls to be placed to the police. He didn't want to be standing in the midst of this scene when the first officers arrived. It would be impossible to explain.

* * *

At a signal from Virginia, Antonio stepped forward, still chanting with the others. He raised his Japanese Samurai Sword and, with one smooth stroke, sliced off Carlos' head which was, in the tradition of the Code, placed in the ring of fire that had been lit to protect the ancients.

A chalice that had earlier been filled with the blood that poured from Carlos' wound was passed from ancient to ancient, each pausing their chanting only long enough to take a swallow. When it was passed to Leslie, she looked at the others with uncertainty. She was concerned about what the taking of Carlos' evil blood into her body would do to the seed growing inside her. Inspired and strengthened by the glances and nods of the other ancients, she drank.

The empty chalice was passed to Morgana, who tossed it unceremoniously onto the headless body still chained to the statue. The body dissolved into a puddle, the residue of death.

The remaining ancients clasped hands once more and began to chant again in their ancient language, a plea that the vampire gods not allow Carlos into the realm of the Prophets, but rather that his spirit spend eternity in the deepest of oceans, fed upon by the bottom dwellers who lived in that eternal darkness.

FORTY-THREE

The few of Carlos' army that survived the battle scattered, abandoning the decaying bodies of their fallen comrades. The park defenders took to the air in pursuit, knowing that all must be destroyed before they could rest.

The ancients, knowing they had accomplished their task and that mortals would soon reach the scene, leapt into the air.

Larry and David rose from their hiding place and found Elizabeth, who was watching the others take their leave.

"It is done. Carlos is gone," was all she said.

The police officer in David took over, creating a need to see what had happened inside the ring of fire. He knew he had seen the figures inside the fire leap into the air and disappear into the night sky, the same as the creature that had killed his mother. He knew with absolute certainty that one of them had been his mother's murderer.

When he reached the blaze, Larry and Elizabeth close on his heels, he put his arm over his head to protect his face and leapt through the fire, feeling the heat only momentarily. Larry hesitated only briefly before following. Elizabeth floated down to join them, having taken the safer route of flying over the flames.

A few feet from the puddle at the base of the statue, they found the disembodied head of Carlos, eyes staring, his mouth open.

Larry saw something floating in the tar and bent to pick it up. Using his already ruined suit as a towel, he cleaned the object as best he could, and stepped closer to David.

"What is it," Larry asked.

"That face," David said. "I'll never forget that face."

"Because of what happened tonight?"

"No, because it's the face of my mother's killer."

"You're absolutely certain?"

"Absolutely. What was it that you picked up over there?"

Larry held out his hand, displaying Carlos' signet. "Have you seen this image before?"

David took the ring and turned it over, studying the odd design. The serpent intertwined with a dragon wasn't familiar to him, but Larry seemed to recognize it. "Can't say that I have. Why? Have you?"

"I have." It was the symbol that had been used as a marker, an image the committee members had followed to guide them to their first meeting with Carlos, a meeting held in the exact location where they were now standing. And after the meeting, he had seen that same image in another location.

He left David staring at the face of his mother's killer and walked around the statue. At the end of each meeting with the committee, Carlos seemed to vanish. After the first meeting, Larry had searched the statue and found a tiny replica of the guiding image etched into the stone at the back. The image on the statue was an exact mirror to the signet ring.

He put the ring on his finger and held it to the image on the back of the statue. The two fit together perfectly, and when he pressed, he felt a small rumble as the back of the statue began to move.

"David! You might want to see this," he shouted.

Elizabeth, who had been watching the mortals, joined them as they looked into the opening that revealed a passageway down into the earth, a circular stairwell carved of stone. David hesitantly ducked and stepped onto the first step.

"Wait," Elizabeth said. The men paused and looked at her. She flew into the air and returned a moment later, her hand clutching a small stack of twigs.

"These are rose stems," she told them, handing them each several. "They are deadly to any vampires we may encounter below."

"Roses are deadly to vampires," David asked incredulously.

"Not all vampires. Only those made by Carlos."

Not sure he fully understood, David tucked the stems she had handed to him into his pocket and began to descend, Larry close behind. When they reached the bottom, they found Elizabeth already waiting, having turned to mist and floating down ahead of them.

"I really wish you wouldn't do that," David said.

"Do what?"

"Disappear and reappear like that."

"I apologize. I forget that your mortal eyes cannot see when I move at such speed or turn to mist."

"Well, it's just creepy."

"Hey," Larry said, interrupting them, "I think the tunnel leads this way." He started off, feeling his way along the wall with his hands. The stone was rough and crumbling in places. Occasional spider webs suddenly hit his face, making him stop to wipe them away.

David followed, using his hands to follow the passageway as well. Elizabeth, able to see in the dark, walked easily, and was amused at the trouble the two mortal men had navigating the path cut through the stone.

After a short distance, she reached forward and touched David on the shoulder, startling him, and nearly making him scream.

"What is it?"

"I sense a presence. It comes from up ahead."

"What kind of presence?"

"The presence of other vampires. There are many near. I should go ahead of you." Without waiting for agreement from the mortals, she sped off into the darkness of the tunnel, returning a few seconds later. Had David and Larry been able to see in the dark, they would have seen the concerned expression on her face.

"They are awake. And they have a victim nearly cornered. Follow me quickly!"

David and Larry moved more rapidly, still navigating by feel. When they reached the end of the tunnel, they found themselves in an immense cavern, the floor containing hundreds of stone pedestals. In the distance, they saw a small light waving back and forth, revealing the silhouettes of dozens of creatures. They could hear Elizabeth yelling, her voice echoing off the carved walls of the cavern.

As they ran in the direction of the light, their feet began to stick to the stone floor. Looking down, they found more of the strange black tar that coated the ground in the park above. Someone must have been down here killing vampires, but who? They exchanged a troubled look, knowing that the person waving the light was in deep trouble, and that they had to do what they could to save the vampire slayer. They plodded through the black goo as fast as they could, until they found themselves at Elizabeth's side.

She was drawing the vampires away from their intended victim, and was calling to the person holding the tiny flashlight, a person whose voice David suddenly recognized.

* * *

Mike was certain he was finished. The approaching vampires had fully recovered from whatever it was that had caused them such pain earlier and were again advancing on him. He had killed several more, thrusting the point of his metal stake into their hearts, but there were still far too many left, and he was exhausted.

The light was having less and less effect on the creatures as their eyes adjusted. Mike would have no defense once that effort failed.

Just when he thought he would be overcome, he heard a howl of pain from the rear of the hoard, a sound similar to the muffled roar he'd heard each time he struck his metal stake through the heart of one of the creatures. It gave him a measure of hope that someone—something—else was fighting at his side.

"Leave him alone!" he heard a voice call out.

The undead turned toward the voice.

"Your master is dead. You will soon share his fate."

As Elizabeth backed away, the vampires following, Mike realized she was giving him another chance to escape. He looked up the shaft, knowing he still couldn't climb the vertical wall. He'd have to find another way out. He didn't know where the woman had come from, but her presence told him there had to be another exit.

"How have you been killing them?" he heard her call.

He hesitated, not wanting to attract their attention by answering. But she seemed to know what she was doing. "I have a metal spike." He looked expectantly at the backs of the creatures. One or two turned around at the sound of his voice and snarled at him, but quickly turned back and faced the woman. "I've been stabbing it through their hearts"

"Very good," came the reply. "The only ways to kill them are to pierce their hearts or slice off their heads."

Mike lunged forward and jabbed the stake into the back of one of the vampires, piercing its heart. "What about crosses?" he said. "I held out a cross and one took it away like it was nothing!" He stabbed another while she held its attention. He assumed she was doing the same from her side.

"Crosses mean nothing to vampires. That's a myth created by mortals. Holy Water is the same. It has no affect on them."

"I suppose garlic is useless, too!" Another vampire fell to Mike's stake.

"Garlic can hurt, but cannot kill."

Then Mike heard a familiar voice.

* * *

"Green! Is that you?" David shouted over the heads of the beasts who faced Elizabeth. He hadn't considered that shouting might draw their attention to him, and he regretted it as soon as he did it.

"Use your roses!" Elizabeth ordered. She was holding the branches out toward the approaching beings, who seemed afraid to get near the roses. They pulled the stems from their pockets and began waving them at the vampires. It had the desired effect of at least keeping them at a distance.

"Chief?" they heard Mike Green calling from his site, trapped behind the ever-shrinking group of vampires. Elizabeth stepped forward, and plunged a rose stem into one's chest while slashing the throat of another with her other hand, before stepping back next to the two mortal men. Larry and David took her cue and lunged with their rose stems as if they fencing foils.

"We're here. Me and the Mayor."

"So the cavalry has arrived!"

The Mayor poked at a vampire and missed as it avoided the rose stem. The Chief slashed the chest of one, causing pain, but did not pierce its heart.

"How did you get down here?" he resumed his conversation with Mike across the melee.

"Climbed down a shaft under the Conservatory," Mike called back as Elizabeth stepped forward and killed another vampire. "I just can't climb back up!"

"Then you'll have to get out this way. There's a tunnel to the park." The Mayor and the Chief lunged in unison into the group of vampires, each of them hitting their mark and destroying one. They were somewhat surprised at the ease with which the rose stem entered the creatures' chests; there was no resistance.

"Are there many left? I don't know how much longer I can last!" Mike said, the strain evident in his voice.

"We're cutting them down as fast as we can," the Chief answered. "The rose stems are working!"

"Rose stems?" His daughter's words came back to him again. "Because they don't like roses. If they were nice people, they would like roses … They cry when they come near our house. They can't go past the rose bushes Mommy planted outside."

Mike reached into his front pocket and pulled out the crushed remains of the two roses he had plucked from the Conservatory display above. There was little left of the broken stems, and the petals were almost entirely wilted, but they still retained some scent.

Cautiously, Mike held the wilted petals out in front of him and stepped closer to the back of one of the vampires. It turned and backed away, a look of fear on its distorted face. Mike stepped back into the recess in the wall beneath the vertical shaft and put his trusty spike in his belt loop while he split the rose petals into two small handfuls.

"Get ready, Chief! I'm coming through!"

He began waving the rose petals in circles around his body. Keeping his back to the stone wall, he started moving around the outside of the group of menacing vampires, thrusting his handful of roses at any who turned toward him. Before long, he had managed to slip past to the other side, where he stood with the Mayor and the Chief.

"You have done all that you can," Elizabeth said to them before lunging forward, slashing the rose stems at another of the hideous beasts that faced them. "It is time for you to go."

"I'm not leaving until every one of these things is turned to goo," the Chief said to her. "I can't have them running around my city."

"Do not worry. I will take care of them. You must leave the way we came. Return to the park."

The Chief looked one last time at the beautiful woman, amazed that such a creature could really be a vampire, and said, "Thank you for helping us save our friend."

She glanced at him and replied, "No, thank you and your friend for helping defeat these evil ones."

The three men ran toward the tunnel. The muffled roars of dying vampires, their hearts pierced with rose stems, continued to issue from the cavern as it disappeared behind them.

FORTY-FOUR

After leaving the park, the ancients gathered at the cathedral and sat on the rooftop, deciding who would track down the rest of Carlos' offspring. None of them knew exactly how many offspring there were. Only Katherine knew for sure, and she was in southern Russia with Stefan, the one pure blood child who had been successfully hidden from Carlos.

They decided that they would all go to see Katherine and Stefan and find out as much as they could about the offspring of Carlos. They could then form a plan for the hunt. They would leave that very night.

Virginia was assigned the task of assembling the remaining non-ancients and setting them free. They had been taught well and lived according to the Code. They were ready to live in the shadows on their own.

Virginia stood on the marble steps in front of the church and whistled. All who had survived the battle, bruised, battered, some severely wounded, gathered at her feet.

She said, "Chicago is no longer a safe haven for our kind. After the events of this evening, we will surely be discovered by the mortals. We, the ancients, have a quest to follow, and I cannot ask that you join us, so you are all now free to go wherever you wish. Those who want to stay with us, be prepared to leave within the hour. The rest of you, know that I will always love you as my children. Wherever I or you go, we are family and we will protect each other. Remember the things I have taught you, and always live by the Code."

Soon it was time to leave. It would be a long journey, not one easily made even for an immortal, so they decided to make use of the mortals' technology. Grant packed his H2 and drove many to the airport, while others flew, being sure to avoid detection by airport personnel. They climbed into wooden coffins that were crated and loaded onto cargo planes headed for southern Russia where they would be greeted by Katherine, one of the oldest of the ancients.

Only Virginia remained behind. Elizabeth had disappeared, and she was worried.

FORTY-FIVE

The aftermath in Lincoln Park turned into a nightmare. The fact that the Mayor had been involved in a major cover up caused a scandal of great magnitude. The details printed in the newspapers were sketchy, at best, but behind closed doors, listening to the Mayor's mad ramblings, Chief of Police David Duncan learned much of the truth. The vampire Carlos and his followers had been close to being discovered by mortals twenty years prior. They were also on the run, hiding from others like them for undisclosed reasons. Carlos had approached some of the city's upper echelon government employees and made a secret pact: His newfound allies would do everything possible to destroy any evidence of the vampires' existence and help them prevent discovery. In return, the vampires would use their powers to boost the careers of the committee members, and would then leave the city, or at least stop killing such a large number of its citizens. The vampire's tactic of threatening the lives of the committee members' families left little choice.

The Mayor never really understood what their power was, but a year later, he was elected Mayor, a position he had dreamed of. And when the mysterious killings suddenly stopped, he was sure they had kept their end of the bargain and had left the city for good. He'd never thought they would return twenty years later.

The press corps rejected much of the talk of the supernatural, dismissing it as delusion and dementia, which was what the psychiatrists were telling them it was. They did, however, latch onto the idea of a cover up, immediately pushing for the Mayor's removal from office, based not only on his obvious insanity, but on the basis of the cover up as well.

As the Mayor began naming members of the cover up committee, it was determined that he was one of only two living members. The Deputy Mayor, filling the seat vacated by Larry's admittance to the psychiatric hospital, set about the task of sorting through the scandal, trying to determine how deep it went.

The events in Lincoln Park were rumored to have been retaliation for something. No one knew what, but it was assumed that it was meant to make a point to the Mayor. No one was ever able to proffer a plausible explanation for what had occurred.

* * *

Detective Mike Green sat in Chief David Duncan's office. As he waited, he noticed things he had ignored, or been too busy to observe, on past visits. They were small things, like the stain on the back of the Chief's chair, the horizontal blinds that didn't close all the way, or the small screws that someone had removed from one of the windows so it could be opened more than two inches. These small details seemed magnified, and stood out to Mike.

He looked down and realized that his socks didn't match. In fact, his shoes weren't even a matching pair. He had one black shoe that tied and one brown slip-on. Oh, well, he thought with a sigh, I'm probably going to be fired anyway.

Everyone knew about his drinking binge a few nights earlier. He had been technically off duty at the time, forced into a short vacation, but with his history of alcoholism, it was grounds for dismissal. Being summoned to the Chief's office at a time when the only current case was the investigation of a scandal surrounding his drinking buddy was not a good sign.

He leaned forward, elbows on the Chief's massive desk, head propped in his hands, and thought about his conversation with Jane the day before, just after Sam's memorial service.

* * *

"I'm not ready to come home, Mike," she said, explaining that she needed more time before she could forgive the hurtful things he'd said, more time to get over the fact that he'd been drinking behind her back. Mike couldn't find the words to respond. He studied his shoes.

"But," she added, "I'm not asking for a divorce." Mike's head popped back up, hopefulness showing on his face. "Not yet, anyway." She waited for a response. When all she got was a confused, sad look, she continued, "But I do want a separation, at least for the time being."

At her words, he felt like she might as well have taken his revolver and shot him in the heart. Losing her would be the worst part of all that had happened. Worse than losing his job. Worse than losing Sam. Worse than losing his own life.

But he understood that she couldn't put up with the things he had done and said. He did not want Meagan to see him drunk. He promised Jane that he wouldn't allow that to happen to their baby. How many broken promises had he made to Jane over their six year marriage? He had no clue, but he was certain Jane had kept a running tally in her head.

Rachel needed some help around the house now that Sam had been laid to rest, and their relatives returned to their own lives, she'd told him. She and Meagan would be moving into one of the spare rooms. It would keep them close to their own neighborhood and Meagan's friends. It would also be convenient for Meagan to see her father.

It was some consolation to Mike that he wouldn't completely lose access to them. They'd be nearby, just not living under his roof. To get them back, he knew he had to straighten up, prove that he was off the liquor for good, and make some sort of reparation for the things he'd said, things his wife certainly never deserved to hear.

Meagan had been playing with some other children, but came running over to Mike. He bent down just in time for her to leap into his arms.

"Daddy! Did Mommy tell you? We're gonna stay at Aunt Rachel's house for a while." The enthusiasm in her voice made him smile.

"Yes, baby. She told me. I'm sorry that Daddy can't stay there with you and Mommy. But I'll be just a few blocks away in our house."

"I know. Someone has to take care of Digger."

Mike looked at Jane, a small smile turning up the corners of her mouth. He was grateful for the excuse she'd manufactured for their child.

"You know that Sam won't be there, either, right?" He was concerned that she might still be watching and waiting for him.

"Yes, I know. Sam died." He was astonished at her matter of fact tone. "The Night People hurt him. But I'm not scared of them anymore."

"Why not?"

"Because they went away." Her tone implied that even a village idiot would have known that.

"You don't hear them anymore?"

"I heard one the other night, outside Rachel's house. When I looked, she was standing there just looking at the house. She was really pretty. She had a long coat." Mike reflected that the description could easily be of Elizabeth. "And she picked one of Rachel's roses. She likes them, so she must be a nice Night Person. But she was leaving. I don't think they'll be back."

* * *

He read about it in the papers. There was a lot of supposition, and a lot of holes in the details, but he knew the truth. He had leaked most of the false reports to the press. The "cult activity" red herrings were as effective now as they had been in the past. And, if he did say so himself, the way he manufactured and planted evidence suggesting that the journalist had been killed because he'd discovered the conspiracy was pure genius. The journalist had discovered something, but hadn't put it all together. With a little creative falsification combined with hints in the proper places, the press eventually made the connection.

The vampires he'd been covering up for all these years were finally gone. Too much had happened too suddenly; it hadn't been just another day in the vampire world.

And the committee was gone, too. The Mayor had been admitted to the psychiatric ward, and the only other remaining living member, named during the Mayor's ramblings, had been found in his office, dead from a self-inflicted gunshot wound to the left temple. Apparently, he'd decided death was an easier choice than facing the press. The Deputy Mayor wasn't going to have much left to investigate.

So he was free. No one would ever know his real identity, or his role in keeping the evidence of vampires away from the collective consciousness of the citizens of Chicago. Maybe one day he'd write a book about it, a sequel to the one he had written ten years earlier and stashed in the basement of the museum. He only wondered why it had taken so long for Tonya Stewart to find the book and understand what it was really about.

About the Author

After spending several years in Chicago, Kaycee Nilson has returned to her native Texas, where she resides with her family. She writes for several websites.

ALL THINGS THAT MATTER PRESS ™

FOR MORE INFORMATION ON TITLES AVAILABLE FROM
ALL THINGS THAT MATTER PRESS, GO TO
http://allthingsthatmatterpress.com
or contact us at
allthingsthatmatterpress@gmail.com